An Adverse Possession

**CALUMET
EDITIONS**

Minneapolis

First Edition SEPTEMBER 2024
An Adverse Possession Copyright © 2024 by R. Newell Searle.
All rights reserved.

This is a work of fiction. All of the characters, names, incidents, organizations, and dialogue are either the products of the author's imagination or are used fictitiously.

10 9 8 7 6 5 4 3 2 1
ISBN: 978-1-962834-26-1

Cover and book design by Gary Lindberg

An Adverse Possession

Newell Searle

**CALUMET
EDITIONS**

Minneapolis

"He meditated on Horatio's appearance out of the mists of the family's collective memory. Thanks to him, I have a mission instead of a career. My destiny is healing people at the mineral spring—once I get the road opened."

~ Robert Hartwell, M.D.

"Now that I got what I want, I'm gonna keep it. Even if him an' me have to go at it like a couple bulls in ruttin' season."

~ Justin Taylor

To Rod Searle, father, farmer, statesman and conservationist—
a hard act to follow.

Also by Newell Searle

Saving Quetico-Superior, A Land Set Apart

Copy Desk Murders

Leif's Legacy

Chapter 1

An October rain beat a melancholy patter on the fallen leaves. In the dim light of daybreak, the three-story house loomed dark and angular against the cloudy sky but for a single light in a first-story window. Inside the house, Boston Meade shuffled a half-dozen clippings into a folder marked *Runyon Mineral Spring ~ Adverse Possession*.

He weighed the clippings in his hand and made a wry face. All I accomplished this summer. A few stories. Dozens of phone calls. Calls that led to more calls. More questions. Fewer answers.

He had readily agreed to help a lawyer find a recently retired farmer in a property dispute. A task of a day or two. After that, he intended to dedicate the summer to drafting a book about a retired forester when he wasn't writing his syndicated column for *American Outlook*. Tracking the farmer took time away from the book and the summer's writing consisted of a half-dozen articles for the *Alton County Statesman*, southeastern Minnesota's largest daily. They were collaborations with Ginger O'Meara, the paper's editor. Though he owned the newspaper, she controlled it because he hired her with a promise to keep his hands off its management. He paused and reread one of his articles:

WHEN YOUR PROPERTY ISN'T YOURS—
Waterford—July 21, 1986.

Robert Hartwell, M.D., of Waterford claims his family has owned the Runyon Mineral Spring since 1874.

According to Justin Taylor the spring became part of his cattle operation when he bought Norman Becker's farm in May 1985. According to Mr. Taylor, Mr. Becker secured title to the mineral spring because of his continuous use of the tract for thirty years.

Acquiring legal title to another party's property is possible under Minnesota law through open, continuous and unauthorized use for at least fifteen years and spending money to improve it. The process is called adverse possession or squatter's rights.

After selling his farm to Mr. Taylor, Mr. Becker left the county and his whereabouts are presently unknown. Dr. Hartwell and Mr. Taylor will present their documents of title in district court on July 28. Meanwhile, anyone with information about Mr. Becker's current location is asked to contact the sheriff.

A brief, economical statement of the case, he thought. Well, most of it, anyway. Good as far as it went. He didn't foresee what was coming. All his career, he tried to observe, connect and report the facts. Once he agreed to help Morris Isaacs, he couldn't pretend to be objective. Undesirable but unavoidable. He couldn't say 'no' so, after he said 'yes,' he couldn't back out. Not after the disputed title turned into a case of probable fraud. He realized then he had become an integral part of the story.

He removed the tortoiseshell glasses, pinched the bridge of his Roman nose and then replaced the lenses. Shaking his head in disbelief, he marveled that a dispute over an obscure mineral spring thirty miles away could blow up into a story as complex as some of his international assignments in Saigon, Mexico City and Beirut. Once he got his teeth into this story, he spent all summer chasing it backward and forward in time until it played out.

What mysterious power draws men to a life on the sea or in the soil, he wondered. Not because there weren't other kinds of work. Certainly not for the money. Farming was dirty, physical labor with great financial risks and damned small rewards. On top of that, the Bureau of Labor Statistics said four of the ten most dangerous jobs were in agriculture. It must be in their soul. Taylor was consumed by his dream of ecological grazing. Hartwell pursued his driving vision of a wellness center. Possessing a piece of land wasn't like owning a car or even a house. Soil was a living thing and losing the farm brought endless heartache—like a divorce or the death of a child. It was existential. He knew families that had lost their farm after four generations. It was a mortal wound. No man owned a farm, the farm owned him. Boston knew he could say the same for journalism. Poor pay, some danger and a profession hard to quit. He rose from his chair and stretched. *Quit bitching. I brought it on myself. No good deed goes unpunished.*

He sealed the clippings into a manila envelope and put that into a folder between several others in the filing case. Then he shut the drawer with a feeling of completion. It was nearly 7:00 a.m. and time to make coffee. Then his phone rang. "Meade here," he said in a soft voice. Then he held his breath as he listened to the caller's brief message. "Thank you for calling," he said softly and hung up the phone. Climbing the stairs, he whispered, "Death be not proud, for thou art not so."

Chapter 2

A pair of Charolais bulls bellowed threats and butted heads as strings of saliva streamed from their gaping mouths. Their heavily muscled forequarters packed the bulk and power of a compact car. Divots of sod flew from their hooves as they jousted for leverage. Their gusts of heavy breathing broke the evening's tranquility. Yet, despite the bulls' grunts and roars, the grazing cows showed no outward interest in the fight for their favor. The butting contest ended abruptly a moment later when a car stopped at the pasture gate.

"Who in the hell...?" the driver sputtered as he got out of the silver Mercedes with California plates. The lithe, blue-eyed man with a golden tan walked to the gate with the grace of a tennis pro. A green street sign indicated this was the Runyon Spring Road but the black and white sign on the gate said: "Private Road. Taylor Land and Cattle Company." Robert Hartwell, M.D., rattled the padlocked steel gate blocking the road. "When... when did this happen?"

He plucked a strand of shiny barbed wire and heard it twang like an out-of-tune guitar. Crossing his arms atop the gate, he rested his chin on them and looked toward his property at the road's end, a mile away. His acreage included the mineral spring that flowed from a cavern in the low limestone escarpment that defined the Runyon Valley. He also owned the abandoned tuberculosis sanatorium next to it. In the low light of a June evening, the pasture brought to mind the baize cover on a billiard table that his late wife, an art curator, once called a Gainsborough landscape. *Felicia was right. It's all of that.*

5

Leaning on the gate, he remembered his first trip to the spring in 1943. He was twelve that summer and, after the state closed the sanatorium, he rode his Schwinn Excelsior bike five miles from Waterford to see it. In his memory, he saw the water issuing from the limestone grotto large enough to stand in. And around it grew a lush Eden of delicate maidenhair ferns and yellow buttercups, sedges and delicate harebells with spotted leopard frogs and blue cliff swallows, orange dragonflies and silver minnows. The waters of Runyon Mineral Spring became the small creek that angled southeasterly across his property and down the valley to the Wacouta River. This eidetic memory of the spring and its fairyland dell had often saved his sanity during his year as a young Army combat medic in Korea.

The bulls continued their truce to stare at Hartwell. He watched the cows as their jaws rotated while chewing their cuds. In turn, they looked at him with large, wet eyes in an expression that struck him as compassionate. Then one of them burped and regurgitated a cud and continued chewing.

He hadn't seen his property in fifteen years but it had since taken on an importance he had never felt before. He remembered leaving Minnesota for the Army as a green kid and returned from Korea the next year as a much older man. Then he thought of the years in San Francisco studying medicine and opening a practice. The blocked road gave him heartache. *Even if the spring hasn't changed, I have. My Minnesota credentials expired long ago. Last year I thought Felicia would recover. She would continue curating art while I treated coronary diseases. Thirty years is all we had.* He wiped his eyes and shook his head. *Goddamn cancer*!

Out of frustration, he rattled the gate in its frame, then he kicked it. At fifty-four, he didn't need more money or want the stress of making it. Ever since Felicia's death, he hungered for a new life with real purpose. *Horatio, I'm here. You told me to come.* How to explain the frightening dream where he met a long-dead ancestor. It defied all reason and science. It had to be a… a what? His great-grandfather knew him as if he had been by his side all his life. *He talked to me when I needed someone. Told me to sell the practice. Come here. Now here I am, shut out of my property.*

6

In family lore, Horatio Hartwell was a Waterford pioneer and a homeopathic doctor who bought the spring and opened a health resort in the 1880s. After his death in 1913, the family leased the resort to the state as a tuberculosis sanatorium until penicillin became an effective treatment. After that, his father leased the property to a neighbor for hay and pasture. The vacant sanatorium was already derelict when Hartwell inherited the property. It had to be more dilapidated now, he thought. Decay, like any disease, had a way of accelerating. It didn't matter. This was to be his future.

Horatio's advice had resonated within him. Not one given to second thoughts, he had acted as swiftly as if doing triage under fire. If his flurry of quick decisions alarmed friends and colleagues, so what? Better to decide now than dither and look back with regret. He sold the practice to his associates and then the hilltop house in the Sunset District. Working through an agent, he bought a new house in Waterford over the phone and then shipped his goods to Minnesota. After unpacking some essentials this morning, he visited the family's graves in the afternoon and then drove on to see the spring—if only he could see it.

Still leaning on the gate, he listened to the courtship zoom of nighthawks in the dusk and the sound called up Horatio's appearance out of the mists of the family's collective memory. Thanks to him, he had a life-giving mission instead of a career. *I'm going to open the road and heal people at the spring. It's my destiny.*

With his gaze fixed on the distant escarpment, he imagined breaking ground later this summer and erecting a modern facility by the spring. Then, a year from now, he would open a center dedicated to wellness and meditation to treat the stress that caused heart attacks, strokes and other coronary diseases.

Turning from the gate, he walked east along the fence paralleling County Road 6. A metal "No Trespassing" sign hung from the second wire every five hundred feet. A lot has changed, he thought, running fingers through his short, silver hair. The valley used to have a half-dozen farms with dairy and hogs and fields of oats, corn and soybeans. Now it was all hay and pasture. The farmhouses were gone but the barns remained. What happened to everyone, he wondered. It looked like the farm crisis took out Norm Becker, too, though he was doing well the last time they talked. He didn't say anything about selling. Hartwell blamed himself for not calling when he didn't hear from him this winter. Then he thought he missed Becker's call because he was too busy with Felicia's dying to notice. The radical changes left him disoriented, as if he had just dropped into Tibet.

"Why is the road gated?" he muttered as he returned to it. "This is a public road. I have a right to reach my property. All right, I'll walk in." He climbed over the steel gate with ease and skirted a nearby group of cows. The bulls large eyes followed him the intensity of radar tracking an enemy plane. Then the largest bull lowered its horned head and sauntered toward him. Its large, wet eyes burned with the violent ardor of a rutting male.

"Hoo bossy," Hartwell cooed in a low voice and walked backward at the same pace as the approaching bull. Then he scrambled over the gate to safety. The bull stopped, shook its massive horned head and expelled blasts of air in a challenge. "That's right, big fella. You're horny and I'm no Pamplona *mozo*. No getting past you. I'll have to get access from your owner."

He got into the car, perplexed he hadn't heard from Becker. They had known each other since boyhood and he passed Becker's driveway every time he went to the spring. Sometimes Norm had joined him. As teens, they went there to share stolen cigarettes and girly magazines. Becker took over the farm after high school and then Hartwell entered the Army. It had been fifteen years since they talked face-to-face. That was at his mother's funeral. But Becker wrote or called like clockwork about renting the tract. *When did we last talk. Must have been a year ago. Norm said some of the neighbors hadn't made it.*

On his way to Waterford, Hartwell vowed to track him down. It would be good to catch up. Taylor Land and Cattle owned his farm so they would know how to reach him. Then he saw an on-coming white pickup towing a gooseneck trailer. The fast-moving rig hogged the road and Hartwell swerved onto the shoulder to let it pass. He glimpsed a dwarfish driver, a black logo on the door and a couple of cattle in the trailer. He watched the rig in his rearview until it vanished around a curve. "*Jesus!*" he muttered. "Minnesota is as dicey as California."

Hartwell owned a new house on a wooded lot along the Wacouta River. As he parked the car, his stomach audibly reminded him he hadn't eaten since breakfast. Then he remembered he hadn't bought any groceries. Too late for that now. Leaving by the back door, he crossed the patio and walked a quarter mile into downtown Waterford on the riverside bicycle path.

The town's appearance amazed him. When he left after high school, it was a small, rural community with one of every kind of basic business and service: grocery and household goods, furniture, funeral, automotive, medical, financial and farm services, a library, schools and churches, bars and liquor stores, a Dairy Queen and a hamburger joint. Since then, gentrification had tripled the population to 16,000. Many newcomers were drawn to the river's bucolic setting and the city's bicycle paths, riverside park and the bandshell where there were seasonal concerts and plays. Executives and doctors settled there and commuted to Rochester only thirty minutes away. Some turned Victorian houses into bed-and-breakfast inns or renovated the formerly vacant brick storefronts into eateries, funky bookstores, art galleries and antique shops. It seemed as exotic as Kathmandu.

Wandering along the main streets, he checked the menus taped in the café windows and thought Waterford's makeover would keep him interested. Most of the cafés he remembered had been replaced by new ones. He entered Gretta's Garden because of its vegetarian entrées.

"Welcome to the Garden," said the tall woman in a peasant dress and embroidered blouse. She tucked a lock of dark hair under the paisley scarf and picked up a menu. "I'm Gretta Green. And you are…?"

"I'm Bob Hartwell. I just moved back from San Francisco."

"Oh, cool. Glad to meetcha." She handed him a menu. "Tonight's special is stuffed bell peppers. Follow me," she said and seated him at a small table.

"Your entrées are extraordinary," he said when she brought water. "It reminds me of San Francisco. Did you grow up here?"

"No. I'm a transplant. Originally from Minneapolis. I spent a lotta years in California. I went to culinary school after ten years in nursing. Opened the Garden five years ago."

"You're a native?"

"Yes and no," he took a sip of water. "Born and grew up here. I liked San Francisco so much I went to med school and settled there."

"You here to take over Harald Nielsen's practice?"

"No. Who's Nielsen?"

"A good doc but he's doing ten to twelve for murder. We need a replacement."

"I'm a cardiologist. You need an internist or a generalist. By the way, do you know anything about the Taylor Land and Cattle Company?"

"Well… it's a cattle company," she said, rolling her eyes with a smirk.

"No, I mean, who owns it. Who's in charge? I own the mineral spring property and the company has fenced me out of it."

"Oh, that's too bad," she said turning serious. "It's owned by a guy named Taylor. He came in from Texas and bought up some farms. He's never been here. Well, of course… he raises meat." Her bubbling laugh had a musical pitch. Then she took his order and turned to greet other customers.

There's a free spirit, he thought listening to her talk to others. She struck him as more a middle-aged flower child than a Minnesotan, but he sensed a good air about the place. He left a generous tip because the portobello bisque, sesame roll and gruyère were light, flavorful and nutritious—as good as anything in San Francisco. Good for the heart.

Gretta's entrées have creativity and healthy wisdom, he thought on the walk home. Whoever she was or pretended to be, he would need someone like her to oversee the food at the center. Someone who combined nutrition with a palate for taste, texture and presentation. When the time came, she might have ideas about possible collaborators.

Hartwell paused at the ruin of a stone gristmill and watched the water tumble over the wreckage of the spillway. The river hadn't changed since he was a boy. It was still sixty to eighty feet wide, hip to

10

chest deep and clear enough to see the pebble bottom as it flowed east toward the Mississippi River. Shaded by trees, it was an ideal stream for tubing, canoeing and fishing. He stood on his patio; grateful he could hear the rapids from his backyard.

Taylor's telephone number wasn't in the White Pages, but the Yellow Pages listed the Taylor Land and Cattle Company. It was now 9:30 p.m. No one would be at the office at this hour. He would deal with him in the morning.

Justin Taylor stood at his office window with the phone to his ear. "Say your name again. *Uh-huh.* An' you say you own the mineral spring. That right?" He listened, surprised at the call. "No, I'm sorry," he said. "That ain't possible." While he listened to the caller, he gazed at the cattle in the valley below him. His 1,800 acres were the kind of range he had dreamed of since adolescence. In it he saw everything his father's Texas ranch had lacked. Minnesota's soil and climate produced more than enough forage to fatten three hundred head of Charolais cattle. "Well, c'mon out if you want," he conceded. "But I'm tellin' you, it won' change a anything."

The office window offered long views of the upper Runyon Valley—most of it his property. His yard was at the bight of an escarpment that curved in two directions and defined the upper valley. The northern rim ran easterly and the other curved away to the southeast. He picked up naval binoculars and focused on a herd of fifty head grazing in a paddock below him. *Nothin' on God's green earth outshines cattle grazin' good grass,. Damned soothin' to hear 'em chewin' their cuds. It's all I ever wanted in life.*

He shifted his focus to another of his five herds dispersed across the valley. Each bunch grazed a paddock of 40 or 50 acres enclosed by a portable electric fence. Seeing the grass inside it appeared eaten to the ground, he glanced at the calendar. "They've been on that patch nearly two weeks. Time to put them on fresh grass." Rotational grazing had the virtue of acting as a complete ecological feedback loop. Grazing invigorated the grass, the cattle's hooves broke up the soil and stirred in grass seeds and manure. It was automatic mowing, plowing, fertilizing and planting. Exactly like what the buffalo did.

Leaving the farmhouse office, he shoved his hands into his hip pockets and basked in the sunlight. On fair mornings like this, he could help but think that ranching was a vacation. He rolled his thickly muscled shoulders and torso that had filled out during the roughneck years in the oilfields. That was an education, he thought, flexing his thick fingers. He had a ruddy face, hooded eyes, a long nose and a steel gray mustache that he brushed with the tip of his fingers. Even without a horse, his boots, Levi's and a silver belt buckle marked him as a cattleman.

His timing had been pitch perfect, he thought. The farm crisis forced farmers into selling. All the land he needed had come up for sale. In just six years, he had bought the land, the cattle and fixed up the farmstead. The barn had a new coat of red paint, the silo wore the black TLC Co. logo and a white rail fence flanked the driveway. After he and the crew tucked the corrals behind the barn, the yard had a clean look. *Still can't believe it. My perfect ranch. From idea to reality in six years.*

"*Hmm umm,*" he hummed, knowing the Gopher State had it over the Lone Star for grass and cattle. By rotating pastures, he grazed cattle from April to late November. And, if anyone doubted his methods, he had records to prove his way made a bigger profit than feedlots.

On his way to the barn, he recalled learning about rotational grazing years ago as a teen in a Four-H program. He had showed has father how it increased the growth of gramma and buffalo grass, but his father rejected it. He said the old ways were the best ways. *Bullshit!* The memory rankled him. *Even at fourteen, I knew we couldn't fatten cattle on jimson weeds, cheat grass and sand sage. Pa woulda got out of debt and kept the ranch if... but, he died broke.* Taylor paused to scuff gravel with his boot and thought of the thirty years of work to get the money for this operation. *Too bad Pa din't live. The cattle are payin' their way an' he mighta believed me this time. Well, if things go any better, I'd think this is a setup.*

He waltzed into the barn and checked on the two calves he quarantined yesterday. They had a virus that caused diarrhea. Without treatment, they might die or fail to gain weight. Seeing both critters on their feet made him smile. Another day in the barn and they could go back to grass. Six months of grazing would bring them up to market weight.

"*Buenos días, Jefe*," Nacho Morales called from the barn's other side. The chunky Tejano foreman's grin gleamed against the dark beard on his tan face. Tattoos on his arms covered long knife scars.

He called Taylor *Jefe*, because he was the boss but more because the honorific was a term of friendship with an equal. The extended Morales family had lived along the lower Rio Bravo since the days of the Spanish. Raised near Nuevo Laredo, Mexico, he picked up his imperfect English in Texas. Like Taylor, he had left his father's *rancho* for the oil fields where they met and became *compadres*. Now the *Jefe* ran his ranch and he trucked cattle to and from Laredo.

"Where are the boys at?" Taylor asked.

"Pablo, he cut hay on Wilkes place. Carlos, he clean shit from the Becker barn."

"Good. Did you unload the bales last night?"

"*Sí, Jefe*." He cocked an eye at the calf. "*Oye, el ternero*, he look good today I think."

"He's better," he said. "Here, you give 'em the electrolyte. I hear a car comin' in. It's probably that guy who claims he owns the mineral spring."

"Oh, what you do?"

"Lay out the facts. That's all I can do."

Taylor walked back to the house as the silver-gray Mercedes stopped beside his white pickup. He shoved his hands into his back pockets and shook his head in amusement at the lean driver dressed in Bermuda shorts.

"Are you Mister—"

"—Hartwell. Bob Hartwell. Thank you for seeing me, Mister Taylor. I own the mineral spring property. I'd like to talk to you about securing access."

"Like I said on the phone, there's nothin' I can do. I hate to say it but... but well, Becker got title to it by usin' it for years. It was already part of his farm when I bought it from him. It's smack in the center of my ranch an' I'm not gonna sell it. B'sides that, the township vacated that road long ago. So, it's outta my hands. I cain't do a thang 'bout it."

"What are you saying?" Hartwell asked, raising his voice. "Norm rented my property."

"That ain't what he tol' me." Taylor opened a folding knife and sharpened a pencil nub. "Said he ain't seen ya in all the years he used the place." He squinted at Hartwell, who was about his height but seemed runty dressed in shorts.

"That makes no difference. We talked every year."

"Not how I heard it. He tol' me he asked if he could graze the place but never heard back. As I understand the law, if he uses the property and you don't sue 'em within five years, he can claim it. And that's what he did. I got proof of title and paid good money for it, too. I'm sorry, but that's how it is.

"I don't care what Norm told you," Hartwell snapped, his blue eyes flaring in anger. "He didn't get title to it. I pay the taxes every year. Where is he?"

"I dunno," Taylor shrugged. "He sold me his place a year ago an' said he was movin' to Arizona. Last I seen of 'em was his Buick and the van leavin' his yard."

"No forwarding addresses?"

"Someplace in Arizona. I got it in my office. Wait here." He returned with a slip of paper.

"Have you heard from him?"

"Nope. He was all business. Just signed the deed and took the money."

"Well, I can prove I own the property. Then I'm going to get the road open and build a wellness center on the old sanatorium site."

"Look mister, that's not a good idea," Taylor said patiently, as if explaining a simple fact to a stubborn child. "I don't want trouble with you. An' I ain't tryin' to be difficult." He folded the knife. "But look around. Buildin' in the middle of a ranch ain't gonna be pleasant what with cattle bawlin' and the smell of cow shit. I can see you're shocked. Naturally. I would be, too. But law is law, understand. Look, just to get

14

on good terms, I'll pay you for a clear title. That way we don't have a dispute. Name a price and I'll cut a check."

"I'm not selling."

"Look, I'm willin' to settle—but on my terms," he said, lowering his voice.

"I see… well, thanks for your time," Hartwell said, clipping his words. "I guess we'll settle this in court." A moment later, he left the ranch in a cloud of dust.

Taylor watched him leave. *He's got more money than he can say grace over. Sure as sunrise, he'll get himself a lawyer.* He lit a cigarette, inhaled deeply and blew out a cloud. *With all his money, why does he want those piddlin' acres?*

He walked around the barn to the tractor shed where Morales and Duarte were hitching a portable squeeze chute to a John Deere tractor. The chute was a wheeled box of steel tubes and panels to immobilize an animal for medical treatment. This one could be towed to a pasture and was strong enough to hold a bull.

"*Buenos días, Jefe,*" Duarte Guzman said, touching the brim of his cap. He was one of the three other Mexicans who worked for Taylor.

"*Buen día, Duarte.* Nacho, what's with the squeeze chute?"

Nacho pushed a lock of dark hair under his cap. "*Las vaquillas…* heifers from Texas," he said, "*…la pulmonia.*" He meant shipping' fever, a form of pneumonia. "They in a corral."

"Good work, Nacho. Okay. *Vámanos tipos,*" let's go guys. Duarte climbed on the tractor and towed the chute off the escarpment by a tractor lane to a corral at the former Otto farm. While Taylor and Morales followed in a pickup, he told the foreman about the Californian. "Offered him money but he din't want it. He's so rich he can strut sittin' down."

Morales grinned and shook his head. "¡*Ay-yi-yi, un rico*! He change his mind, I think." Then he spit out the truck's side window.

"Wish you were right amigo. I think he's gonna lawyer up. Go to court. He's stubborn."

Duarte stopped at the corral with two heifers and backed the chute up to the gate. He unhitched and parked the tractor to one side. Then he opened the back of the chute while Morales and Taylor guided a heifer into it. As the animal entered, he dropped a bar over its neck. Morales pulled a lever that pressed the chute's sides against the animal and held it still. While the heifer stood, Taylor inserted a vial of antibiotic into a syringe. After a quick jab, Duarte released the sides, raised the bar and the animal capered back to the herd. Then they vaccinated the second heifer.

"I hope there ain't any more with fever," Taylor said. "All the same, keep an eye on this one." He lit a cigarette with satisfaction. "Not bad. They'll git better faster outside. That's the virtue of grazing. God is on our side. Let's check the other herds."

"*Jefe*, what you do about that hombre?" He spit again.

"Show him the papers. That oughta convince him against goin' to court." He turned his gaze all around the valley lush with grass and clover. "I wanted a place like this since I was a nubbin," he said, brushing his mustache. "It's what I wanted for our place but my old man wouldn't budge." He dragged on the cigarette, dropped it and then crushed it under his boot. *An' my timin' was perfect, he thought as he got into the pickup. I had oil money to buy land fast an' cheap. Now that I got what I want, I'm gonna keep it. Even if the rich guy an' me have to go at it like a couple bulls in ruttin' season.*

Chapter 3

"Adverse possession—my ass," Hartwell sneered on the drive back to his house. "Just wait until I find Norm. He'll hear from me over this. I'll hire a lawyer. I'll sue them both if I have to." But where did Becker go? Taylor's claim might stand up if he couldn't find him. No—that changed nothing. He checked his watch, subtracted two hours for California time. Yes, his lawyer would be in the office now. He plugged a phone into the patio jack.

"I can't help you with that," Mike Bottomer told him. "I don't know Minnesota law anymore. Look up Morris Isaacs in Featherstone. We were law school classmates. He's sharp."

"What else can you tell me about him?"

"Ten years as a deputy attorney general. He's a modest and unassuming man but don't underestimate him. Some who did are still serving time."

Sounds like the man I need, he thought and phoned Isaacs for a late afternoon appointment. Then he dialed directory assistance and asked for the number of Norman Becker at the address Taylor gave him. For what seemed a long time, he heard nothing but the operator turning directory pages. There wasn't a listing for Becker at that address or in any of the surrounding towns, she told him. The reply took away his breath. *What*! *I've been robbed... my future is... there's no way... I hope Isaacs has a detective who... If he doesn't...*

He filled the rest of the day unpacking utensils and linens. At mid-afternoon, he drove to Featherstone for the 4:00 p.m.

appointment with Isaacs. As far as he could see, the city hadn't changed in the last twenty years. The downtown blocks of brick Romanesque buildings were as he recalled them. The Louis Sullivan bank with its terra cotta decor anchored one end of the city green and faced the Federal-style courthouse at the other. There were new fast-food shops, big box stores and one-story office blocks at the city's margins. Otherwise, the city seemed unchanged. It even had angle parking without meters.

He walked down the block to the yellow brick Heath Building and rehearsed the case in his head. *Taylor can't claim my land. Either Norm pulled a con job or Taylor doesn't know the law.* Bottomer gave him the impression that Isaacs ran a high-powered law firm. Probably high cost, too. No matter. He sounded like a man who could settle this with a few phone calls. A sign in the Heath Building lobby listed an insurance agency and a copy shop on the ground floor. Butler Design Services and Isaacs Law were on the second floor. His expectation of a powerful, multi-attorney practice shrank with each creak of the wooden staircase.

Isaacs welcomed him into the simple but comfortable private office with a large wooden desk, a matching credenza and filing cabinet, and three upholstered chairs. The shelves behind the desk held rows of statutes and law books. One wall had a window above the credenza. The other wall held citations. His framed Saint Paul College of Law diploma reminded Hartwell that Isaacs was a night school lawyer. Then he remembered that Justice Blackmun and Chief Justice Burger also graduated from that school.

"Doctor Hartwell, I'm pleased to meet you," Isaacs said, extending a hand and waving at the chairs. "Please, sit down."

As they shook hands, he appraised the attorney as a man of obvious good health. His whiskey-colored eyes radiated warmth if not kindness. The linen suit coat seemed out of step with the current mode of pin-striped power suits and suspenders. With thinning hair and rimless glasses, he seemed the epitome of a semi-retired, middle-aged man. Bottomer warned me not to underestimate him, he reminded himself. This ordinary appearance might be a ruse.

"Mike called and told me a little about you," Isaacs said, sizing up a fit man with ice-blue eyes and a thin nose. "He and I go back a long way. Hart-well—what a perfect name for a cardiologist. Oh, would you like a cup of Nescafe?"

He declined. Instant coffee seemed like another sign this attorney was on the back side of his best years. "I understand you used to be a deputy attorney general."

"Oh, that was ages ago," he said, dismissing it with a wave of his hand. "A lifetime ago. I went to law school on the GI Bill. After a few years with a big firm, I went to work for the attorney general. Now he's a federal judge. Fritz Mondale took over and promoted me to deputy in 1961. He's a great man. A shame he isn't our president. I left the AG's office after ten years and moved down here. Now I do contracts, wills, estates—that sort of thing. It's a simpler life and closer to my favorite trout streams. Fishing is good for my blood pressure. Now, how may I help you?" He laced his fingers together and peered over the top of his glasses.

"I own the Runyon Mineral Spring north of Waterford. A man named Taylor bought all the land around mine and fenced off the town road. When I talked to him this morning, he told me Norm Becker sold him my property as part of his farm."

"Oh, and how does he explain that?" Isaacs scowled at this.

"He said Norm got title to my land by adverse possession. He bought it as part of Becker's farm."

"Does he have documents?"

"He didn't say."

"Tell me about the road. Is it public or a driveway?"

Hartwell hitched about in his chair. "The town road is public. Or used to be. It runs for a mile from County Road 6 to my property. Becker and another farmer owned the land on either side of it. Their driveways were about halfway up. Taylor bought both farms."

"Did your renter have permission to use your property?"

"Yes. We signed annual contracts for hay and pasture. That is, until last year."

"Can you prove it?"

"I have the notarized contracts."

"Do you have them with you?" Isaacs asked with barely contained excitement.

"No. They're in transit from San Francisco. My papers will be here in a week or two."

"Good. If you paid the taxes and have notarized contracts, there is no way that Becker or Taylor can claim ownership of your parcel. What are you going to do with the property?" he asked, spreading his hands.

"Build a wellness and meditation center. My great-grandfather had a health resort there before it was a tuberculosis sanatorium."

"Oh, yes. I recall the sanatorium. That was before my time but I've heard about it."

"I suppose the town board won't open the road unless I prove ownership. And Taylor will object to a road through his farm. He didn't strike me as the accommodating type." He studied Isaacs' face and saw the lawyer's eyes light up. Yes, he thought, appearances *are* deceiving. "Before we go farther, I want to hire you."

"Thank you, I'll be happy to represent you."

"Good. What's next?" Isaacs seemed more competent than the office trappings suggested. "I assume you have an investigator to work on this."

"*Ah*, no private detectives here. I'm afraid we'll have to do the legwork ourselves."

"I see... oh well, all right."

"Now, get in touch with Mister Becker if you can—"

"—I tried. Taylor gave me his Yuma address but there's no phone listed for it."

"Give me the address. Meanwhile, research the road. Look for records that it is a dedicated public right of way. You personally need to know that. When you've done that, contact the township clerk and ask about its status. Chances are he's a farmer and will be hard to reach during the day. Ask him if the board went through the process of vacating it. As a property holder, you should have gotten a notice of abandonment.

"I got notices in the mail from time to time but none for abandonment."

"Frankly, I doubt they vacated it," Isaacs said as he scribbled a note. "If they did, you could file a petition to reopen it." Then Hartwell borrowed his pen and scribbled a note. "We also need an abstract of your property, copies of your tax payments and other proofs of unbroken ownership."

"I see… so, looks like I'll be busy all week," he said, irked that he had to do most of the grunt work.

"Oh, I don't think it will take long," Isaacs said easily. "The courthouse has copies of your tax and property records. So, let's meet next week. Meantime, I'll make some calls."

Hartwell got into the car and saw it was after five o'clock. The courthouse had just closed until Monday. "*Damn!* Now I'll lose two days. I hope we can clear this up in a week or two." He stopped at the Featherstone IGA. It was larger than the Waterford Piggly Wiggly and might offer a wider variety of products. Disenchantment came quickly. The IGA carried the standard Midwest staples of wheat breads, dairy, meats and fresh, canned and frozen vegetables. It didn't have the sushi, king crab, baguettes, mangos and avocados he took for granted in San Francisco. Ready-to-eat frozen entrées repelled him. He picked up yogurt and soft cheese, butter and eggs, and pushed his cart to the produce section.

"*Bob*?... Bob Hartwell… is that *you*?"

The voice startled him. Turning, he stood face-to-face with a blonde woman about his age. She was impeccably made up and shapely in heels, designer jeans and a silk blouse. He set a cantaloupe in the cart beside the Romaine lettuce as he racked his memory for her name.

"Yee-es, it is," he said. "*Uh… uh* Rita, Rita Lustig? What a surprise!" He swallowed a lump in his throat. *Omigod… haven't seen her since high school!*

"Yeah, it's still me," she said, flashing a bright smile and squaring her shoulders in a way that drew his attention to her bust. "I'm Rita Docker now," she said, taking his hand.

"You're still as lovely as… How marvelous to see you!"

"And you look great! I really like that silver hair with your tan. So, the last I heard you were living in San Francisco. What brings you back?"

"I arrived two days ago," he said, taking her proffered hand. The adolescent eagerness in her voice told him she was the Rita he once knew. "Guess I'm like a salmon returning to home waters. Have you lived here all this time?"

"Pretty much. I knocked around a while after high school. Got an accounting degree and came home, you know. You remember Gerhard Docker, don't you?" She cocked her head and he noticed her penciled eyebrows. "He owned a couple electronics stores."

He nodded, not because he remembered but to encourage her to tell him more. *Wow, a familiar face. At least one old friend remembers me.*

"Well, he hired me as an accountant when I was in a tough spot. Well, you know how it is… one thing leads to another and…" she said, excited and beaming. "Well anyways, we married even though he was older. We had twenty-five good years. He died three years ago. And you… I can't believe a handsome guy like you has been single all this time."

"No. My wife died last winter. We had thirty years…" he said, feeling the emotion squeezing his throat. "After that, well…" he coughed. "I decided to start a new chapter."

"So-o-o… you're going to practice medicine here then?" She continued to hold his hand in both of hers. "Maybe take the vacancy at the clinic."

"No. I came back to turn the mineral spring into a wellness center."

"That's interesting. As I remember, your family used to own it, didn't they?"

"They—I still do. Right now, I'm dealing with a guy named Taylor who claims he owns it," he said with a dash of temper. "That won't stand after I take him to court."

"Oh for…" she said, letting go of his hand and knitting her brow into a scowl. "Justin Taylor is my husband. He's… I'm sure if you talk—"

"—I tried this morning. If there's middle ground, I missed it. Sorry, I hope that won't come between us."

"No way! I hope to see more of you," she said, giving him another bright smile and taking his hand again. "In fact, we're hosting the annual barbecue for the cattlemen's association. It's on the Fourth of July. Quite the deal. We'll roast a whole beef outdoors, rain or shine. Justin will give tours of the ranch. I *want* you to come. See for yourself what he's doing. Once you meet him he's—"

"—We've already met," he said firmly. "I doubt I'll be welcome. Thanks all the same. It's good to see you Rita," he said, now eager to end the connection.

"Don't be a stranger then," she cooed. "It's good to see you… I haven't forgotten all the fun we used to have." She winked and sashayed toward the checkout counter.

He exhaled with relief as he watched her. Omigod… Rita. After all these years… He shook his head. Hasn't changed. Same dazzling smile. Same pretty face oozing come-ons. Still sways her ass when she walks. Like waving a red cape at a bull. He remembered when merely looking at her gave him an adolescent hard-on.

So, she married Taylor, he thought on the drive home. One or the other must have a hidden side he missed. *She was a goodtime girl. A risk-taker. No thought for the consequences. But we did have fun.* He couldn't help grinning at the memory of losing his virginity to her at fifteen. *Why did she marry Taylor? She's a cougar—even in high school. A boy-toy is her style.*

Chapter 4

"Meade," the man barked into the telephone. Shifting the receiver to his left hand, he toweled the perspiration from his morning run. "Good to hear from you, Morrie. What's up?" As Boston listened, his pale gray eyes narrowed behind the tortoise shell glasses. A compact man of forty-two, he had the patrician looks of a young Spencer Tracy. He dropped the towel and jotted notes. "Sure, I remember Taylor... well, his name anyway. He bought some farms in foreclosure. Yeah, now I know who he is. So, what's this about?" He swiped a wrist across his damp forehead and listened as Isaacs filled in what he learned from Hartwell. "*Jeez*, I haven't thought of that place in ages. Adverse possession, *huh*. Sounds like that could be an interesting story."

He listened a while longer, shifting from one foot to the other. "How long will this take?" he asked, wary of further commitments. "I've got to write my columns for *American Outlook* and there's a publisher who'll give me an advance on the Nielsen book." He listened some more. "Okay, I can give you a couple days but I don't want to get bogged down."

He knew Isaacs wouldn't ask unless he was in a tough spot or suspected something amiss. No matter how intriguing, he didn't have time for Isaacs' client. On his way upstairs to the bedroom, he worried the gig could become a black hole sucking up his time. He shed the shorts and turned on the shower. *Morrie's a friend. The least I can do is see what's up.*

He shampooed his dark hair and then toweled himself dry. His soft chinos and a polo shirt were a far cry from the private label power suits he wore in Chicago as a magazine executive. And trading the BMW cabriolet for a Jeep Cherokee proved far more practical in winter and dispelled the idea he was a big-city snoot. Despite these changes, however, he was still adjusting to the rhythms of Featherstone after twenty years in Chicago.

He was the third generation of Meades to live in the Queen Anne house atop the low ridge overlooking Featherstone. From the wraparound veranda he enjoyed an expansive view of the town and the undulating countryside of southeastern Minnesota. On this morning, the groves and farmsteads, cornfields and pastures, marshes and ditches created a tapestry of varied textures in shades of lime, avocado, basil and mint. The azure sky pastured a few puffy, lamb-like clouds. This vista gave him a sense of his place in the world. There wasn't another like it anywhere.

But beyond the view, he drew inspiration from the 29,000 neighbors and townspeople he had privately derided as hicks in his college days. He now accepted the fact that he was one of them and not the urbane sophisticate of his youthful pretensions. After twenty years of reporting national and international events for *American Outlook*, he wrote a weekly syndicated column that interpreted the news through the lens of Featherstone. In doing that he discovered a born-in-the-bone satisfaction limning the effects of great events on the lives of ordinary people. The Runyon Mineral Spring held the potential to be such a story.

Boston and Isaacs made a friendship the year before when they worked at saving Leif Nielsen's farm from his brother's schemes. After that adventure, it was hard to say no to a friend as competent as the mild-mannered attorney who still liked an occasional criminal case.

"I'm not sure what to make of this," the lawyer began as Boston settled into a chair. "My client owns the Runyon Mineral Spring and rented his land to a neighbor. The neighbor sold his farm to Justin

Taylor last year with a claim he got title to the spring through adverse possession. He says he has a document to back it up."

"So, it's a case of squatter's rights?" He jotted a note.

"Yes. You can gain legal title if you use someone's property long enough without permission or payment. Minnesota has a stringent test. It's usually a case where someone makes a trail across your property or puts fence just over the property line. Most of the time it's small potatoes but in this case, it's a quarter section."

"It sounds clear-cut. What do you need from me?" He was still wary.

"We're looking for Norman Becker. It's possible he committed fraud. Whether deliberately or inadvertently, we don't know. I want your help locating him." Isaacs rubbed his chin. "Becker's farm was worth say, two hundred fifty thousand dollars. Add in the mineral spring and it was worth at least three-hundred-fifty thousand. He left a forwarding address but there's no phone there."

"So, you mean he sold and vanished?"

"It seems so."

"So, why me? It's not like I'm unemployed," Boston said and laughed.

"I know. My client has lived in California for thirty-five years and doesn't know anyone. But you have a network of contacts around the country. And, besides that, you have a talent for connecting odd facts into a clear picture. Something about this case… Can you help me out?"

"Well…" He drew a breath and swished his mouth about while he considered the arrangements he had made to spend the summer outlining a book about a deceased forester and his land ethic. "It happened last year and Isaacs was one of the main actors. The publisher offered him an advance if he saw an outline. He shrugged. "All right Morrie," he said, ambivalent. "If it were anyone but you… I just hope it won't take more than a week."

"Me, too. This client is hot to trot on construction."

He thought about the case on the drive home. The client needed to prove he owned the tract and Isaacs needed to find Becker. That would clear things up. It was either a mistake or a fraud. If it was a fraud, it would be catnip to that retired prosecutor. And it was just interesting enough that whether he helped Isaacs or not, he would wish he had. Either way, he guessed he would make himself miserable. Despite his drive to start the book, it couldn't overcome the seductive call of an investigation. He parked the Jeep under the oak in front of his house. Then he sat behind the wheel and wondered how much time he could spend on this project. *A week... two? Oh, what the hell! It's fun to work with Morrie.*

A white border collie with black ears ambushed Boston at the front door. Jester's eagerness always made him smile. Ginger and her dog brought cozy energy to the three-story house when they moved in eighteen months ago. He had hired her for the editor's chops despite lingering and mutual distrust from a romantic break-up twenty years before. Their brush with death on a murder case matured them to see beyond their old grievances. After a chaste year of sharing the house and earnest conversation over daily meals they now shared a bed—a step Ginger gleefully proclaimed as "living in sin."

The boxy house had warmed during the afternoon and the humid air seemed viscous. He thought a tureen of chilled vichyssoise might be ideal for supper. Though it was only 2:00 p.m., he began preparing it. He enjoyed cooking as an art. Ginger didn't have time to do it, and her minimalist repertoire consisted of salads, brown rice and chicken—healthy but dull. When he had the time, he prepared something elaborate like *coq a van* or *boeuf bourguignon* with *tarte tatin* or crepes from a Julia Child cookbook. He discovered a good meal helped Ginger shake off the day's stresses. Sometimes it acted as an aphrodisiac. Tonight, perhaps.

He opened the kitchen windows and then chopped, cooked and pureed the leeks, onions and potatoes. While the vichyssoise cooled in the refrigerator, he sat in the den tucked under the staircase and outlined an approach to finding Becker. Hearing Jester run to the front door he knew Ginger's Subaru was coming up the hill. A moment later, the front door banged open followed by, "What's that aroma?"

28

"An investigative news story," he called from the den. "I'll tell you over supper."

They sat side-by-side at the small dropleaf table on the veranda set with vichyssoise, baguettes, camembert and pears. As the sun sank, they gazed at the countryside in the luminous glow of the low evening light. Sunlight flared off the copper courthouse dome and the steel the water tower. Ginger's chestnut hair had golden highlights. He admired the sharp profile of her freckled nose. When she smiled, her amber eyes sparkled with a mischievous glint. A spitfire by nature, she was sometimes a case of spontaneous combustion. Yet he knew her impulsive yin balanced his stoic yang. Lithe and supple, she looked to be thirtyish instead of fortyish. He chalked that up to daily prayer, yoga and AA meetings. With a quick wit, a sharp tongue and fierce drive, she often proved herself to be the irresistible force more than equal to him as an immovable object.

"Say, this is terrific soup," she exclaimed. "Lucky me. I can afford to keep both a dog *and* a manservant!" They laughed out of gratitude for the second chance at love. Fate, chance, destiny or God's will had brought them together exactly when each felt most in need of the other. He had never met another woman like her. Nor wanted one.

"So, what's this investigative story—something your brother suckered you into?" Her eyes danced with amusement. Jack Meade, his adopted brother, was the county sheriff and her favorite foil.

"Nope. Morrie Isaacs has a client with a problem."

"What's that got to do with you?"

"The client owns the Runyon Mineral Spring. He rented it to someone named Becker for pasture. Becker claimed ownership by adverse possession and sold it along with his farm to a guy named Taylor. Then he disappeared."

"What's your role in this melodrama… as if I couldn't guess." She raised her eyebrows.

"Find Becker. Morrie suspects a case of fraud."

"Oh, so you're hunting another missing man. *Hmm*. How are going to do that, write your column and work on your book?"

"Limit my involvement to a few phone calls," he said. "And how was your day?"

"I spent an hour with Mama," she said and some of the good cheer faded from her face. "Same story as always. She didn't recognize me."

"Dementia is a thief."

"Yeah. It robs both of us," she sighed. Two decades after Mama disowned her, Ginger returned home sober, unaware of her mother's dementia. So far, all hope of reconciliation had hit a wall. Mama didn't recognize her youngest daughter. Instead, she asked for her oldest, a nun named Meghan. "We recited the rosary as usual but it's a reflex. I called Meg and gave her a run-down. She wants to see Mama so I invited sis to stay here over the Fourth of July. I hope that's okay."

"Of course! I suppose I'll have to move into my old bedroom so—"

"—Oh, Jeez Louise!" she snorted, rolling her eyes. "She knows we share a bed. And what happens under the sheets. Nuns are realists. Anyway, thanks." She puckered her lips in an air kiss.

Chapter 5

Featherstone's streets were filled with Monday morning traffic when Hartwell returned. He grumbled when he couldn't find parking within two blocks of the courthouse. Amid the pedestrians he thought he was back in California. He paused outside the courthouse to admire its architecture wrought in local dolomite. From the copper dome to the portico and the cream-colored columns, the builders didn't cut corners in the pursuit of magnificence. Standing in the rotunda. he craned his neck to look up into the dome. He realized Horatio was alive when this was built. A lot of farmers and shopkeepers taxed themselves to build something to rival the state capitol. He hoped the wellness center would evoke similar admiration.

The county supervisors, city mayor and the council had offices in the left wing. The sheriff, country attorney, judges and courtrooms were on the right. The offices he wanted—auditor, assessor and recorder—were straight back. He got in line expecting the service equal to the building's magnificence, a notion that faded quickly while he waited in line. *C'mon, c'mon, pick up the pace,* he said to himself, quietly snapping his fingers as the clerk sleep-walked through his job. Then it was his turn.

"Oh, we don't have copies of your taxes, here," he said. "You can get them in the annex. Just follow this corridor and turn left."

He entered the annex irked at wasting fifteen minutes in line for that tidbit. A sign told him to take a number. Meanwhile, the clerks chatted with each other or the customers. No one seemed in a hurry and he wondered why the taxpayers tolerated such dawdling service. Then a clerk called his number. He ordered his documents and waited a half-hour until he got the photocopies. The clerk said, "Have a nice day."

The morning was nearly gone when Hartwell crossed the city Green to the Alton County Historical Museum in the former Masonic Temple. He cruised past the displays of Native American pottery, pioneer tools, German Bibles and World War I uniforms. They struck him as credible exhibitions on a budget. The library had a collection of old maps and he ordered several photocopies of Runyon Township. Then he lost himself in the photo collection looking at advertisements for the Runyon Spring Health Resort. He ordered several photocopies.

With the documents under his arm, he felt as if the project were now something more tangible than a dream. He could now prove his title. That would upset Taylor but too bad. *He's out the hundred grand he paid for my place. That's his problem. We're both victims of a fraud.* Passing the Green's monument to the county's war dead, he stopped and saluted the bronze Union soldier atop the plinth—respect from one veteran to another.

After his morning run, a shower and a shave, Boston sat on the veranda with a second cup of coffee. If he didn't caffeinate himself now, he might be tempted to drink the acidic instant swill at Isaacs' office. *Most adverse possession cases are too mundane to notice but this one… it's got Morrie excited so it must involve a plausible crime—fraud.* Then he drove into town to meet with Isaac. This might be interesting he thought as he trotted up the stairs to the law office.

"Boston, meet Doctor Bob Hartwell," Isaacs said. "He's the client I told you about. Care for coffee?" The doctor already had a cup of Nescafe. He declined and shook the doctor's hand.

"Glad to meet you," Hartwell said. "I remember when your father published the *Statesman*. I understand it's yours now … Morrie, is this my whole team?"

My whole team! The question immediately soured Boston. *Who is this rich, pompous ass?* "Morrie, exactly what do I add to this party?" He ignored the doctor.

"I need your probing mind and national contacts," Isaacs said with the smile of a sage. "We want Becker to tell us what lies behind his adverse possession claim. We can't ask him until we find him."

"Is this something criminal?" Boston spoke directly to Isaacs.

"We don't know," Isaacs said. "Taylor says Becker claimed ownership by adverse possession and gave him a notarized statement. Taylor took his word for it. Bob can prove Becker contracted to rent his land. That negates any claim of adverse ownership."

"Do you really need Becker to disprove the adverse possession?" Boston asked, looking for a way out.

"Technically, no. But Bob deserves an answer. Then there's the question of fraud and who committed it."

"And the road?"

"Taylor bought the farms on both sides of it. He thinks it devolved into a driveway. In that case, blocking is a legal misunderstanding, not a crime. If Bob's claim holds up, and I think it will, continued blockage becomes dispossession," he said spreading his hands. "So, once Bob proves his ownership we can get the road opened. Taylor deserves to know if he was defrauded. There are legal remedies but they're possible only if we find Becker."

"I told Taylor I thought he had been defrauded," Hartwell said. "He didn't blink. Just offered to pay me to quiet any dispute. I said I wasn't interested."

"Tell me about Becker," Boston said, turning to Hartwell.

Hartwell seemed momentarily startled. "Well, our families knew each other. I've known him since I was a kid." He said Becker was two years older than he was. They used to go to the spring as teens but Hartwell said he rarely saw Becker after he was drafted. They hadn't met face-to-face in fifteen years but they talked a couple times a year by phone."

"He was a dairy farmer?"

"He had a herd," Hartwell said, sipped the coffee and set it aside. "He raised corn and soybeans for the market and rented my land for hay and pasture."

"Can you tell me anything else about—?"

"—I expect you to find him by next week," he said in the tone of one accustomed to saying '*stat*!' "I intend to break ground this fall."

"Hold it," Boston snapped, his gray eyes now as steely as November clouds. "I don't work for you. I'm *not* a detective. I'm a columnist for *American Outlook*. I'm here as a favor for Morrie. That's all."

"Well, if it's money, I can pay you and then I—"

"—No, I'm not for hire and won't take orders from..." He exhaled. "Look Hartwell, I have a full-time job writing a syndicated column. I'm also working on a book. My personal deadlines come first. Is that clear?" As he said it, he saw a red flush creep up Hartwell's tanned neck. He knew he shouldn't have set him on his ass in front of Morrie but better to set the boundaries now. *All right, so he's pissed. Not used to hearing anything but 'yes doctor, yes doctor'. Any guy that entitled won't fit in here. Glad he's not my client.*

Isaacs cleared his throat. "Bob, it's best if Boston takes his cue from me and—"

"—I see... And I'm supposed to sit on my ass and twiddle my thumbs?"

"As your attorney, it's my job to call the plays. Second, you're a stranger here. Your full-time job is introducing yourself. That way people may tell you about Becker. No one will help you until they know you. Focus on what's in front of you. Your case will be driven by facts, not construction deadlines."

The doctor pulled a long face and nodded. "I see... All right."

"Sure you don't want some coffee?" Isaacs asked.

Boston shook his head. "Doctor, your family's connection to the spring is historic. Your plan for the center is newsworthy. A story is a good way to introduce you to the county. I'll talk to the *Statesman's* editor. I'm sure she'll run it. If you like, we can do an interview now."

"Interview about what?"

"Who you are, your family's history, the health resort, your plans and challenges for the center. They're news, aren't they?"

"Yes but... but if you publish the paper. Why can't you commit to running the article?"

"It's a long story," he said with a relaxed smile. "I promised her a free hand when she came aboard and—"

"—Besides that," Isaacs interrupted, "…they live together. Don't worry. It will happen."

The meeting broke up an hour later, and Isaacs realized Boston and his client were too much alike to be comfortable teammates. Each was a solo player and Hartwell was a prima donna. Keeping them separated would get the best from each one. He trusted Boston, but the jury was still out on the doctor.

Hartwell went home and slammed every door in the house on his way to the patio. "*Damn it*," he cursed softly. "What a goddamned mess!" It had looked so simple in California. Just return to Waterford, hire an architect, clear the site and let out the construction bids. Then, in a year, stage the grand opening of the Runyon Spring Wellness Center. Instead of meeting with an architect, he had a night school lawyer defending his title and fighting to open the road. And he had to do the grunt work himself instead of developing his plans.

He took a long 'I'm feeling sorry for myself' breath. Who is Meade? Some washed-up reporter who couldn't cut it in Chicago? He won't pull any weight. Isaacs means well but he doesn't show any signs of success. Not like the guy Bottomer said he was. No rush to get it done. At this rate, opening the road could take years.

He plugged the phone into the outside jack, flipped through the Yellow Pages for the names of the township supervisors and called the town clerk. His wife said he was still in the field and suggested calling later that evening. With nothing else to do, he slipped his pager onto his belt in case the clerk called while he went uptown to eat.

"Hi-ya, Doc," Gretta called as he entered. The note of pleasure in her greeting erased some of the moue from his face. The café was momentarily empty and she sat with him. "So, howya making out with the red meat company?"

"It's a struggle," he said, startled by her directness. At this moment, he wanted to set aside his troubles and enjoy the hazel-eyed woman who exuded genuine warmth through the smoky eyeshadow. Despite her make-up and bohemian garb, Gretta struck him as authentic and could be attractive in the appropriate attire.

"What kind of food will you offer your patients?"

"Well, I haven't gotten that far but..." he said, surprised and wondering if his plans excited her or if the question was simply small talk.

"The right food is critical to everything you want to do," she continued with the authority of knowledge. "No offense, but most docs are ignorant of nutrition. Just look at how they eat." She shuddered. "They know even less about flavors. I can see you're not one of them."

"Once my immediate problems are over, I want to talk to you about food."

"Right on," she said, raising a fist. "Any time, Doc. I'd love to have that conversation. You've got an exciting idea. I want to stand in solidarity with you."

"Thanks, I'd like that," he said, amused that her hippie talk lightened his mood. Then he ordered lobster bisque and a Caesar salad. "Your food is so good. Wish you'd join me."

"I appreciate the sentiment, Doc, but I can't eat with the customers. It's rule of the house—I made it. But thanks for the thought all the same."

"*Uh*, Gretta, do me a favor. Don't call me Doc. Call me Bob."

"Right on, Bob," she said and returned to meet a customer.

Gretta was savvy, he realized on the short walk home along the river. She was an outsider who found her niche. Easy to talk to and transparent. A little too countercultural for his taste but he thought they could collaborate on healthy food. Plenty of time to test that idea.

He paused at the ruins of the gristmill dam and watched some kids float the rapids on inner tubes. The wet T-shirts clung to their lean bodies and the water's rush drowned their shouts and squeals. Then he continued walking with memories of times when he and his pals skinny-dipped in quieter pools outside town. Nice to know some things hadn't changed.

*
**

It was twilight when the town clerk called Hartwell. After a moment of introductions, he asked about opening the town road. The clerk directed him to Justin Taylor. "He owns it."

"I have talked to him, but he seems to think he owns my land and refused access."

"Sorry 'bout that but there's nothing I can do. I hate to tell ya, but you're too late," the clerk said apologetically. "The road was abandoned years ago. Turned it over to Otto and Becker as a common driveway."

"Not so fast!" Hartwell snapped. "My lawyer will prove I own the property. That means Mister Taylor was the victim of a fraud. Minnesota law prohibits the town from land-locking my property. So, there is a legal duty to give me access. To back that up, I've got maps that show the road as a public route."

"Township records are the only documents that matter. Look. I'm sorry about your property but you're an outsider. That's not how we do things here."

"I want to see records that you abandoned the road. Where and when can I do that?"

"*Uh*… you can't. You're not a resident of the township."

"*Bullshit*! I'm a property owner… a taxpayer. That gives me a right. Besides that, when did you send the public notice of abandonment?"

"*Uh*… notice? *Uh*, that was years ago."

"I don't' think so. I've got a copy of every town notice for the last fifteen years. Now, either I see the records or my attorney will serve you with a subpoena."

"If that's a threat—and that's what it sounds like—it's stupid on your part," the clerk said, abandoning civility.

"See you in court," Hartwell snapped and hung up. *Bastard*! He brewed tea, thinking it would calm him. When it didn't, he called Isaacs and relayed the conversation in staccato bursts. "I retired to live a tranquil life," he chattered. "Now I'll have to play hardball."

"You have my sympathy," the lawyer said in an even voice. "That's why I retired. For what it's worth, the law is on your side. But it may take a little time to work for you. So, patience is your long suit. You *will* win in the end."

Chapter 6

Hartwell felt cooped up despite the spacious lot and large house, immobilized by legal barriers and his status as an outsider that kept him from making plans. He ripped open a packing box and removed some dishes. So far, he felt as if he were fighting with one hand tied behind his back. Isaacs wasn't aggressive enough. He had no staff or investigators except Meade. The doctor stacked the dishes on the counter. He thought about retaining a different lawyer. Then rejected the idea. He couldn't prove anything until his papers arrived. That would be another week. He hoped Meade would find Becker before that.

When unpacking bored him, he walked into town to escape some of his worries. *Not good to stay penned up. Raises my blood pressure. Cause heart trouble—even in me.* Though it was a short walk along the river, he relaxed going up and down the blocks and checking the menus of the other restaurants. Someone said The Cleaver had good food but the meat-heavy entrées didn't appeal to him. The smaller cafés featured hamburgers, sandwiches and hoagies. He turned a corner and entered Gretta's Garden.

Seated at a small table, he relaxed with ginger-lemon tea amid the chatter of the other customers. On reflection, things weren't as bad as they seemed. Isaacs knew his way around. Meade was all right except for his ego. Things will work out, he told himself. But not necessarily on his timetable. Meanwhile, he could cultivate Gretta. She might have a tip about how to fit in.

"Thank you," he said as she served him the portabella-gorgonzola panini. "At the risk of seeming forward, I would love to have a longer conversation with you. Is there a time when that is convenient?" In her eyes he saw a glow of pleasure at being asked.

"Oh you're not forward. I take Tuesdays off. So after midmorning is good for me."

"I see… Okay, I'll check my calendar and see what we can arrange."

"Any time. I'd love to hear more about your plans."

He paid attention to her easy way with people. It was informal but gracious, even with those she didn't know. A good quality in a collaborator. No pretentious airs—at least none that had seen.

Rita entered with another woman. She saw him and he noticed the way the women exchanged glances as they approached him. It reminded him of high school girls who shared each other's sweaters, secrets if not ex-boyfriends.

"Bob, I so happy to see you," Rita said. "I hoped our paths would cross."

"Hello," he said, rising to his feet. He didn't want to prolong their meeting, especially not after the come-on in the IGA. She used sex to get what she wanted in high school and he doubted her skill had dimmed with age. He wondered if she told Taylor about their romance. Bragging about her conquests was another side of Rita. Relations with her husband were complicated enough without throwing in jealousy.

"Bob, this is Madeline Barnes. Maddie, this is *Doctor* Bob Hartwell. We went together in high school. He's just moved back from San Francisco."

"I'm happy to meet you," he said, captivated by Madeline's dark, soulful eyes framed by sharply arched eyebrows like wings in flight. "Please join me." he said, unable to look away.

"Maddie is my best friend," Rita said, taking charge as if the mistress of ceremonies. "She's my financial adviser. Knows everybody in Waterford, too. Involved in everything, aren't you? I can tell you she knows the movers and shakers. You two oughta get acquainted."

"Yes, I see… Thanks," he said, grateful for Rita's suggestion. He quickly pulled a chair out for Madeline. "Tell me about you," he said as he seated her. Her dark hair framed a heart-shaped face with a short nose and full lips. Small, golden hoops adorned her ears.

"Did you grow up here?" He felt his palms begin to sweat.

"I came from California. Sonoma to be exact. I don't have a big backstory," she replied in a soft voice. "I graduated in finance from U-Cal Berkely, worked for a vintner and then moved here ten years ago."

He listened, wishing to be alone with her. Her gentle, liquid voice, sincere in its timbre, formed words that seemed to come straight from the heart. Felicia was like that and Madeline radiated a similar authenticity. In an instant, his mind filled with the many questions he wanted to ask her until he was struck tongue-tied.

"Bob, did I mention Justin is hosting a barbecue? I did, didn't I?" Rita interrupted. "Please come. It'll be quite the deal. And don't let Justin put you off. I told him you're all right. That we've known each other a long time. If you get to know him, you might find a way to work this out then."

"Did you know Norm Becker?"

The question startled her. "Not really. I doubt he would recognize me. Why?"

"Well, your husband said Becker got my property by adverse possession and sold it to him. But that's not true. He rented the property. Our contracts prove adverse possession is impossible. I don't know what Norm thought or did but if he said he owned my land it's untrue. I'm afraid he pulled a fraud on your husband."

Rita squirmed in her chair and glanced sidelong at Madeline. "I guess I don't know about that," she said. "Justin bought Becker's farm before we married. I'm not involved in his business," she said abruptly and got to her feet. "I'm sorry Bob, but you guys will have to work it out. Maddie and I have to talk over some money matters. So, please excuse us then. But come to the barbecue if you feel like it."

"Thank you but *uh*… what kind of barbecue is it… I mean, who's coming?"

41

"Oh you know, friends like Maddie, the neighbors and cattlemen. It's a field day to show off the benefits of rotational grazing. There'll be tours. It'll be a good way to know Justin."

"I'll come if I can," he said but didn't mean it. "Madeline, a pleasure to meet you."

As the women walked toward a distant table, Rita glanced over her shoulder and they briefly made eye contact before she passed beyond his line of sight.

He finished the panini and tea and left without looking back. Rita gave him the jitters. He recalled how she used to keep him doing whatever she wanted. If she told Taylor they were old friends, it was like her to tell her husband she had invited him to the barbecue. He wondered if she was playing them against each other. But why? It made no sense. Taylor struck him as one who expected blind loyalty if not obedience. *Not Rita's style. If she's shopping for a new conquest, it won't be me.*

Hartwell walked home thinking of Madeline. Then it hit him like a brick. Widowed six months and already thinking about another woman! *How could I do such a thing? No one can replace Felicia.* His shame lasted a few minutes before his thoughts returned to an inventory of Madeline. A petite woman. Heart-shaped face. Midforties. A few silver strands in her bobbed hair. Looking into her eyes was like drinking a cocktail he couldn't get enough of. Rita was still a minx but not Madeline. She was genuine and personable, self-contained and assured. Her reserved air was a little mysterious but it added to her beauty. He entered his house, looked up Madeline's phone number and wrote it down. *Madeline is going to the barbecue. So am I.*

"What kind of person is Bob?" Maddie asked when she finished reviewing Rita's finances. He didn't come off like the men she knew in Waterford. There was gentleness in his interests and the words he used. "You've known him a long time, haven't you?" she said, pushing a lock of dark hair behind her ear.

"Well…" Rita said, surprised at the question. "We dated in high school. The Army drafted him after graduation and we both moved on after that. I didn't see him again until last week. He's still good looking and gentle but not as shy. He intended to be an engineer."

"And the Army was the gateway into medicine."

"I guess so." Rita paused and giggled. "In high school I taught him about biology—you know, birds and bees." She beamed. "Anyway, we learned that together."

Madeline frowned. "He seems like a good man but I noticed sadness in his eyes."

"Yeah. His wife died last winter. I think he needs a sympathetic friend."

"Is that you?"

"God, no. I've got too much trouble with Justin and so does he. Besides that, I get a feeling he wants some distance from me. I don't know why, but it's there. However, he needs a friend." Their lunches arrived and they ate in silence for a minute before they resumed talking about other things.

Madeline left when they finished but Rita lingered over coffee and stared at a poster on the wall. *I'm a fool with men. Gerhard ignored my slutty past and loved me for me. Then he left me a lot of money. It was fun being the merry widow. But Maddie was right about Justin. His country boy charm was an act. He loves cows. I need a friend as much as Bob does. I'd go with him in a heartbeat if only… if only he had returned right after Gerhard died.* She lingered on the thought and sipped her coffee. *Quit dreaming. You'll never marry Bob. Not now. Not ever.*

Rita left Waterford in her red Mustang and drove for an hour along the winding rural roads of the Wacouta Valley. She came to the junction with the Great River Road running along the Mississippi River and parked in a pull out. Standing by the railing, she watched tugboats muscling barges down the river. Riding the river would be fun, she thought. River or road, she wanted to keep going but this wasn't the time to leave. Not yet. Still too much to do. Turning around, she drove toward home and the wall of dark clouds piled on the western horizon. *Justin thinks I will transfer my money to his account. I won't. That's when the storm will break.*

Smelling sweat on her blouse, she stripped and, stood in the shower. She stayed longer than necessary in the spray and she imagined her marital problems swirling down the drain. Then she dabbed herself dry, applied skin cream and put on a silk robe that felt cool in the heat. Meanwhile, Justin came inside and sprawled on the sofa, pleased with his flattering profile in the latest *Minnesota Cattleman*.

"*Mmm*. I like your smell babe," he said as she entered the living room. "Lookin' at you gets my pecker hard. Let's—"

"—Down boy. I'm done sweating up the sheets with you."

"Hey, men have conjugal rights, you know. Old violins play the sweetest music."

"Forget it. I'm not in the mood for fiddling," she said over her shoulder on her way into the kitchen.

"Hey, what'd Madeline have to say?"

"We're solvent," she said over her shoulder. "Solvent but the farm carries too much debt for the projected cattle sales."

"She's a scaredy cat. I know more about money than you or Maddie. Big money comes from taking risks. Besides that, she don't know nothin' about cattle. I'm all right. Did you combine out funds today?"

"No, I didn't."

"When's that gonna happen?"

"*Never*! I told you—I'm not gonna do it. She believes it's a bad idea from both our standpoints. I agree with her. You keep yours and I'll keep mine. We'll contribute equally to the household expenses just as we do now."

"*No*!" He threw down the magazine and jumped to his feet. "No. I told you… a man and his woman should have only one account. And no secrets. And that's how it's gotta be."

"Yell all you want. I won't do it." She turned and stared into his eyes. He had a loud bark but she didn't believe he would bite.

"All right, sugar. Let's drop it for now. You look so sexy I'd plow through a stump looking at you." He winked at her but she turned her back.

Chapter 7

"Clouded future for Runyon Mineral Spring" led the June 21 issue of the *Statesman*. Boston's article introduced Hartwell as a Waterford native whose family once operated a health resort at the mineral spring. It described his vision for a wellness center and Taylor's claim to the same property through adverse possession. Ginger's editorial said a case of adverse possession raised fundamental questions of property rights for every rural resident.

The story and editorial pleased the doctor but he still thought Isaacs was moving too slowly. *Wait, wait, wait. The law's on my side. Why delay going to court? I can't afford that. A frigging waste of time.* Meade hadn't found Becker and that bogged down things even more. He exhaled to expel his frustration from jumping through hoops. *I should be calling the shots!*

Seated in a patio chair, he listened to the rapids until his temper cooled. Then he tried to put himself in Taylor's shoes. If he were the cattleman, he guessed he would stick to his claim since he paid for it. Becker was gone and he wouldn't want to admit being taken in by a fraud. *No, if I were in Taylor's shoes, I wouldn't give in. So... the sooner I go to court the better.*

Putting himself in Taylor's shoes clarified his thinking. The cattleman's attorney could easily claim he abandoned the property. That claim might be stronger if he couldn't describe it property in detail. Isaacs had never been there. And he hadn't seen it in fifteen years. If nothing else, it was time to refresh his memory of it.

"In fact—I'll go right now." He let out a happy "yip" at the idea of crossing Taylor's land uninvited. *So what?* It felt like giving the man his middle finger. "*Fuck you!*" he crowed as he laced his hiking shoes and picked up a rucksack with trail mix, a canteen and a camera. He glanced at the phone and considered asking for permission. Then he locked the house and got into the car. Asking was tantamount to admitting the validity of Taylor's claim.

Hartwell drove north out of Waterford on County Road 5 and turned east onto County Road 4 that separated Taylor's woods from a tract of state-owned hardwood forest. After two miles he pulled onto the shoulder. A broad winged hawk lifted off a fencepost and circled above him when he got out of the car. Leaning on the barbed wire, he reconsidered the wisdom of trespassing. Pointless. Besides, two miles of woods separated him from Taylor's yard. He crawled under the fence and moved down the swale along the edge of the trees with the easy stride of an inveterate hiker. The exercise loosened his stress and he felt his case would turn out all right.

The swale ran south to the lip of the escarpment where it poured through a cleft in the ledge and cascaded thirty feet to the valley floor. He pause a moment on the ledge and then scrambled down the muddy chute and under the fence at the northeast corner of his land. Hartwell hiked along the belt of trees at the base of the ridge. He noticed the hayfield was choked with uncut alfalfa and weeds were invading the ungrazed pasture. After a mile, he crawled through the fence that had kept Becker's cattle out of the spring and the sanatorium.

The small cavern amplified the spring's gush and the sound sent shivers down his back. Water emerged from a crack in the limestone ice cold and gin clear. It filled the narrow channel choked with watercress and flanked by ferns and sedges, buttercups and violets. It appeared much as he had recalled it. Dropping to his knees, he cupped water in his hands and lapped it like a kitten. Its taste was something he had never forgotten.

He wiped his eyes and shrugged off the rucksack. "I'm back," he sobbed and his shoulders trembled. Seated on the sedgy ground among the wild iris, he saw it with a boy's sense of wonder. "I was born for

46

this," he whispered, repeating Horatio's words over and over. "Destiny chose me for this."

Hours passed as he sat by the spring and imagined the people who used to come to the resort to restore their health. And then to the sanatorium at a time when tuberculosis killed thousands of Minnesotans each year. It was one of many state sanatoriums that treated the infected by isolating them and providing sunshine, fresh air and a good diet. Horatio was ahead of his time, he mused. Tuberculosis was once the biggest killer. Now heart attacks, strokes and hypertension take a greater toll. He thought it ironic that modern treatments still relied on fresh air, a healthy diet and relaxation. The evolution from health resort to sanatorium to a center for wellness and meditation seemed natural. Destiny was real.

As he recalled, the sanatorium housed about 100 patients with a medical staff that lived in cottages. Those houses were hauled away during World War II but the concrete foundations lurked in the undergrowth. The sanatorium was the decrepit shell of a rectangular two-story brick and wooden building with a sagging roof. It had thirty-two windows on each side and double openings for doors at either end. None of the windows had glazing and all the doors were gone. The patchy shingles on the wooden mansard roof reminded him of toupees. He had hoped to incorporate some parts of the original building into the new one for continuity's sake. Studying the building as he would a patient, he saw there remained little to salvage. Still, he could reuse some of the bricks as a palimpsest of the past. That meant the center would take more time and materials than he first thought. Removing his cap and rubbing his head, he wondered if it was worth the cost. Taylor was willing to buy him out but there weren't other places like this one. *Is this a pipedream—a fool's errand? No. I'm the fourth generation dedicated to the health of others.* "No, by God, I won't let this fail!" he shouted and heard his words echo from the wall.

The afternoon was well advanced when he entered the building. Floorboards groaned and glass shards crunched underfoot. Broken bottles, crushed beer cans, cardboard cartons and piles of leaves littered the spaces that were once rooms. Faded graffiti marked the interior walls. Where the plaster peeled off the lathes it left behind the repulsive sight of a flensed corpse. The wooden staircase appeared too decayed to climb. Continuing down the corridor, he thought it miraculous that no one had torched the building. Still, there was so little to salvage.

He searched among the weeds around the building for the three stone basins where patients had soaked in mineral water. Finding one, he cleared away the accumulation of dead grass, weeds and sticks. The basin was intact and could be used once it had new plumbing to bring in water. With fists on his hips, he surveyed the site. *All right. I'll rebuild. It's what Horatio wanted.*

The doorway at the building's west end seemed larger than the others. Either Becker or Taylor enlarged it, judging by the tire tracks that ran from the doorway across his property. He walked a few hundred yards along the tracks to the new gate and saw the tire marks continued across Taylor's pasture and up the escarpment to his yard a half mile away.

Entering the sanatorium, Hartwell noticed Taylor or his men had cleared the leaves and trash from the floor by the enlarged door. Squatting, he plucked bits of hay from the cracks in the floor boards. He brushed away some tufts of dried grass from the doorstep and sat to consider a puzzling question. Taylor owned five barns. All of them were closer to his cattle than the sanatorium. Storing hay inside it made no sense. And if Taylor owned this property, it seemed odd he didn't pasture cattle there or cut the hay. Then he gave up because it didn't matter. Taylor was trespassing.

Morales noticed a flash of sunlight off something shiny at the sanatorium. It was too far to see clearly so he entered the office and focused the binoculars. *Oye, el rico con el Mercedes*, he thought as he watched Hartwell leave the sanatorium and walk along the tracks to the gate and then return to the sanatorium.

As the foreman, he knew what *Jefe* expected of him. Getting into a gray GMC pickup, he bounced down the escarpment to the gate trailing a cloud of dust. He opened the glove box, removed an automatic pistol and stuck it in his pocket. Then he passed opened the gate and strode toward the building.

"¡*Oye*! *Estás no permitido… largese!*" You aren't allowed he yelled in Spanish.

"This is *my* property," Hartwell yelled back, planting both fists on his hips. "I have a right to be here."

Morales approached. *No. No permitido. Mueve tu culo. No retorno*, he yelled back, meaning get your ass out of here and don't return. "*Si no…*" He patted the pistol butt and spit.

"Your gun doesn't scare me," he sneered. "I was a combat soldier. I've killed men." Then he casually slung the pack over a shoulder and gave the foreman his back. "I'll be back. Next time, I'll bring the law."

With his hand still on the pistol butt, Morales watched him saunter away. ¡*Maldición*! Goddamn-it he said under his breath. He resented the man's cool show of contempt. He glared at Hartwell's back until he vanished among the trees along the escarpment. Then he returned to the pickup. *El rico* presented a serious problem.

Hartwell felt himself bursting with anger as he sauntered along faking an indifference he didn't feel. When he knew Morales could no longer see him, he released his rage in a furious jog to the crevice. The sun set before he reached the chute and he scrambled up the escarpment in the twilight. It was dark when Hartwell arrived at his car tired, dirty and out of breath.

"Isaacs will hear about this," he hissed over and over as he drove. "I ought to call the sheriff, too." Driving cooled his anger enough to suppose the foreman was just carrying out orders. He couldn't blame him for that. The man didn't know the facts. But unresolved anger dies slowly and Hartwell's rekindled on Monday morning. The foreman had threatened him. Or tried to intimidate him. He was determined to file a complaint when he pounded up the Heath Building stairs faster than usual. Isaacs met him at the landing.

"Good morning, Bob, how about—"

"—One of Taylor's men ordered me off my property," he said. "He had a gun—"

"—Did he point it at you?"

"No. It was in his pocket but he patted the butt. How do I file a complaint?"

"Hold on, hold on," he said, raising both hands. "Is his property posted? Did you ask his permission to go in?"

"Yes, it's posted. Signs everywhere. And, no, I didn't ask permission."

"So, you trespassed on his property." Isaacs studied him, firm in his assessment of the doctor's impulsive streak. "Sit down. I wouldn't file a complaint considering Taylor believes your property is his and that you trespassed. This will only complicate your case."

"He's using the building for something. I got photos."

"Good. Now, you have retained me to resolve your case. I'm working to bring it about. It will move quicker if you avoid confrontations and take direction from me," he said in a parental voice. "Next time, ask permission to enter. If he denies it, we have one more reason to press him. Either way, it hurts his case. Don't let trespassing undermine yours."

Chapter 8

Boston thought Becker's former neighbors h knew where he had moved to. There would be Christmas cards, letters or phone calls. All the farmers within the Taylor's quadrangle had left Waterford. His next best hope was asking those who lived across the county road from Otto and Becker. They had to know where the Beckers went.

"Who are you calling?" Ginger asked that evening as she passed the den.

"Becker's neighbors. They might know where he is."

"So, you *are* getting into an investigation, aren't you?"

"Yeah." He removed his glasses. "I'm calling strangers. Not as thrilling as it was interning for the *Statesman*."

"I remember. You were full of yourself, then. I like you better this way." She went into the living room to read.

"It's a crapshoot. I've got a sick feeling it will take a while. No idea what I'll learn—if anything." He dialed anyway, knowing even one call could lead to another and then another. No one had all the answers. Or any answers. Or only more questions.

A man answered and asked who was calling.

"Boston Meade. I'm trying to reach Norm Becker or Hans Otto."

"Oh? What about 'em?"

"Do you know where either moved to?"

"Why do you want to know?"

"Either man can clear up some questions about the status of the town road."

51

"I don't know where Norm is," he said, easing his tone. "Couldn't believe he'd sell his place. He left without saying a word. Not even goodbye. He told me once they might go someplace warm, like Arizona someday. Maybe buy one of them motorhomes so he and Velva could travel all the time. That was a couple years ago. They sent us a postcard from Kansas City. Said they retired and were on their way. He never ever hinted at anything like that, though. Last I saw was his car leaving early one day with a U-Haul truck behind it. Otherwise, I don't know."

"And Otto? Any contact with him?"

"No. Don't know where he's at. His kids live in Arkansas." The man cleared his voice.

"What can you tell me about him?"

"Good people. We were friends but we were a closer with the Beckers."

"How is it that Otto left?"

"Well, like the rest of us, he was mortgaged for operating loans. A bad deal after land values tanked and interest rates rose. He was in a squeeze, that's for sure. Ya know, he coulda made it if his cows hadn't a died. That's when he went under. Then Taylor bought his place. Hans told us he was going south, gonna live with his kids until he could buy a place. He felt bad over losin' his farm. That was the year after Wilkes left and Scribner died. We couldn't believe it. After each sold out, Taylor knocked down the houses and burned up the wreckage."

"What about the road to the old sanatorium—was it in regular use?"

"Well, hell yes. Every day. Graveled and graded every coupla years. It's that gate. A real sore point with some folks, includin' me. Since he owns all the land behind it I don't see any point to fussin' about it."

Last night's brief call didn't give Boston what he wanted. He made a date with Becker's neighbor on the south side of Runyon Valley. Talking face-to-face he might learn more. On his way, he stopped at the Runyon Spring Road where cattle grazed behind the gate. The road appeared in good repair. Satisfied, he drove on to the next mailbox and up the slope to the yard. From atop the yard, he saw all the farms that used to belong to Larson, Scribner, Otto and Becker. He got out of the Jeep and into the humid air filled with the odor of hog manure and the squeals of feeding pigs.

"Nice to meetcha," the stocky farmer said as he galumphed toward him in unbuckled goulashes. He had a pink face and held out a huge paw.

"Thanks for the invitation."

"Not at all. So, let's go in the house," he invited. "We can talk over coffee then." The farmer left his rubber boots outside but the faint odor of hogs followed him into the kitchen. "Wish my wife were home. She mighta had something to add."

"Your corn and beans look good," Boston said, nodding thanks for the coffee. "See any improvement over last year's prices?" Grain prices had nothing to do with Becker but such questions usually created rapport. "And how about hogs?"

"Can't complain. It could always be worse, ya know. Hogs futures are pretty good right now. As for corn… well, I've seen worse, I guess. At least the interest rates are dropping a little and prices are up a bit. 'Bout time, too. It's been a tough five years."

Each took a gulp from their coffee mugs. Boston set his down first.

"As I said, I want to get in touch with Otto and Becker. Do you know where they are?"

"No, damn-it. Me and Norm were really close friends. I mean thick—or so I thought," he said, lacing his calloused fingers together. "Hans and his woman were fine, too. But we and the Beckers… well we had Sunday night dinners, played canasta and took some vacations together. He never hinted he was gonna sell. And didn't need too neither. He had money and no debt. They never said goodbye. My wife still isn't over Velva leaving like that."

"Did he ever talk about retiring or what he would do?"

"No. Say, what's with all these questions?"

"I'm trying to help the owner of the mineral spring get access to it."

"Oh for… it's that damned gate." The farmer leaned back.

"That's part of it. I'm told Becker got title to the tract after using it for thirty years. By adverse possession. Then he sold it to Taylor."

"No way!" He scowled. "That don't sound like somethin' Norm would do."

"That's why we want to talk to him. Clear it up."

"*Hmm.* Don't sound like him at all. He told me he was rentin' it but, well…"

"The owner can prove he rented it so he still owns it but he can't get access—"

"—That's because Taylor owns all the land on both sides of that road and chairs the town board, too. Just between you and me," and the farmer dropped his voice, "I s'pect he got a quiet okay to gate the road. But that's my opinion."

"So, you had no idea they intended to move?" he asked, surprised at the revelation.

"Nope. One day in May of last year, I seen their car and a big box truck pull onto the county road and head for Waterford. The gate went up a week or so later. Taylor sold Norm's dairy cows and auctioned off the machinery after harvest."

"Did you hear from them after that?

"Got a postcard from Kansas City. Real short message. Somethin' like, 'Sold the farm. Retired. On our way.' That was it. Never another word. No Christmas card, nothin'. I just don't understand 'em leavin' like that. I feel betrayed, ya know?"

"Do you know Taylor?"

"Not really. Met him a time or two at a Farm Bureau meeting. Can't say I know him. Just the same, I don't…" he shook his head and looked away "He's got a… well, you can tell he wasn't raised in Minnesota. Anything else?"

"Not right now. I'll let you know if I hear anything about Becker."

"Thanks. I'd appreciate that. Come back anytime."

Chapter 9

"How was your day?" Ginger asked as she entered the kitchen where Boston was chopping carrots. He didn't reply or even turn his head. The taut muscles in his jaw combined with his intense concentration told her he was sitting on something. *Stuffing it, as usual. He still can't let it out.* "*Hey*! How was your day?" she asked, louder this time.

He looked up, scowled and pulled his face in on itself. "I wasted the whole day looking for a lead to Becker." He set the salad bowl and steaming casserole on the table. "One dead end after another." He threw up his hands and returned to the kitchen, muttering to himself.

"Why don't you call the movers?" She tossed the salad and ladled some beans and rice into a bowl "The company might have a record of where they went. It's just a suggestion," she added in a softer voice, "…it might work."

"Why didn't I think of that?"

"Because you're too locked inside your head. Geez Louise, loosen up will ya."

He knew she was right as soon as she said it. Of course, the movers would know. His early morning call to the U-Haul 800 number entered a holding queue. Waiting for the next available agent felt like entering a lottery. Someone might answer or not. Minutes ticked by and he regretted taking the assignment. A huge waste of time, so far. With the receiver cradled on his shoulder and ear, he scribbled notes on a chapter for his book. Finally an agent answered.

"This is Boston Meade. I work for a Minnesota attorney. He needs to contact one of your customers as a witness in a legal matter."

"I'm sorry, sir. Customer information is confidential."

"But it's a legal matter."

"I'm sorry. I can't give you that information without a subpoena."

"Okay. Let's work something out. How about you contact the customer, give him my number and ask him to call me?" He held his breath.

"Well… all right. Give me his name and your number. It might be a week before one of us gets back to you."

Boston fidgeted for several days as he waited. He snapped at Ginger when she urged him to practice patience. Hanging around the house while waiting for a call added to his irritation. When he couldn't stand waiting, he called the U-Haul agent. "This is Boston Meade, I—"

"—Oh… yeah, I was about to call you. Sorry, we've been swamped. It's a busy season you know, Lots of moving. Yeah, Becker ordered a twenty-six-foot box truck and—"

"—When was that?"

"*Uh*… May tenth of eighty-five. Picked it up in Rochester. Paid with a cashier's check."

"From what bank?"

"Cornerstone Bank of Rochester. He never dropped the unit in Yuma. It's still missing."

"Did you report it to the police?"

"Yeah, per routine. It hasn't turned up."

He hung up, stumped. He fished out the address Taylor gave Hartwell and called directory assistance in Yuma. He hoped a different operator could find Becker. Then he listened as the operator scanned through the directories. There was no Norman Becker listed in the greater Yuma area including the towns of Wickenburg, Tonopah, Gila Bend and Tortilla Flat. Boston slammed down the receiver. Was it time to throw in the towel?

He took his crankiness and a glass of iced tea to the veranda. "*Yugh*," he muttered at the air heavy with the afternoon's humidity.

"It feels like buttermilk—definitely oleaginous." Then he took some cheer at the sight of the approaching blue-black thunderclouds. He raised his glass in a salute to the storm and hoped it would bring a cool wind to flush the heat from the house. Thunder rumbled far off with a sound like rocks rolling down a chute. Minute by minute, the thunderclaps got louder, lightning ripped across the sky and the daylight dimmed to an early dusk. Light rain pattered softly on the veranda roof and then Ginger arrived. The shower became a torrent in her short dash between her car and the house.

"*Ugh*! I'm soaked!" she cried.

He leered at her standing there in a wet, semi-transparent blouse. "You've won the wet tee shirt contest."

"Oh, fuck you!" She raised her middle finger and rushed inside. After a change of clothes, she returned blotting her hair with a towel. "Well, how was today?"

"Like yesterday. I'll bitch about it over supper," he said and led her to the table as the wind whipped the rain into gray sheets.

"Oh, leftovers, my favorite," she said and poured herself a glass of sparkling water. "You were going to bitch about…"

"Becker is a missing person's case." Boston stabbed his salad for emphasis. "He didn't tell anyone he was leaving. Didn't say goodbye. Sent postcards from Kansas City. He rented a U-Haul van with a cashier's check and never returned the van. There's no Becker in Yuma. He's covered his tracks."

"So, if he's not in Yuma…?"

"I don't know. Here to Yuma is a four-day drive."

"What do you think?" She knit her brows and nibbled on salad.

"Everyone said he was in good financial shape. But people in trouble usually hide that sort of thing. At least at first. He sold his farm and Hartwell's land with it. Either something happened to them between Kansas City and Yuma or the Yuma address was a dodge so they couldn't be followed. It makes sense if he in fact pulled a fraud. So, I have to consider the possibility they assumed new identities and settled elsewhere. I'm leaning toward that theory."

He and Ginger cleaned up the dishes and then she left the house for her weekly AA meeting at the Lutheran church. It was still raining lightly at 9:00 p.m. when she returned, relaxed but tired. "Learn anything?"

"No. It doesn't make sense," he said. If the Beckers are living somewhere else then they weren't who everyone believed them to be."

"I know this," she said, looking him in the eyes and shaking her head. "You won't rest until you find them. Or what happened to them, will you?"

"Guess not," he conceded. "But I'm done with it for today."

"Good. Let's go to bed so I can work on your libido. You'll feel better in the morning."

Boston woke at dawn in a chipper mood after Ginger's ministrations. He jogged a mile and a half along the county road below the house as far as the crossroads at the House of Truth, a rural tavern, and returned. He fixed their breakfast while she said her prayers and worked through her yoga routine. It was still early when she headed to the *Statesman's* office and he returned to his den and the phone.

A fast-growing retiree Mecca like Yuma had to have a lot of realtors, he thought. One was all he needed. Directory assistance surprised him with the numbers of a dozen large realty agencies. His first three calls went to answering machines.

"Gladstone Realty," someone answered. "Let me help you find a new home."

"Thanks. I'm Boston Meade, a private investigator in Minnesota." *Private investigator?* The words popped out of his mouth without a thought. "I'm looking for a couple who said they were moving to Yuma. I can't find a phone number. They're needed here on a legal matter."

"You mean, they're in trouble?"

"No. Witnesses in a civil matter. Will you double-check an address for me?"

"Sure. Give me the address," the realtor said, excited.

"It's 48115 Yaqui Drive. Norman Becker. He would have bought it in early May of eighty-five. I could be mistaken about the house number."

"Hold on, I'll look at a city plat." The realtor put down the phone and Boston heard paper rustling. "Yeah, there's a Yaqui Drive all right, but it's in one of those subdivisions that didn't pan out… know what I mean?"

"You mean dirt streets and vacant lots in the chaparral?"

"Yep. Desert Shores is in receivership. Savings and loan crisis killed it. Call Sunburst Federal in Phoenix. They're the receiver. They'd have a record if those folks bought a lot."

The call to Sunburst Federal became a series of automated responses with instructions to press one for home loans, two for… and on through options he didn't want. After an hour, including twenty minutes on hold, he talked with an actual person who transferred him to someone else who asked if he owned property at Desert Shores.

"No, I'm an investigator tracking someone who may have bought a lot there. We need to contact that person for a civil matter in Minnesota." He gave him the address on Yaqui Drive.

"I'm going to put you on hold while I check," the agent said. "*Don't* hang up."

Private investigator. Didn't take long to call myself that. But that's what I've always been. He clenched his teeth and listened to a loop of dumbed down Beetle's tunes. The agent returned a few minutes later.

"No one named Becker bought that or any other lot. I'm sorry."

"Can you tell me if anyone owned it?"

"Nope. No one. It never sold."

Jester galloped to the front door, followed by "I'm ho-*ome*—I'm hong-*gree*." Ginger kicked off her flats and entered the den barefoot. "Hi, lover." She gave him a kiss. "How was your day?"

"Dialing for details," he said with an exasperated sigh. "Or dialing in desperation. Or dialing for dead ends. The day got away from me. I haven't started supper. Sorry."

"That's okay. I'm hungry but not for anything hot or complicated—unless it's *you*."

"Thanks," he laughed. "I got sidetracked. How about a fruit salad…? I can cut up a watermelon, cantaloupe and some Colorado peaches."

"Perfect. Let me make supper. I can tell you're frustrated. You've had another one of those days," she said, trotting up the stairs. Five minutes later she returned in a spaghetti strap summer dress. *He can be so hard to read,* she thought while slicing the fruit. *Never know what's going on inside. If he'd just open up. Quit living in his head. At least he noticed this skimpy dress. That's encouraging … maybe we… two nights in a row*!

"Anything wrong?" She buttered a slice of rye bread and took a bite.

"Nothing except this Becker business is getting darker."

"How can it get darker?"

He took her hand and led her to the porch. "Here's the dark stuff. The Beckers said no goodbyes. There's no house at the Yuma address. They didn't even own a lot. No one did. And the U-Haul vanished. So, either they have taken a new identity or something happened to them or… or I don't know squat. The only motive for hiding seems to be selling a bogus claim of adverse possession. That's the only reasonable explanation."

"Why do you say it's dark?"

"Everyone who sold to Taylor was bankrupted by a disaster *except* Becker—or so I'm told." He arched his back and then resettled in the rattan chair. The Beckers weren't in financial trouble. At least, so their friends say. So—"

"—Is it possible the Beckers were working with Taylor, somehow?"

"I never thought of that! If they were, it would explain a lot of things."

"I have a feeling you're going to involve the *Statesman*. Just remember our agreement," she said, guarding her editorial prerogatives as foreplay more than power play.

"You read my mind. But not yet. I haven't talked to Jack. He won't touch it until there's something solid. Right now, what I don't know is growing faster than what I do know—which isn't much."

"I know your instincts are good. Keep me posted, but no surprises—"

"—Well of course not," he said, scowling at her.

"All right. How about you stop sleuthing for tonight. You haven't played the piano in weeks and I feel like singing." She grabbed his hand and led him to the baby Steinway in the living room. "It might make you human again. After that..."

The polished Steinway surfaced memories of his mother, who taught him to play. He had accompanied Ginger during rehearsals for the high school musicals and then didn't play after he settled in Chicago. When he returned at his father's death, he poured his grief into the keyboard until he found his heart again. Just touching the keys soothed him.

"Any requests?" He cocked an eyebrow at Ginger. Her musical tastes ran to 1960s Patsy Cline and 1970s Carole King. He preferred Duke Ellington and Cole Porter.

"Play anything you want," she said. "You need a release."

He riffled the keys. She smiled and sang Gershwin's "Embraceable You."

Chapter 10

With the Fourth of July two days off, Ginger set out for Saint Paul to pick up Sister Meghan. If anyone could nudge Mama into seeing her, it was Meg. She tried to recall the last time they had spent four days together. At least ten years ago—before rehab. *Just after she pulled me back from… I'd be dead but for her. Mama brought me into the world but sis gave me life.* Then, tuning the car radio to a country station, she belted out songs with Loretta Lynn and Willie Nelson, feeling young, free and hopeful.

Anticipation swelled in Ginger's throat when she pulled up to the college convent and saw Sister Meghan Theresa O'Meara waiting on a shady bench. Dressed in a plain taupe skirt and jacket with a wooden cross, the stout woman with plain features looked every inch a nun. Ginger hopped out of the car, the nun rose from the bench and the sisters hugged and swayed with happy squeals and laughter. Then their words tumbled out of control as both tried to talk at once.

"I see you're happy," Meghan said, catching her breath. "It's obvious that living with Boston agrees with you. I'm glad—for both of you. I'm looking forward to seeing him."

"Well, he's all worried over the fact that we're, *uh…* you know… living in sin!" Ginger giggled and Meghan joined her laughter with a whinny. "You'll find him… *uh…* changed. He's not the stuck-up, arrogant ess-oh-bee you remember."

"I'm not surprised. You've changed, too. So have I. " She shook her head. "We're such different women."

"Oh really... how so?"

"You are a pixie, a Tinkerbell, a soul bursting with passion... always in motion. And me, well, I'm an overly contented, middle-aged sociology prof."

"*Ha!*" Ginger laughed. "Underneath it, you're the serious one. Always turning over the rocks. You call a spade a spade."

"Well, that's true but, if you disrupt my complacency, I'll thank God for that."

Then Ginger asked if she had heard from or seen their older brothers. "I get Christmas cards but not much news," she said with a sigh. "I don't remember when I last saw Cletus or Sean. Not since I got sober."

"I talk to them from time to time," Meghan said. "They're happy. Both have jobs since they retired from the Marines."

"That's more than I knew before," she said and turned off the four-lane to enter Featherstone. "I sure wish I could see them. Well, someday..."

Boston stepped off the veranda and welcomed them with a wide smile as Jester burst out the door. "Sister Meghan, our house is your house—and our dog is your dog."

Meghan took his outstretched hand and pulled him into a hug. Then, looking him in the eye with a scowl, "I don't want to hear 'sister' or 'Sister Meghan.' Just call me Meg. I want to feel like I'm part of a regular family."

"Suits me. Let's go inside," he said, picking up her satchel.

Ginger noticed her sister gawking at the huge house with its wraparound veranda, corner turret with leaded windows and second story dormers. Until now it was a house she had only seen from the road below. Once inside, she gaped at the living room and the massive fireplace, Persian rugs and the wide curving staircase that swept to the second floor.

"Come on, sis, let's get you settled." Ginger put her arm around Meghan and walked her to the guest room. "While we're doing that, my manservant will prepare our supper."

"You always believed you'd live here," Meghan said later as they sat on the veranda and watched the evening shadows spill across the countryside. "Now you do. Your dream has come true. And Boston, what are you doing if you're not running the *Statesman*?"

"Staying out of Ginger's way and—"

"—and making my life comfortable." She blew him a kiss.

"Look, I know you two have a lot to catch up on," he said, rising from the rattan chair. "I'll do the dishes and say good night. Meg, I'm glad you're here."

*
**

Up at daybreak, Boston made a large pot of coffee, set out cups for the sisters and took his mug to the veranda. With his feet on the railing, he listened to the jays and pheasants, hogs and cows greet the rising sun. Then a cup rattled in the kitchen followed by soft footsteps and the squeak of the screen door behind him.

"Good morning, sweetheart," he said tenderly without looking back.

"*Mmm*. Thank you. I never hear sweetheart in the convent."

He bolted out of the chair feeling a warm flush on his cheeks. "I thought you were—"

"—Oh, sit down," Meghan said, waving her hand. "It's time to get over your fear of nuns. We aren't really supernatural, you know— not unless you want us to be." She dragged a chair close to him and they drank coffee quietly as the countryside awoke. "You're good for her, you know." She patted his arm. "You give her stability. She's sober, happy and finally the person God created her to be."

"Thanks, but you did more than anyone. She's a force of nature who's good for me, too."

"As you know, we're from a dysfunctional family." She said, staring into her coffee mug, her brow furrowed. "Daddy was a weak, happy drunk. Mama was and still is unforgiving and harder than flint. She was determined to have social status and tried the only way she knew… make her sons become priests. So, they rebelled and joined the Marines," she shook her head. "Then Mama insisted that Ginger and I take the habit. Well… you know how that turned out."

"Do you regret the habit?"

"Not one bit. My life has a purpose and stability."

"Are you in touch with your brothers?"

"Yeah. More now that... well, family ties take on greater importance as you get older. They're married, divorced, remarried and have children and grandchildren I've never met. I want to see them. I haven't seen Mama in four years... that's terrible, I know." She lowered her voice. "We're going to see her today. If you're comfortable, tell me how it is between Ginger and Mama. I'm worried. Ginger's troubles have always been tied to Mama's disapproval."

He thought about what to say. A barn swallow pipped and dipped in front of them. "She's still hurt that Mama hasn't said her name and always asks for you—her nun. She accepts it because she can't change it."

"I'm glad she's realistic. Mama will see both her girls, but I worry about her reaction."

"What's the worst that can happen?"

"Mama has a spiteful side," she said, grasping her cross.

"Ginger told me that, too. Many times. Two years ago she asked me if it was immoral to pray for an end to Mama's suffering. You know, not asking for a miracle but for a swift, peaceful end... in God's good time, of course. I was in my own misery then. And not knowing what to say, I said her choice to suffer along with Mama while dedicated to her welfare seemed Christlike. I think we learned that in catechism. Anyway, Ginger can face anything."

"You did learn that in catechism. Thank you for being her, her... What are you... companion, friend, lover? What are you two?"

"Explorers."

They laughed together.

"How about pilgrims," Meghan suggested.

"That works, too. We are mapping a relationship one day at a time."

Hearing Ginger in the kitchen ended the conversation. She joined them, still in her pajamas. "What are you two doing... talking behind my back, I suppose."

"Well, of course," Meghan laughed. "It's more fun that way. Your manservant needs new glasses, though. He called me 'sweetheart' thinking it was you. Should've seen him blush."

"Do you want breakfast now or after prayers," Boston said to change the subject. "I assume you two will have prayers."

"Let's eat after prayers. Aren't you joining us?" Meghan asked.

"I'll listen while I'm cooking," he said. The sisters stayed on the veranda. From the kitchen, he heard them begin, "In the name of the Father, the Son…" Without thinking, he crossed himself, surprised and then embarrassed that he had responded to the liturgy he thought he had all but forgotten. That's the thing about Catholic formation, he thought. It goes so deep nothing can eradicate it.

A half-hour later, they sat down to breakfast and Meghan said a prayer. Then she looked at them with a twinkle in her eye and started telling nun jokes with the timing of a stand-up comic. She kept them in stitches with stories of convent life until Boston imagined her in a Chicago club. Of course, she would be funnier in the starchy black and white habit. When she finished joking, she said a prayer of thanks and the sisters left for the nursing home giggling like schoolgirls.

He spent the morning cleaning the kitchen. When the women didn't return for lunch he took it as a hopeful sign and mowed the lawn. Then he weeded the flower beds, grateful for a mindless respite from seeking Becker. It was nearly 5:30 p.m. before the women returned as boisterous as sailors on shore leave.

"We painted the town!" Ginger cried in triumph. "We ate at the Streamliner, went by the school and stopped at Holy Name to see Father Frank. Then we stopped at the *Statesman* so I could do a couple chores."

"It was great!" Meghan agreed. "I love the family photos in your office. You do resemble your father. I see it in your profiles."

"Thanks," he said, grateful she saw only the physical likeness to his father. Professional comparisons hadn't always pleased him. As he carried a pitcher of lemonade to the veranda he thanked God their day wasn't an emotional train wreck.

"Oh, get yourself a whiskey," Ginger said. "This is a celebration."

"That's okay," he demurred. "How was Mama today?"

"A miracle," Ginger cried with misty eyes. "A miracle, a fucki'—"

"Hey, watch your language, your sister is present—"

"—Guess where I learned it?" The women laughed.

"Tell me about it," he said and lit the charcoal to grill chicken and sweetcorn.

"Yeah well, Mama did a double take when we entered her room. Her eyes had a flash of light I never saw before. A spark of recognition. She saw *me*! And—" Ginger's voice cracked.

"—Mama said, 'my girls, my girls,'" Meghan continued. "She didn't call my name or Ginger's but she said, 'my girls, my girls.' That's something."

"I'm glad," he said in a husky voice. "A real miracle. This *does* call for whiskey—Irish."

"Good," Ginger said. "Fix one for Meg—and get yourself a Kleenex!"

He wiped his eyes on the way to the liquor cabinet, astonished at his tears of joy. Mama's coldness was an open sore in Ginger's life, a pain he could do nothing to lessen. In his tears he recognized that he had suffered with Ginger deeply but unconsciously. The realization gave him joy that he did suffer with her. Then he returned to the veranda and handed a glass to Meghan.

"It's Tullamore Dew," he said and raised his glass to them both. "An old Irish toast for ye—and Mama," he began. "Always remember to forget the things that made ye sad. But never forget to remember the things that made ye glad." They touched glasses. "*Erin go bragh!*"

Much later, when he and Ginger were in bed, he asked again how she felt.

"I can't put it into words," she said, snuggling next to him. "It's holy. It's a miracle, but it's not a cure. She might revert tomorrow. But she saw both of us—that means she saw *me.*"

He kissed her cheek. It was moist and salty.

Chapter 11

Jack Meade looked forward to summer because it meant barbecue and barbecue meant far more than grilling meat. As the orphaned child of a mixed-race Creole couple, preparing the meat and the sauces constituted a liturgy that resurrected childhood memories. The aroma of slow-cooked pork and brisket revived memories of his parents' voices as they prepared the sauces from unwritten recipes passed through the generations. When the Meades adopted him, he joined a white family whose notion of barbecue was limited to grilled meat sprinkled with salt, pepper and Worcestershire sauce. Fortunately, Mother Meade coached his youthful experiments blending chilis, garlic and molasses. He was fourteen when he hit on the mix of flavors that matched those of eidetic memory and tears of joy burst from the well of his soul. The rich, subtle flavors brought to life the spirit of his parents. Preparing the meat was as sacred as a Sunday Mass of joyous unity.

He entered the kitchen at daybreak humming to himself and did a light-footed dance. Then, he tested the mixture of paprika, salt, brown sugar, garlic, pepper, onion, and chiles that had steeped all night in the ceramic bowl and pitcher he inherited from his mother. After a quick taste, he added a little more paprika and garlic. After tasting the hot sauces steeped in beer, he smacked his lips, made a face and added several more dashes of hot sauce for the heat he wanted.

Rubbing the seasonings into the pork shoulder and ribs gave Jack the sensation his French, Spanish and African ancestors were watching him from the hereafter. The realization raised goosebumps along his muscular arms. Today of all days, his heart beat with pride as the custodian of their unique sapor.

His dusky complexion stood out in Alton County's population of pink-skinned descendants of German, Scandinavian and Polish immigrants. The long-ago schoolyard taunts of "Sambo" ended in third grade after he and Boston bloodied some noses. His popularity soared in adolescence when he led the Featherstone Falcons in back-to-back state football championships. Now he was serving his third term as the county sheriff. Despite the unspoken but still palpable racial prejudice in Alton County, he lived with a soulful sense of being fully himself—a Creole baptized Jacques Baptiste Dubois. Barbecue gave him a born-in-the-bone feeling of authenticity as a man of several races and cultures, even if being that man wasn't always easy.

He snapped on the kitchen radio while he rubbed the meat and hummed as The Supremes sang "Someday We'll Be Together."

"Jack!" Kris called from the bedroom. "It's too early for that."

"Okay, sorry." He took the meat, the sauces and the transistor radio to the backyard. Rocking to the music of Lionel Ritchie and Marvin Gaye, he taught his sixteen-year-old son Ben how to rub the meat and lay the fire. The brick smoker was his own construction and served as an altar where he grilled. When the charcoal glowed, he added hickory chunks and closed the lid for an hour until the hardwood coals attained incandescence. He reveled in the hiss of the pork striking the hot iron grate. It was just 9:00 a.m. The meat wouldn't be ready until mid-afternoon.

Kris slept in, a luxury for an emergency room nurse and then got up for a cup of coffee while still in her robe. She was a force in her own right with a soft heart for Boston. He and Jack were "her" men and neither seemed entirely complete without the other. She was a fearless mother, spouse and sister-in-law who took either man to task with equal ferocity. Loving Jack included loving Boston—and now Ginger.

Looking out the window, she smiled at the sight of Ben focused on the art of turning the meat so it cooked evenly. Her children would be culturally rich, she thought. Jack was instilling Ben with his heritage of Creole traditions, just as Kris was instilling Lily with her family's Polish traditions. That was a challenge because her thirteen-year-old daughter was a sweet child one moment and a willful adolescent the next, depending on her mood.

Marriage wasn't on her mind when she met Jack in a university psychology class. But she fell for his warmth and gentleness as much as his good looks. When the time came, her parents resisted, wanting her to "marry her own kind." She defied them, saying he was a Catholic and, therefore, her own kind. Blue-eyed grandchildren and Jack's barbecue soon convinced Pa and Ma Kaminiski that he was one of their own.

When the guests arrived, Jack took Meghan's hand in both of his and honored her request not to call her sister. "Are you really a nun?" Lily asked,, looking askance at Meghan. "You don't look like one."

Meghan laughed. "Yes, I am, Lily. Nuns exist to serve. We are best known by what we do, not by what we wear."

"Oh," Lily said, blushing. "I didn't know."

"Jack," Ginger said. "Meghan is doing criminology research. It might tie into your graduate studies."

"Really. I'd like to hear more about that."

"I teach sociology," Meghan said. "We have a grant to study the norms of prison culture. We're trying to identify the influences that return women to crime after release. We interview them at the prison. Most are convicted of theft or fraud. That makes it hard to find good jobs. Women have it hard enough even if they haven't been inside. So, there are both internal and external influences that lead them back to crime."

"I want to hear more but... *uh*... right now, I've got to get back to the meat. I know it's Friday but I hope you'll eat barbecued pork. C'mon boys," Jack said and headed toward the backyard. "Head's up," he yelled, tossing his brother a can of beer from the cooler. Then he opened one for himself.

"Smells great," Boston said, peering into the smoker. "How soon?"

"Another three hours or so."

71

"*Three* hours! My mouth is watering already." He pulled the tab on the can.

"Well, how is sleeping alone again with a nun under your roof?" Jack snickered.

"It's not an issue. Meg knows the score. So does Father Frank. I'm glad Meg's here. They saw their mom yesterday and she acknowledged Ginger existence."

"Well, hallelujah! I know it's been an open wound."

"Yeah." Boston took a slow swallow of beer. "I know you're off duty but I'd like your thoughts on a problem—"

"—*What now*? Another crime I don't need to know about." Jack squinted with a sparkle of humor in his dark eyes.

"I don't know," Boston said and recounted Hartwell's problems.

"I read the article. He needs a lawyer and Morrie's a good one."

"Well, Taylor chairs the town board and the clerk won't let Hartwell read the minutes."

"Oh Taylor. I know who you mean. Big guy. Came up from Texas. Lotta dough. Top bidder at some sheriff's sales. A lotta folks hate him for it. Envy, I guess." He lay in the hammock and squinted at Boston sprawled in a lawn chair. "So, what are you working on if not the road?"

"Morrie asked me to find Becker to clear up the question of adverse possession. The real question is whether he defrauded Taylor by selling him property he didn't own. There's no sign that the Runyon Spring Road was abandoned but Becker has vanished. His neighbors say he left last year without a goodbye. He left an address in Yuma that has turned out to be a vacant lot in a bankrupt project. Becker never turned in the rented van."

Jack sat up. "So, this is at least a missing persons case."

"Maybe. They left in May of eighty-five."

"Is it possible they had a fatal accident somewhere?"

"They left with a big truck and a car. Some friends got postcards from Kansas City but nothing after that. With two vehicles, it's not likely both died in an accident." Boston scratched his head. "Looks like the Yuma address is a dodge and they've settled elsewhere. It's possible they left in a rush before Taylor could discover the fraud. Then changed identities."

"*Hmm.*" Jack got up slowly and turned the meat. "All right, I'll have a deputy make some calls—as a favor. The more you can tell me, the better. Just don't drag me into it until you've got something solid."

"It's a deal," Boston held up the empty can as a request for another beer. "Midday and I'm already at the booze."

"That's not booze—that's a sandwich in a can. We'll hit the booze later. And don't worry about Ginger. She's tougher than you are."

"That's a fact."

Chapter 12

A steady stream of cars and pickups followed the pasteboard signs directing them to the Cattleman's Barbecue. A sign at the driveway said: "Taylor Land and Cattle Supports Future Farmers of America." Teens in polo shirts with 4-H and the FFA logos parked the cars and directed visitors. Most of the guests came as couples dressed in jeans, high-heeled boots and pre-creased straw hats. Small groups of guests enjoyed the valley view from the edge of the escarpment. Others gathered at the open bar and the barbecue pit where meat sizzled and smoked over a large bed of coals.

Taylor greeted his guests with a wide smile beneath his mustache. He wore a short-sleeved white shirt, high-heeled boots and a Stetson. "We'll start the tours in a few minutes," he said over the murmur of people enjoying themselves. Rita flitted from group to group like a butterfly, chatting easily but always casting an eye for arrivals. Hartwell stood out as he walked down the driveway and into the crowd dressed in crisp chinos and a ballcap embroidered with Redwoods National Park.

"Bob! Bob," Rita called. "I'm so glad you came." Heads turned toward Hartwell. She took his arm and stroked it. "I insist you relax and have a good time. You're among friends." Like many of the other women, she wore jeans, boots and a form-fitting blouse. "Justin is leading tours now. So, I hope you two can talk later then."

"Maybe," he said without conviction.

As she led him from group to group, she introduced him as *Doctor* Hartwell, her friend and a native who had just returned home.

Her introductions didn't mention why he returned or that he owned the mineral spring. When someone asked whether he was practicing in Waterford, he said, no, he was retired.

Now that he was at the barbecue, Hartwell wished he hadn't come. Seeing Madeline was the motive but she wasn't there and Rita hung on to him as if he were a trophy. It felt like a blind date arranged by someone who wasn't his friend. Then he recalled that Rita had always been that way. At fifteen, he couldn't get enough of her nubile body and she played on his adolescent lust to get him to do what she wanted. After forty years, he found her mature foxiness provocative and still exciting. *Same sexy, Rita. She opens the door to her legs and waits for me to cross the threshold.*

Rita brought him to the barbecue pit just as the tour wagon arrived. "Justin, look who's here."

"Oh, yeah you're—"

"—Bob Hartwell. Your neighbor who owns the mineral spring," he said loud enough for the others to hear.

Taylor pressed his lips together and nodded but didn't extend his hand. Neither did Hartwell. "Nice of you to come," Taylor said evenly and pointed to the roast. "Be sure to enjoy some beef 'fore you leave. The bar's over there. Drinks are on me. If you stick around, let's you and me have a little talk." He turned on his heel and climbed aboard the wagon. "C'mon up, folks. The next tour leaves now."

"You see, Justin's a little rough around the edges but he's not impossible," Rita said as she walked Hartwell to the bar. "I rarely touch alcohol now, but you go ahead." They each ordered club sodas and then sat in the shade. "It's been a long time," she said gently. "There's so much to catch up on."

Hartwell relaxed a little as they recounted their lives since high school. Time had been kind to her, he thought. She had a smooth face and eyes that still flashed indiscreet suggestions. The false eyelashes were a bit much but she still had a great figure. Rita was still the goodtime girl he knew but more experienced now. Romping with her might still be fun but what a colossally disastrous idea.

"The year after graduation I had an oopsie," she said, breaking into his thoughts. "I got preggers by a guy who was a total shit. I didn't want anything to remind me of… so, I went to a doc in Minneapolis that I heard about… a kind of specialist." She looked away, her expression rueful, before she continued. "It was immoral I suppose, but you know… I learned from that." She shrugged. "Our educations are a collection of our mistakes with lessons learned."

"I see… and I'm sorry," The confession stunned him. "I had no idea that happened."

"I would've kept the baby if it were yours," she said, looking down. "I know you would've been a good father. Does this shock you?" She looked up, her brows knitted.

"No. I've heard many kinds of confessions… I'm glad you recovered."

"Keep this to yourself. I don't want Justin to know." Then her expression brightened and she told him about getting an accounting degree and working for Gerhard Docker. "Well, you know the rest now. He was sweet, funny and mature. That settled me."

"Children?"

"A son, Barry" she said with a faraway expression. "A sweet, funny kid. He joined the Marines. Why, I'll never know. Killed in Beirut three years ago." Rita pressed her lips together and hugged herself. "That was six months before Gerhard died." Then she rolled her shoulders as if to free herself. "Now, enough about me. What about you?"

He told her that his service as a combat medic convinced him to study medicine on the G.I. Bill. He said San Francisco was idyllic before the city was overrun with drugs and weirdos. Then he told her about Felicia and her death from cervical cancer. "Life felt empty after that. I wanted to start over. That's when I had this dream that the mineral spring would become a meditation center. Have you been down there?"

"No, I haven't." Rita touched his hand.

"You should. Then you'll understand. It's a good place for people to restore their emotional and physical health. That's why I'm here—to build a meditation center."

Rita touched his hand again, this time lingering at his wrist and renewing his suspicions. Then she looked away with a strained expression. "I understand why you want your property back. I wish I could help you but…"

"It's not about wanting it back. I never lost it. What I want is access." He hoped frankness would win her support. "I hate to think Norm cheated your husband but how else to explain it? Whatever he did or didn't do, he never got legal title to my land. I'll prove it in court if necessary."

"You're as stubborn as I remember, that's for sure," she said, shaking her head. "So is Justin. This ranch is all he's ever wanted. And well, I still care for you Bob. And I care a lot. I don't want to see you get hurt. This could get ugly."

"It's already ugly. Your foreman threatened me a couple days ago when I went there."

"Oh for… that Nacho. You know, I wish… Oh, there's Maddie," she said, jumping up and waving. "She was hoping you'd come. I'll leave you two. It's time to go back to being the hostess. See you later then." Her fingers caressed his shoulders as she walked behind him and left him confused.

What's she up to? He wanted her as an ally but she was signaling something else. *Playing me off against her husband? Start a fight? Wanting to hook up on the sly? It's clear she wants me—but why? Whatever it is, I don't want any part of it. I came to see Madeline.*

Chapter 13

Madeline offered her hand and Hartwell held it until she gently broke loose. He was pleased to see she didn't wear a wedding band. Single, widowed or divorced—it didn't matter. Some adroit conversation would answer those questions. It was enough to be with her, look into those dark eyes and hear a voice that invited deep listening. He said little to avoid interrupting her.

Everything about her electrified him, especially her eyes and voice. Her stylish jeans and calico shirt were expensive but not flashy. *She's about ten years younger than I, but not too young. What am I doing?* He was suddenly conscious of sizing her up for something long-term. Felicia died six months ago and thought he should feel ashamed to be window-shopping already. He knew he wouldn't be looking if he were still in San Francisco.

"This isn't my usual crowd," Madeline said as they walked to the bar. "I came to see Rita and you. Who knows, I might pick up a new client."

"Not my scene, either. I came because of you," he said and laughed. "As for a client, I'll need someone with your skill once I'm settled. But let's talk business another time."

"Rita said you were classmates. What was it like being teens in a small town?"

He took off his cap. "Well, did you ever see the movie *American Graffiti?*"

She nodded and laughed. "I loved that movie, as silly as it was."

"Well, it was nothing like that… except in our fantasies. It's what we dreamed of…"

"Oh really, like what?"

"Oh, something beyond corn and hogs and a ten o'clock town curfew."

"Tell me about you," he began, hoping to turn the tables. "What was it like being a teen in California?"

She smiled. "Nothing like *American Graffiti*. I grew up in Paso Robles north of L.A. and had the usual experiences. You know, dances, first car, experimented with weed, that sort of thing. Went to college in Berkeley and got a degree in finance. I eventually worked for a vintner in Healdsburg, Sonoma. But I told you that, didn't I?"

That's a résumé not a revelation, he thought. He soon noticed her frustrating habit of answering a question about her past with another question. At the same time, she kept him on the hook to reveal himself a little more. Madeline's simple, oblique questions extracted personal information without explicitly asking for it. Her skill made him feel noticed but gradually cautious. He pressed on, knowing he lacked her finesse in questioning but hungry for clues. She gave him nothing about past or present lovers, husbands or children. He asked about her parents and received a vague answer, as if she scarcely knew them. Other questions about her personal life were deflected. Knowing her will take some time, he thought. But it will be time well-spent.

"Let's go on Justin's tour," she suggested. "I dressed for the occasion." A tour of rotational grazing didn't appeal to him but he agreed just to please her. As he climbed aboard the wagon, Morales turned to look at him from the tractor seat. Their eyes met for an instant, just long enough for the Tejano to flash a smug sneer. Cattlemen climbed aboard and Taylor last of all. Then the rig started along the track off the escarpment.

The cattleman said his 300 Charolais cattle were divided into six herds of fifty to sixty animals. Each bunch grazed on a different part of the ranch. Smaller herds were easier to move from one grazing unit to another. "I've got two bulls in each herd. Well boys, with odds like that, it looks like the bulls drew a pat hand from a stacked deck." The men guffawed but Hartwell saw Madeline's expression pinch in disgust. He was only half-listening to the virtues of rotational grazing when the wagon passed along the fence separating Taylor's land and from his.

On an impulse, he asked, "Why aren't you grazing that tract?"

"Glad you asked," Taylor said with an easy smile. "Now folks, on your left, you'll see the Runyon Mineral Spring tract. The spring comes out of a little cave there and starts a crick runnin' through the property. Grazin' cattle in there would ruin the spring and the crick. That's why it's fenced off... to protect the fragile *ee*-cology."

Hartwell nodded, disappointed his question didn't produce the discomfort he had hoped for. Meanwhile, Taylor talked about keeping records and recited exact figures on how much rotational grazing increased the volume of grass. More grass meant he could graze more animals per acre for a net return higher than other methods of feeding cattle.

"How do you figure that?" A husky cattleman next to Hartwell called out in a challenge.

"Glad you asked." Taylor conceded that land and fencing were large up-front costs but so were feedlots. Grass and feedlot cattle were worth about the same per pound at the market. Feedlot animals reached market weight quicker but at a higher cost. His animals grazed for nine months of the year so he didn't buy feed. A pasture was a healthier than a feedlot so he spent less on vet bills. Eating grass-fed beef was healthier and tasted better. "You'll notice that at lunch."

Taylor jumped off the wagon when the tour stopped in a lush patch of grass and clover. Knee-deep in fescue, he said that confining a herd to a small spot for a short time forced them to eat everything. That suppressed weeds and promoted new growth in grass. He rotated each herd to a fresh unit every two to three weeks. He dug into the soil with his hand. "See how loose the soil is. Heavy rains like the one last week just soak in. No puddles, no run-off. Rest-rotation grazing is a natural feedback loop."

Hartwell noticed that Taylor spoke with heart-felt conviction that his method of raising beef was good for animals, people and the earth.

The doctor thought it possible he had been wrong about the cattleman. It was possible a better man lived beneath the tough-guy exterior. Protecting the spring for ecological reasons fit in with Taylor's land ethic. What if that was really his motive. He might retaliate by rallying conservation groups with a save-the-spring campaign. It would complicate the design and construction of the center. Then what?

After the tour, Hartwell and Madeline shuffled along the line of serving tables where the caterers piled their plates with cooked beef, Cole slaw, cornbread, baked beans and watermelon. He looked at the food knowing it was more than he could eat. Especially the lean beef. But his attention focused on Madeline. *She is fascinating. It's her composure, her aura and how I feel when I'm with her.*

They sat facing each other across a narrow table and she asked how he became a cardiologist. "It came to me in Korea. I was an infantry medic and had to keep guys from bleeding to death. Naturally—"

"—That takes a lot of courage. Treating men in combat when you can't shoot back."

"Oh, I was armed. North Korean snipers targeted the medics because it demoralized the men. I was a rifleman as much as a medic. They shot at me and I shot back. Now, working for a vintner sounds fascinating. Tell me more."

"Well, accounting is accounting wherever you are," she said with an easy smile, as if to brush off the question. But he persisted.

"Oh, c'mon. You had to like something about the job. What was it?"

"Okay. It was more than bookkeeping. I learned a lot about wine, how it's made, the rootstock for the grapes, pruning and a thousand other details. It's an ancient agriculture. That's what fascinates me. That's what makes this tour interesting, too. Tell me more about the center."

"This is family lore. Sure you want to hear about it. My great-grandfather Horatio was a homeopathic doctor who bought the mineral spring and ran a health resort before it became a tuberculosis sanatorium. He appeared to me in a dream just after Felicia's death. It was a low point for me and he urged me to create a center for wellness at the spring. I needed a new purpose so, here I am."

Hours slipped away as she listened with her chin resting on folded hands. "You have a mission that's bigger than you. It's admirable and important. I look forward to hearing more as you go forward." She glanced at her watch and rose from the chair. "Oh, it's so late. I've enjoyed the afternoon, Bob. I hope we meet again."

He stood, too. "I'll walk out with you," he said as they headed toward the driveway. Then Rita called after him. He stopped, though he resented her intrusion.

"That's okay," Madeline said, taking his hand. "Talk to her. I'll see you again."

He stood in the driveway looking after Madeline until she left.

"Well, you two really hit it off," Rita said with a smile as she sidled up to him. "I'm sorry for watching. Maddie is a special friend. I'm protective of her."

"Protective from what?" he asked, annoyed.

"Not from you. It's a long story and I'm not free to… she's had some…unhappy experiences with some men. If you see her again, be gentle. She's… I don't know, fragile in a way. I can't say more, but I don't want to see her hurt."

She took his arm. "I came over because Justin wants to come to an understanding."

"Understanding—what understanding? I understand everything. Either he or Norm is trying to defraud me of property. It's as simple as that."

She looked away with downcast eyes. "I hate being the go-between but he's too proud to approach you. It's… you need to talk to him." She led him to where the catering crew was packing the left-over meat. Taylor waited with his arms crossed.

"Let's take a little walk," he said and nodded toward the edge of the escarpment behind the house. "I want to show you somethin' that might make things clear."

The men went behind the house where they could see the gloaming fill the lowlands. Taylor stood in the day's last shaft of sunlight with his hands jammed into his back pockets. "I bought those woods for hot weather pasture. It also protects the deer and turkeys."

"I see… that's commendable," Hartwell said, wondering what his point was.

"Ain't that a purty sight?" Taylor pointed to a herd of white cattle in the valley where the sunlight gave the grass a silken sheen. "As fine a ranch as y'all can find anywhere. I put seven miles of fence around it. A couple more miles inside it. Invested a bundle in land, fencing and Charolais stock."

"It is lovely," Hartwell agreed. "Especially at this time of the day. I'm a cardiologist and agree with you that grass-fed beef is healthier that feedlot meat. And I can understand why you don't want a road through it. From your perspective, my ownership is an inconvenience."

"Well now, that's a real nice way to put it," he said as dusk snuffed out the shaft of sunlight. "Your plans will wreck everythin' I built. I cain't run this place with a public road through it. An' I cain't put together another ranch like this, but y'all can build a meditation center anywhere. As we say in Texas, first in time, first in right."

"This isn't Texas," Hartwell said. "And if it were, I'd be first in time. The mineral spring has been in my family for a century. Mineral springs are rare. I have no intention of relocating. It looks like Norm pulled a fast one and sold you land he didn't own."

"I don' believe that Becker would do a thang like that. Everbody says he was as honest as the day is long. Sayin' he pulled a fast one don' cut it."

"It is a fraud and I can prove it. County records show that I paid taxes on my land every year. I also have notarized rental contracts signed by Norm. And township records will prove the road wasn't abandoned."

Taylor crossed his arms. "What's your point?"

"Just this," Hartwell snapped and locked eyes with him as choler rose in his throat once more. "I returned home with a plan to use my property and won't be suckered out of it. Or get run out by your pistol-packing foreman. I'm a Korean War vet. I served under fire—have you?"

The cattleman shuffled his boots and cleared his throat. "Look Hartwell, lawyers will cost us both a bundle. Let's settle this quietly. Name the price. Your land is worth five hundred an acre. That's eighty grand. Throw in the spring and it's worth a hundred-fifty grand."

"You keep your money and I'll keep my land."

Taylor let out a breath of exasperation. "All right. Go hire yourself a lawyer. What's the old sayin'… a fool and his money. Before we're through you won't have money or land."

"Neither will you."

Chapter 14

Becker's closest neighbors didn't know where he went and their interviews left Boston with more questions than answers. Everyone was indirect. None made accusations but all were clear in their dislike of Taylor. Less clear were their reasons for dislike. Because he had lots of money when they didn't or it could be for other reasons. His gut said they knew more than they told him. Farmers were proud men and he needed at least one of them to talk straight. He considered who else might be in Becker's circle of associates and groaned at the idea of starting a new line of searching.

Tapping into farmer networks wasn't like getting into business and political ones. Rural networks were less formal and more personal rather than organizational. Over the years, he learned that women often talked openly about things their men would not. Often, the women confided in their pastors. A pastor might know who was in trouble and why. Rural church membership still reflected its immigrant origins. The Irish and Poles were invariably Catholics. Otto sounded German so he might have been a Lutheran. But Waterford had four congregations of different synods. Becker sounded like an English name and he might have belonged to the Congregational or Episcopal congregations. Or an evangelical one.

Waterford's Yellow Pages listed eighteen congregations. He picked up the phone questioning whether he really wanted to do this. It could take a day or two or three. So far, chasing Becker had eaten up over a month of his time instead of working on the Nielsen book. Well, what the hell. He dialed the first number. And then another. He left a half-dozen voice-mail messages before he connected with a Lutheran pastor who said the Ottos used to belong to his congregation. Losing them was a blow. The pastor gave him a phone number in Fayetteville, Arkansas. Well, that's something, he thought.

The evening call surprised Hans Otto but he recognized Boston's name because he had continued his subscription to the *Statesman*. After the introductions and small talk, Boston laid out his reason for calling. Otto said Becker was a close friend but he hadn't heard from him.

"Becker left in May of eighty-five," Boston said. "When did you leave?"

"October of eighty-four. After I moved, Norm sent us a Christmas card. We talked on the phone a couple times that winter and then nothing. So, he musta buckled under the pressure."

"Pressure? What pressure? Tell me about that."

"Well, Taylor's not a guy to take no for an answer. He wanted all the land inside those four county roads. When a fella was in financial trouble—and we all were—he'd make us a lowball offer. We all said no 'cause we didn't wanna sell. Now and then he'd stop by and say the offer was still on the table. A shame to pass it up. Every time he bought a farm we lost a friend. After you lose enough friends, stayin' on starts to feel pointless. We all love our farms but havin' friends who share your life makes it worthwhile."

"Tell me more about how Taylor works."

"A couple years ago, things were really bad for sure. We were all mortgaged to the neck. Couldn't borrow any more against our land. All it took was a small problem to sink ya. And if the barn burned or the cows died and you couldn't pay on your loan, well the bank would move in and shut ya down. We all felt helpless. And there was Taylor just waiting for a fella to go under. Then he'd make his offer. You could fight foreclosure but no tellin' how much you'd get. Or take his offer in cash. Seeing old friends and neighbors go… well it was depressin'. That made it easier to think of sellin' out, ya know. End the misery. When things got bad for Wilkes he took to drinkin' an' beat up his wife. She left him an' he lost the farm a few months later, anyway. Scribner lost his place to foreclosure. Next day, he drove himself into an abutment. Killed him."

"Anything suspicious?"

"Nothing you can prove. Just too much bad luck in a small area."

"Did the Beckers have family?"

"No. He and the wife didn't have no kids. Far's I know, he was an only child."

"Do you know if Norm belonged to a church?"

"*Nah*. He said they were full of hypocrites. He might be right."

"Did the town keep up the Runyon Town road or was it your private driveway?"

"Graded and graveled it regular. At least 'till I moved. I was clerk of the town board until Taylor arrived. Then Peterson ousted me in the election of eighty-two."

"So, the town maintained the road until at least eighty-two?"

"*Yee*-up, that's right. It wasn't used a lot but we kept 'er up. After I sold it, Norm was the only farm he hadn't got. That and the mineral spring. Suppose he's got it by now—"

"—No, he hasn't. The owner is proving his title and trying for access."

"Good for him. I wish him luck."

"We need to talk to Becker. He sold the mineral spring as part of his farm. Said he got title by adverse possession."

"*Whaaat*? Run that by me again, wouldya? There was no reason for him to sell. He wasn't in trouble debt-wise. He inherited money in addition to what he made. I know for a fact he rented the mineral spring piece. Claiming squatter's rights don't square with his reputation."

"That's what we want to clear up. He's the only one who can tell us. Thanks for your help. I'll call if I hear news of him." Boston hung up thinking he had hit another wall. Becker was in good shape financially. He had good friends. None of them believed the adverse possession claim. Except for the Kansas City postcards, no one had heard from them in a year.

He started Saturday morning on the veranda watching the rising sunlight crawl across the countryside. Sparrows and robins sang in the trees behind the house. He heard a gang of crows raging in a distant grove, cows bawled and then a tractor started. He leaned back in the chair, opening himself to daybreak.

"Are you all right?" Ginger asked later, looking into his face. "You tossed all night. What's eating you?"

"I'm okay. Last night's call with Otto raised more questions. I just couldn't fall asleep. The neighbors are edgy talking about Taylor. At least, I think so."

"Like afraid?"

"No, not exactly. They don't want to do business with him."

"Got any ideas?"

"None with facts behind them."

Ginger watched him start down the hill on his daily run. *He won't let go until he knows what happened. His virtue and his vice. Once he gets his teeth into something...* She shook her head and whispered, "God grant me the serenity to accept the things I cannot change..." knowing his stubbornness was one of them.

Chapter 15

The gentle, all night rain continued with no let-up insight. It was the kind of mid-summer soaker that made farmers smile and kept them out of the fields for a couple days. Boston took it as an opportunity to talk face-to-face with those who lived across the road from Taylor's farm. He made appointments over the phone and the farmers said come out anytime. They would be around all day. He set out for Waterford through the steady showers and stopped at the Glynn farm across the road from what had been Arne Larson's dairy.

"C'mon in out of the wet," Glynn called. He was a short, compact man with a child's guileless blue eyes. They half-faced each other at the kitchen counter over cups of coffee. "Rain just when we need it," the farmer said. "Corn's ready to tassel. So, we'll have a big crop."

"Won't a heavy yield just add to the surplus and keep down prices?"

"Yeah, I 'spose so but ... regardless of prices, I don't know any farmer who wants to raise a poor crop. Prices are one thing, satisfaction is another."

"I want to talk about the mineral spring road," Boston said. "Is it public or just the private driveway for Otto and Becker?"

"Becker and Otto used that road," he said. "Now and then, other folks used to get water from the spring. You know, home remedies. It was graded and graveled regular."

"When was the last time you saw that?"

"What the heck are you gettin' at?"

91

"The mineral spring owner can't get access to his property. Taylor says the road was abandoned."

"The hell it was! That road's been used forever or we woulda gotten notice. They graveled it three years ago. It's got new culverts. I don't like that gate across the road but I got enough worries without making trouble over it."

"Any ideas where the Beckers went?"

"No idea. Wish I did. I miss 'em. Hell, the big shot's bought out all the folks I cared for. We had a tight little neighborhood 'til he showed up. He don't go out of his way to socialize."

"That's what others told me. What can you tell me about Larson's barn fire?"

"Oh for… sweet Jesus. One helluva fire. He had a loft full of hay so she burned hot and fast. I run over to help when I seen the flames. It was raining. Arne had already let out the cattle. He had registered Holsteins, too, and no way to milk 'em. The barn was pretty-well gone by the time the fire trucks showed. After the insurance paid out, he said between debt and equity, he couldn't borrow enough to start over."

"How long after the fire did he sell out?"

"Oh, it took a few months. The herd went first. Then machinery at auction. After that, he and Doris moved to Wisconsin."

"You know what started the fire?"

"No. The insurance adjuster said it was lightning. He never really investigated, though."

Boston made a note to ask Larson about that.

"I'll tell you something else but don't use my name—"

"—I won't. Go on."

"I raise a few Angus calves for the market so I know the business. But Taylor's operation is a strange one," he said, scratching his head.

"Oh, how so?" He was hoping for this kind of hook.

"Well, he's got lots of cash but I can't see how it comes from selling steers."

"Why is that?"

"Cattle prices are low. What he's sold isn't enough to account for the money he's spent."

"I heard he made a lot of money in the oil fields." He made a note of Glynn's skepticism. Something more to investigate.

"Well, I 'spose that's it. I guess I'm suspicious 'cause he bought out the neighbors. Well maybe… but a guy who gives as much as he does to the Future Farmers club can't be all bad."

It was still raining when Boston arrived at the next farm. He heard polka music coming from the barn. Entering, he met the dairyman washing a stainless-steel milking machine. The farmer snapped off the radio and wiped a wet hand on the overalls before offering it. He waved Boston to a seat on a square straw bale and hitched around another to face him.

"There's been a lot of change in this part of the county," Boston began. "I'm interested in knowing why so many farms so close together went under. Did you know Ray Purdy? I haven't talked to him yet."

"Oh you bet, know him well. A good friend, too."

"I hope to talk to him. What should I know about him?"

"Poor Ray never got a break in his life. Hard luck from the get-go. Still a boy when he took over the farm after his dad died. His two kids died of rubella. He went big into growing corn when prices were good. Unfortunately, he didn't have the acreage he needed to make real money. So he hocked the farm to buy a self-propelled rig for custom harvesting. As soon as he bought it, the price of corn went in the tank. Hardly anybody had money to hire custom combining."

"So, that didn't work out."

"Nope. He had a few jobs but it wasn't enough. Don't know how it coulda been worse."

"What happened?"

"A couple lug nuts on the combine's front drive wheel come off and sheared the bolts. Happened in a field. Getting parts took forever so he missed the harvest. After that, he couldn't make payments and the dealer repo-ed the rig."

"In foreclosure after that?"

"Oh, for sure. He said Taylor offered to buy his farm earlier. Ray couldn't see a way out, ya know. Not after repo. I tell ya, bad luck followed him like a cloud."

"Where'd he go?"

"He lives in a mobile home park in Waterford. I can get you his—"

"—Thanks, I appreciate that. Was Taylor interested in your farm? It's a nice spread."

"That's a curious thing. He don't want land with a road through it. As soon as Becker left, he put up the gate."

"I know the owner of the spring tract. He's got a clear title but no access."

"Well, good for him. Just be careful. I think Taylor plays for keeps. He's got a Mexican foreman. A sneaky guy. The kind who'd knife ya in the back."

Another mile and Boston pulled into a yard where a limp, black Missing In Action banner hung from the flagpole. The farmer's wife met him at the door and called her husband, who was napping. Boston accepted her offer of coffee to be polite though he drank little of it.

"Hey there, nice to meetcha," the beefy farmer said. "God made rain to give us extra zees, that's fer sure." They sat at a Formica kitchen table by a window with gingham curtains.

"I noticed your MIA flag," Boston said. "I traveled with the Marines as a reporter. I'm sorry for your loss."

"Thank you. We think about him every day. Wish we knew what happened…" and his voice trailed off. "Now, what can I do for ya?"

"I'm trying to catch up with David Wilkes. Can you tell me where he went?"

"Last I heard, he lives in Iowa with one of his kids. A good fella but… too bad about him and the wife. That's alcohol for ya. We weren't as thick with 'em as with Purdy."

"How was it he left farming?"

"He was hangin' on, him and his wife … well, he was depressed and drinkin' an'… well, let's just say she left. Then his cows started foamin' at the mouth and a lot of 'em died—like overnight." He snapped his fingers. "Those that lived didn't give much milk. That's 'cause they ate water hemlock. Deadly stuff in the spring but most cows avoid it."

"Is that when his cattle died?"

"No, it was later in the season. Coulda been in the hay I guess."

"So, that forced him out of dairy?"

"Yeah. He had debts like the rest of us. Milk prices were down then, and interest rates were up. He couldn't make it without the weekly cream check."

"And Taylor made him an offer?"

"Yep. The farm went up for sale. The sheriff... say, is he related to you?"

"My brother, by adoption."

"Well, some of us pooled our money hoping to buy it back for him but Taylor got the place. We're still sore about it. Same for the others he bought out."

"It's strange he didn't try to buy out the mineral spring tract."

"Yeah. We wondered if they're in cahoots or somethin'."

"No. The owner is fighting for access. Has the township kept up the road?"

"Hell yes! Say, what's with all these questions? If you're some kinda investigator, I say you're barking up the right tree here. That's all I'm gonna say but you're on to somethin'."

"Well, it's unusual to have so many farms in a small area—"

"—I see where you're goin'... somethin' fishy, that's for sure. None of those men woulda sold if you offered 'em straight out. Those farms have been in the family for three, four generations. Becker held out 'cause he had more money than us but..." he shook his head.

Sensing he had gotten all he could, Boston said, "Thank you. We'll talk again."

"You betcha, you're welcome any time."

Morales thought he recognized the driver as the Jeep passed him and turned in at the Glynn farm. The foreman drove on to check on the woods. There were no cattle there at the moment but the grass looked good enough for grazing during the hottest weeks of July. Seeing the Jeep at the next farm, he parked where he could watch the driveway. He lit a cigarette and wondered why the newspaperman was talking to the neighbors. *Jefe* won't like it, he thought. An hour passed before the Jeep left the farm. He followed it as far as Waterford and then returned to the ranch. He wiped his feet on the sisal doormat and entered the office. The cattleman looked up.

"*Jefe*, I see Meade stop at three farms. Stay an hour. Each one. Then I follow him to town. What we do?"

Taylor drew a long breath. "I dunno, yet. No way of knowin' what the neighbors are tellin' him 'bout me—if anything. I don't care what they say but I don' want it in the news. Leave him alone for now. If I think of somethin', we'll talk."

"Okay, *Jefe*," he said and turned to the door.

"*Un momento*, Nacho. There is one thing. Find out where he lives."

Chapter 16

Boston lounged in a living room wing chair with a lapful of reporter's notebooks. Becker's neighbors hadn't given him anything definite. Little more than indirect comments. Comments about Morales proved nothing except prejudice against Mexicans. "It's not enough," he muttered in frustration. "I need something definite… something on the record. Something for Jack."

Ginger looked up from her needlepoint. "What are you mumbling about?"

"The interviews. The farmers chalk up their losses to bad luck. It's like they want to blame Taylor but won't. I've got to have something more than someone buckled under pressure or there's something fishy or I'm on to something but won't say what that is. No! I need something solid to share with Jack!"

She stood behind him and wrapped her arms around his shoulders. "I know you won't drop it. So, what can I do, lover?"

He reached up and pulled her closer. "Just be yourself. That's all I need."

"Why don't you just ask them—what do you really think caused your disaster?"

"It's not that easy. Not like asking a congressman for a quote. These guys hardly know me. Direct questions tend to make them leery. They blame themselves for losing the farm. It's a source of shame. That's why so many get depressed. Open-ended questions work better."

"Would they say if they thought their experience would help others?"

"Yeah… they might. That means committing to a series. Am I on assignment?" He looked up at her with a grin.

"No. A stringer on spec. Show me a story." Then she laughed. "Same rules as before."

"Thanks, sweetheart, but don't let the editorial power go to your head." He decided to start with Ray Purdy.

He found Purdy's house at Prairie View Park on Waterford's south side. His gray double-wide prefab home and a dozen others sat in a new park where most of the trees were saplings. Everything about it suggested a frugal life on a tight budget. After last night's phone call, he wondered if this was worth the time. He wondered if the old farmer was an addled geezer. Then a bald, older man in a plaid shirt opened the door and called him in.

"Set down, set down," Purdy said with enthusiasm. "The missus went to church for some women's deal. Now, tell me what I can do for ya. Coffee?"

He took a cup to be polite and then ignored it. "As we talked last night, these are fast-changing times on the farm. I'm talking to retired farmers to collect the lessons that could help younger farmers weather hard times."

"Glad to help but ya know, when I sold, I figured it was time I got outta farming. It's a young man's deal now, that's for sure. Used to be all ya needed was muscle and hands-on training. Now ya gotta be some kind of finance wizard with the money an' have a business plan an' a marketeering plan and besides that, ya need more than a hunerd 'n sixty acres to stay ahead in the game."

Purdy tended to ramble and Boston had to guide him back to the point. The man seemed lonely for company in addition to his wife. Finally, Boston asked how so many farmers in a small area could go out of business so fast.

"Ya know, that's a strange run of bad luck, that's fer sure. Larson was unlucky. That fire was either lightning or damp hay catching itself on fire. Wilkes and Otto," he shook his head. "Bad luck. Some cows died from eatin' that damned hemlock. The rest didn't give good milk."

"Water hemlock?"

"Yeah, there's a lot of it along the cricks an' ditches. Any wet spot has it. Probably baled some in his hay. And poor Scribner, he took his troubles real hard, too. Barely hangin' on as it was. He got stinking' drunk after the sheriff's sale and drove into an abutment. His wife got an insurance payout but… We all figure he did it on purpose. That's real sad." He shook his head.

"I understand you had troubles with custom combining."

Purdy nodded. "Oh for sure… That Massey-Harris was a money eater."

"Anything suspicious about it?"

"*Nah.* My mistake was buyin' a used one. Cheaper for me but I bought all its problems. Din't see 'em 'til too late. Hard to get parts. That's what done me in."

"How were your dealings with Taylor? Was he fair, a good man to do business with?"

Purdy glanced at the ceiling. "I don't like sayin' bad against anyone that I can't prove but… I never want to do business with him again. Or the folks he hires."

"What about the folks he hires?"

Purdy fidgeted in his chair. "To put it plain, it's that Morales fella. He ain't white. Ya don't know what he's thinkin'. Made me uneasy. Ya seen his scars? Ya don't wanna turn your back on him, know what I mean? Prob'ly knife ya."

I am getting somewhere, Boston thought on the drive home. Purdy was the second man to mention Larson's fire, water hemlock and Morales. Farmers tended to be cooperators. Collaborators. They rarely went after each other. At least openly. So they weren't going to accuse a neighbor. Not directly. Larson moved away so maybe he would be more direct.

He called Larson who was cautious at first but opened up after hearing that he had talked to Glynn and Otto. After some general chatting about farming, he asked Larson about the fire.

"I can tell you it wasn't lightning," he said in a tone that carried the weight of conviction.

"Meaning?"

"The insurance guy said it was lightning 'cause it wasn't electrical or spontaneous combustion."

"But you don't think so."

"Couldn't a been. I saw the flames before the storm hit. I shoulda asked the cops to investigate but, well, I had a herd and no barn or milking equipment. Just had to let it go. And there was moneybags with his goddamn checkbook!"

"Was it a good offer?"

"*Pfui*! Not at all. Just the best I could hope for and stay off welfare."

"Think it's strange the only hard luck farmers all lived inside those roads?"

"Yeah. Bad luck didn't exist 'til he showed up. He made a lowball offer for the farm. I said no. Wasn't interested."

"Were the others treated like that?"

"Yeah, as far as I know. Every year, somebody who said no had a disaster that sunk 'em. Now, does that sound like coincidence to you? Don't to me."

"You think it was arson?"

"Either that or act of God—and I'm not accusing the Almighty. The insurance adjuster said the policy would pay off faster if it was lightning. It just wasn't enough to start over and I was already mortgaged." Larson cleared his throat. "I can't prove arson but... but you can draw your own conclusions. Just don't say I said it."

A few minutes later, Boston called an Iowa number and asked for Wilkes. He felt the man's resistance as soon as he said who he was and why he was calling.

"I don't wanna talk about it," he said. "It don't matter anymore. It's done. Talkin' about it..." he exhaled loudly. "Talkin' about it just brings back the pain. Don't do me no good to get worked up since the heart attack."

"Can I ask you about Norm Becker?"

"Sure. Great people. How are they?"

"That's just it. They sold to Taylor last year and vanished."

"*Whaaat*! That can't be. I don't believe it. He was well enough off that he didn't have to sell—especially to Taylor! Now they're missing... no one's seen 'em?"

"Exactly. No one's heard from them. It's like the ground swallowed them."

"Now that *is* strange. Even if Norm sold, he'd never sell out to Taylor. He told me so."

"Can I ask how you feel about Taylor?"

"When you find Norm, ask how he feels. Whatever he says, that's how I feel. Okay?"

Boston signed off. Nothing. Hints, indirect accusations but no facts. Taylor bought seven farms in five years on the cheap. Except for Larson, not one clear accusation despite a suicide, a missing couple and three farmers who have moved.

Chapter 17

Madeline filled Hartwell's thoughts in the days following the barbecue. Nor could he stop comparing her with Felicia. Closing his eyes, he saw them as alike in poise, confidence and elegance. Sometimes they morphed into a single image. When he was with her, he felt like the man he had been when Felicia was alive. It was dreamlike, as if his wife hadn't really died but taken up residence in a younger body. Now and then he told himself that rebounds were tricky. It wasn't her youth that attracted him. It was her being, her poise, that sense of herself. Still, be careful. Yet, self-admonitions didn't keep her from his thoughts.

He dialed her number and he thought she sounded happy to hear from him. After a few minutes of conversation she agreed to join him for dinner on Friday night. He hung up happy she said yes, and happier that he felt no pangs of infidelity to Felicia's memory.

To be sure, Felicia was all he could have desired in a life companion. Wise, sexy when it suited her but also down-to-earth and practical. He replayed from memory a conversation a few days before her death. *'Do you think you'll marry again,'* she asked. *'No, I don't think so,'* he replied. *'I think it best that you do. Your spirit needs a companion.'* He shook his head and sighed. *I'm a doctor of every heart ailment except a broken one. In that, Felicia was wiser than I am. Maddie is like her. The kind of woman she would have chosen for me.* Friday's date couldn't come soon enough.

"I've looked forward to this all day," Madeline said as they drove to the Café L'Oiseu, a French bistro along the river that boasted

Burgundian cuisine. The *maître'd* in black slacks led them to a table and put the wine card in front of him. The waiter would be right with them— *biantid.*

"It's good to be with another Californian," Madeline said.

"I'm a native son. My great grandparents were among the town's original settlers. Beneath this tan, I'm Minnesotan through and through, doncha know," he laughed and gave her the wine list. "Please, you choose."

She smiled. "Thank you. I will. *Hmm...*" she ran her finger down the list while whispering the labels. Then she chose a wine from a French village she had visited. They both ordered *coq au vin.*

"What brought you here? Why you want to leave Sonoma?"

"For work reasons," she said, shifting in her chair. "I left the accounting firm because it bored me. Working for a vintner looked glamorous. And it was at first. Then the owner promoted me to a management post. After that, he hinted that I owed him special attention after hours. He was married but..." she grimaced. "The job paid well but the hassle wasn't worth it. I came here ten or so years ago and have done well since the Rochester crowd moved in. I still can't picture you and Rita together in high school. You are so opposite."

"That was a long time ago. We were different then. Kids, really. Her marriage to Taylor makes things awkward between us."

"*Hmm,* I can imagine." She fingered her wine glass.

He turned the conversation and asked about her hobbies and interests while they ate.

"I like the single life," she said, resting her chin on folded hands. "I have time for the Waterford Chorale, I chair the Alton Women Rising group. It supports women who accomplish things they thought were impossible. Seeing them succeed is satisfying."

"But, isn't it lonely? I mean, don't you miss the presence of others around you? Solitude is something I don't like. Having a house all to myself without—"

"—What are your hobbies?" she asked and took a spoonful of chocolate mousse.

"Well, there's tennis, hiking, chamber music concerts and reading mysteries. I used to play the banjo for anyone who cared to listen."

She laughed. "I like all of those things—except the banjo!"

Afterward, they walked along the river and sat shoulder to shoulder on the bench by the wrecked dam, transfixed by the moon's sinuous reflection dancing where the water curled around a chunk of concrete. Then they walked to his car in the dark.

"Maddie, I've really enjoyed this evening," he said when he stopped in front of her house. "This is the happiest I've felt in months." He toyed with the idea of a kiss but thought it was too soon. "I want to see you again."

"Yes. Of course," she said, getting out of the car before he could unbuckle his seatbelt. "You don't need to walk me to the door," she said with a smile. "Good night. And thank you."

That was quick, he thought as she walked to the house and disappeared inside without a look back. If that wasn't a brush-off she came darned close to it. She's careful. *Chalk it up to whatever happened in Sonoma. Rita said she was fragile. I'll play the long game.*

He sat on the patio and replayed the evening. Madeline had asked about his vision for the mineral spring property, "if you get it back?" The question had made him cringe. He had said he still had title to it and wanted to resolve the dispute peacefully but doubted the possibility. When he said the case might go to court, she had nodded and said: "Justin isn't one to back down. You are a good man. I hope you win," she said earnestly. "You radiate integrity. Because of it, I feel something's about to blow. I don't want to see you hurt."

Hartwell called Madeline several times after the dinner date and some conversations lasted more than an hour. Afterward, he felt drunk on her voice. The more they talked, the more he felt she embodied Felicia. And the more she seemed like Felicia, the more he wanted to see her. Was she for real or a projection of his need? Only one way to know. Ask her out again.

She accepted his invitation to a picnic in Limestone State Park where three branches of the Limestone River joined. It was a half-hour south of Waterford and popular with birdwatchers in May, leaf-peepers in October and campers and fly-fisherman in the months between. She squealed in surprise when the road plunged into the park's deep glen and then fell into silent awe at the cream-colored cliffs rising above the river.

He set the wicker hamper on a rustic table in the half-empty picnic ground. She spread a checkered cloth and laid out a spread of brioche sandwiches, fruit, cheese and chilled wine. The river sang a soothing chuckle over the stony shingle and a kingfisher chattered on a limb above the water. He told her how he had loved camping there as a kid.

"It's magical, " she agreed, gazing at the valley.

"I'm glad you like it," he said, trying without success to catch and hold her gaze. She seemed aglow with pleasure but he suspected her delight had little to do with him. She wasn't shy, timid or afraid, of that he was certain. Though she spoke candidly, he felt she was also holding him at bay. They made fleeting eye contact and, for an instant, he caught a faraway look, a soldier's thousand-yard stare, which might be grief, loss or pain. "Are you all right?" he asked in alarm.

"Oh yes, I'm fine," she said, flashing a sudden smile. "Why?"

"Just a feeling. The look in your eyes. Like you're about to cry."

"Oh, no, nothing like that. Just that this is so beautiful, it's... it's almost painful to look at. Let's hike to Chimney Rock," she said, gathering the luncheon leftovers. "You told me the view is terrific."

"Of course," he said, convinced he had seen real pain and her explanation wasn't the truth. It was anguish and knowing that touched him deeply. She is holding in some excruciating pain, he thought. He would do anything to relieve it if he knew its cause. However, remembering Rita's caution that she was fragile, he knew better than to ask about it.

They hiked single file along the shady riverbank, stood shoulder to shoulder on the plank bridge and looked at the trout lurking in its shadow. Then they ascended the ridge by switchbacks. The view from Chimney Rock was worth the climb but it didn't bring them together as he had hoped. Though she grasped his hand for a pull up the steeper pitches, she let go immediately after gaining her footing. He had hoped for a lacing of their fingers or a sign of attraction. Instead, she kept to herself, cautious and covertly on her guard. Nor could he clear his mind of the pain he saw in her eyes. Whatever caused it, it was private and he guessed it was something from her past. He let it go. In time she would tell him with the moment was right. After that, they clambered down another trail to the car.

Their conversation flowed easily on the drive back to Waterford and he wanted to believe they were drawing closer. When he stopped at her house, he hopped out first and opened the trunk. Madeline took the picnic hamper from his hand and held it in front of her.

"Thank you for a beautiful day!" she beamed. "You're such fun to be with. Let's do it again, sometime."

He said good night, deflated and perplexed that another date had ended without a hug, a kiss or even a lingering conversation. Instead, she gave him a kind, firm but earnest good night. Maybe I intimidate her, he thought. She had never married but he had a thirty-year union. Patience, he told himself. Later, sitting on his patio, he believed Madeline's warmth and friendliness were genuine but her candor puzzled him. *Her candor keeps me at a distance. Wards off intimacy. She like a chess player. Reads my moves before I make them and has a counter move in place. Just what is her game?*

Madeline liked Hartwell's calls and company, but today's picnic left her questioning herself. "Well, Maddie," she said, tossing her soft hat onto a chair. "What are you going to do about Bob? He's wants you." She opened a window and let in cooler air. "He isn't hiding his interest. What am I going to do about that?"

She began by taking stock of the pluses and minuses. He was over fifty but still youngish. Their difference in ages wasn't a problem. His eyes had a light that was gentle and empathetic. Perfect for a man who had to give grave news with gentleness. Good eyes for a doctor. His friendship was worth having but she didn't want a mate so... but she didn't finish the thought.

What do I feel? The question had become more difficult to answer with each date. She paced about the room wishing she could put it all on a spreadsheet. Sort it into a column for assets and debits and then balance them. But emotions didn't work that way. *I made that mistake before. I won't make it again.* She thought of life as an investment portfolio. It had diversity to balance the familiar and comfortable things against unexpected disasters, trust against uncertainty. She was earning more money than she ever thought possible. And she had a diverse circle of interesting friends. *What is my life missing that only Bob can provide?* She drew a breath. Nothing came to mind.

The evening star caught her attention. Standing at the window in the darkened room, she looked at Venus and remembered the few times she had drifted into a romance. She ended all of them before intimacy. "Oh, Maddie," she whispered. "This has gone on too long. I should have nipped this in the bud." She sighed. *I enjoy our dinners, the walks by the river and the lectures at the library. Breaking off would be easier if he had a glaring flaw. But he doesn't. He's mature, honest, kind and sensitive. Good qualities in a friend... everything I should want. But—he's like a plate of brownies and I don't have impulse control. We aren't lovers now but it's only a matter of time. Then he'll make a move. What then? I can't... not and be true*, she told herself and thought of Sonoma.

Chapter 18

The sheriff and his chief deputies had offices in one wing of the courthouse along with the county attorney, district judge and a courtroom. The rest of the force had offices in the annex behind the courthouse. It wasn't ideal from a teamwork standpoint but Jack liked his large office with a window on the Green. It had a small worktable and comfortable chairs, a bookcase and filing cabinet instead of his predecessor's rack various rifles, shotguns and pistols. State and national flags stood in one corner and a large print of ducks landing in a marsh hung on the wall behind his desk.

The officer knocking at his door had peach fuzz cheeks, a two-year college degree and certification. Detective Sergeant Mary Kasson assigned him to look for reports on the Beckers in other states and sent him to Jack's office for a briefing. He entered wearing a crisply pressed uniform and stood erect before the desk. "You wanted to see me, sir?"

"Close the door," he said. "Don't worry. You're not in trouble— or are you?" And then he laughed. "This is confidential. You'll report directly to Detective Kasson and me on this." He handed the deputy a sheet of paper with information about the Beckers, their car, its license plate, when they left Waterford and the Yuma address they gave to Taylor. It also included the size and make of the U-Haul van and its license. "We think they vanished south or west of Kansas City."

"Are they wanted?" He could scarcely hide his eagerness.

"We don't know. Check with the state police between Kansas City and Yuma. Look for speeding tickets, new car registrations, fatal accidents, anything."

"In other words, this is a missing persons case."

"Yeah. In a manner of speaking," he said, nodding. "It's part of a larger puzzle that I can't go into now. Keep it to yourself and report to Mary or me."

"Yes sir, I will sir."

He liked the rookie. Despite his youth, he seemed disciplined and took the initiative without over-reaching. On top of that, he didn't have loose lips. By the time he lost the peach fuzz, he might make corporal. Detective Kasson chose him for the assignment because she thought he needed the experience. He recalled when he was a rookie twenty years ago and Mary took him under her wing. She taught me a lot, he recalled on his way to the water cooler. Then he turned to the day's quota of paperwork.

Deputy Peach-fuzz returned a week later. "What did you find," Jack asked.

"Nothing. No records of the Beckers in Iowa, Kansas, Texas, New Mexico or Arizona. On my own, I checked with Wyoming, Oklahoma, Colorado, Utah, Nevada and Nebraska in case they took an alternate route. Nothing. Sorry."

"Don't be sorry. Eliminating a set of possibilities narrows the search. Good work."

"Where should I look next?"

"For now, go back to your regular duties and keep this under wraps." I could keep Deputy Peach-fuzz busy all summer, Jack thought after the rookie left. No evidence or information about the Beckers. He wrote some questions on cards and stuck them in the file he had just started. It was one thing to vanish in a car but quite another to vanish with a car and a vanload of furniture. It begged a question: If the Beckers were so well-liked by the neighbors, why did they leave without a goodbye?

Boston jogged with an easy lope along the county road below the house that curved around the end of the ridge. He ran west for a mile and a half and turned back at the House of Truth. Daily runs kept him fit and the exercise often loosened the odd thoughts lurking at the back of his mind. Today he sought insights on Becker but nothing came to mind.

Approaching his mailbox, he noticed fresh tire tracks just off the shoulder as if someone had parked there. The spot gave everyone a clear view of his house. Four cigarette butts littered the ground. All were the same brand. He wondered how long did it take to smoke four. A half-hour at least. The butts weren't there yesterday morning, he was certain of that.

He considered his discovery as he walked up the hill to the house. Then he shook it off. There were a lot of reasons why someone would park there. Teens making out on a late-night date came to mind. Or a farmer checking the soybeans in the field across the road. Someone could have emptied the car ashtray. It had nothing to do with him. Right now, he had to find Becker and the five farmers who sold out after a catastrophe—if those were catastrophes. Knowing those particulars might open leads.

Three readings of his interview notes revealed nothing new or overlooked. The leads were intriguing but inconclusive. The cattleman had used the farm crisis to his advantage but he didn't cause it. He bought each farm with cash just before it went up for auction. Farmers sold because he made the best offer but his ready money made people suspicious. His neighbors didn't like him but rural residents were slow to accept newcomers. They blamed him for breaking up a network of friends. Was any of that important, he wondered and then shrugged it off. *I'm supposed to find Becker, not second guess Taylor.*

He spent the morning in the *Statesman's* newspaper morgue looking for the cause of the foreclosures but found nothing in the weekly notices. Then he turned to the Tuesday editions that devoted two columns a week to news from Waterford. A small item reported the fire that destroyed Larson's barn. A later story said Wilkes sold his farm after a disease killed some cattle. An obituary said Scribner died in an auto accident shortly after he sold his farm. Another story said Scribner and Otto lost dairy cattle to convulsions. Boston paused. Purdy said the cattle died from eating water hemlock. Time for another talk with Otto. Meanwhile, the morgue's ambient dust made him sneeze and worked into his skin until it itched like poison ivy.

He went home and compared ownership maps of Runyon Township. A dozen of the township's ninety-six farms changed hands between 1980 and 1985. The seven farms Taylor bought were the only ones adjacent to each other. The rest were scattered. Five of the seven sold because of catastrophic losses. Concurrence isn't a cause he told himself, but there wasn't another pattern like it anywhere.

Damn it! I should have seen it before. Seven farms fell, one at a time like dominos! Like Germany's conquest of Europe from Austria to France. Hartwell's tract in the center is like Switzerland. This is strange. I need another opinion.

A phone call and he was on his way into town to the Commerce Bank, a brick building with faux Greek columns supporting its pediment. "Well, well, an emissary from the Fourth Estate," Emery Daniels rumbled and his gravelly voice filled the dimly lit office. "Always good to see you. Sit down, sit down. Tell me, what can I do for you?" The old banker in a tweed suit peered at him through large glasses from beneath a hedge of bushy eyebrows.

Daniels had owned the bank since the Depression. Like an owl, he said little but often saw obscure things lurking in balance sheets and cash flow statements. His discrete shrewdness led many businessmen to consider him a sage. Though he never accused anyone directly, Boston had learned to trust the old man's questions as sagacious hints about where to look for answers to touchy questions.

"This is off the record," Boston said. "I need a second opinion on some facts I've gathered for Morrie Isaacs."

Daniels nodded. "I read the article about Hartwell's troubles. How I can help you?"

He told Daniels how it started out as a small favor to help Isaacs and it had since opened into a bottomless pit of questions for which he had no answers. Becker vanished but the neighbors said he wasn't in financial trouble and had no reason to sell his farm.

Daniels coughed, cleared his throat and sipped some water. "And so, knowing you and Morrie as I do, you both think there is more to this than a claim of adverse possession."

"You've heard of Justin Taylor, I assume," he said. When the old man nodded, he continued. "He bought nearly eighteen-hundred acres around the Runyon Mineral Spring tract. What's fascinating is that he did it in five years and paid cash."

"Do you see something suspicious in that?"

"Not on its face but he did it buying out farmers after each suffered an incredible loss. I'm struck by the pattern of failures. No similar pattern exists elsewhere."

"And?" the old man asked. "Tell me more. I'm not grasping your drift."

"There's a predictable pattern to his purchases. He buys one farm. A year later, an adjoining neighbor has a financial disaster. He buys that farm and the next year a neighbor has a burned barn or sick cattle and so on. He buys them just as they are about to go into foreclosure. Four county roads enclose his ranch. The mineral spring tract is in the center and he claims he got that from Becker through adverse possession. Hartwell's got the goods to disprove that. Taylor's neighbors are careful about what they say."

"*Hmm.* In other words, you suspect this Taylor had something to do with the disasters." Daniels peered at him with rheumy eyes.

"It's too synchronous, too pat to be happenstance."

"Let's see... *hmm...* eighteen-hundred acres at current prices... *hmm...* that's about one-point-six million dollars. And you say he paid cash. *Hmm.* I would have heard if he borrowed that much from banks at this end of the state. So, the ranch isn't his money source. It's other banks or another source."

"I think it's the latter but I don't know a lot about the cattle business."

"Well, cattle prices haven't been high enough to make that much money in five years. These days, they're lucky to break even."

"So, I should look in another direction," Boston said. He knew that if Daniels suspected something he would throw out a lead or a question and trust him to follow up. It had always been that way between them.

Daniels removed and wiped his glasses. "From what I hear, the farmers you mentioned ran good operations. They might have restructured their debts if rising interest rates hadn't cost them so much equity." The banker cleared his throat. "I think you're on to something. I'll keep my ears open and let you know."

He thanked Daniels and left, chewing on the inside of his cheek. *He's come to the same conclusion I have. Not accusing anyone... just nudging me. That means there's more to this.*

Chapter 19

It's dangerous to know too much, Boston thought on his morning jog. It's more dangerous to know too little but I still don't know what I don't know—and that's the most dangerous of all. The pattern of farm disasters ahead of Taylor's purchases looked highly suspicious. It now seemed odd that no one noticed them before. Then he thought it best to keep that under wraps. An accusation wasn't proof and if he were wrong, it could hurt someone including him. All the same, it was a grim picture to share with Morrie. But only with him.

"I hope this isn't stealing time from your book." Isaacs said as Boston entered his office.

"It is, but that's on me. This case has gotten under my skin. You know how it is. I can't leave it alone. Some questions scream for answers," Boston shook the offered hand vigorously.

"Yes, I know. That's another reason why I left the AG job. All those questions I couldn't answer pestered me like poor relations. So, what's on your mind?"

"I want your opinion on stuff people told me in confidence. I'd prefer that you don't share it with the good doctor. I haven't seen any sign he has either discretion or good judgment."

Isaacs nodded with a wry smile. "Of course. Go on."

"I interviewed the farmers who live adjacent to Taylor and talked to as many of his victims as I could—"

"—Victims, *hmm.*"

"They're suspicious of him but tight-lipped. There's an unspoken fear he'll retaliate if they accuse him." Then he outlined the sequence of disasters. "I haven't talked to Jack in a few days so don't know if he has anything about Taylor's past in Texas or Oklahoma."

"Do we have evidence the disasters weren't happenstance?" Isaacs asked.

"Yeah, but the questions exceed the answers. Not enough for an investigation."

"Did you get any leads out of your interviews?"

"They tend to chalk it up to bad luck. Larson doesn't think the insurance company did a thorough investigation but that's as far as he'll go. If Purdy suspects anything, he didn't let on. He seems happy to be out of farming. Otto says water hemlock killed his cattle. I'm going to see a veterinarian about that."

Isaacs raised his eyebrows. "You are all but suggesting Taylor caused the disasters. Say, sabotage? If so, we could be lurching toward a criminal case."

He nodded. "It feels that way. But I have nothing to back it up. I talked with Emery the other day."

"Well, what wisdom is he dispensing? Oh, by the way, I have a coffee maker now. No more Nescafe, care for a cup?"

"Only if it's already made," he said. "Otherwise, don't go to the trouble on my account. No sugar, no creamer." He accepted a cup more out of friendship than need. "Long story, short, Emery thinks much as I do and that's reassuring. At current values, he thinks Taylor may have spent one-point-six million to buy his land. He doesn't know of any banks that have lent that much to one borrower so—"

"—You think the money comes from another source?"

"That's what he thinks and so do I."

"There's no crime in that, as suspicious as it looks."

"Sure, but a single farm failure or scattered failures aren't unusual. Look at the sequence of disasters that hit five adjacent farms. It strains belief to call it happenstance. The pattern doesn't occur anywhere else. It looks methodical. Lundstrom and Becker, the first and last sellers, are the only ones who didn't suffer disasters."

"Going to be hard to prove anything, but I tend to agree with you."

"Then there's this… Becker left quietly but sent post cards to a couple neighbors postmarked in Kansas City. He said he sold the farm and retired. The address in Yuma doesn't exist and the Beckers never turned in the U-Haul."

Isaacs blew out his breath. "I see what you mean."

"There's more," he said. "Taylor told Otto it would be a shame to turn down a generous cash offer for his farm."

Isaacs nodded as he took notes. "There's nothing straightforward in any of this."

"None of the neighbors like Taylor. Some of it is envy and some is because he's an outsider. They blame him for breaking up a group of friends. So far, I haven't heard anything solid against him."

Isaacs nodded. "I agree. He could have taken Becker's claim to the spring's title in good faith. Afterall, Bob wasn't around and Taylor saw Becker's cattle on the tract. Saying he got by adverse possession would seem credible."

"That leaves us with two ways to look at this," Boston continued, feeling energized by his friend's agreement. "Becker saw his circle of friends go under. At some point it's possible he saw no point in staying. Knowing Taylor wanted his place, he sold the mineral spring with it and disappeared." He screwed up his face as he thought. "On the other hand, Becker's friends said he didn't like Taylor and would never sell to him. That could be a projection of their own bias. The information we have both supports and questions Becker's honesty. That leaves us with two possibilities—the Beckers are in hiding or they're dead. In either case, we don't know where."

"Let's keep this between us," Isaacs said quickly and wiped his glasses on a kerchief. "As you've noticed, Bob is impatient. His ego and impulsive streak make him a loose cannon. I don't want him shooting off his mouth. A careless accusation could unleash something akin to a lynching—or a libel suit."

"One more thing," Boston said. "I think I'm being shadowed. Someone followed me when I did the interviews. The other night, someone sat on the road below my house long enough to smoke four cigarettes."

"What precautions are you taking?"

"We've got a dog. I've got a revolver and can…"

"I know you can shoot… just don't go there."

They heard the outside door to the Heath Building open closely followed by the rapid footfalls of someone pounding up the stairs. Isaacs retrieved an accordion folder from his desk drawer. The doctor burst through his door a moment later.

"How about a cup from Mister Coffee?" Isaac offered. "What's new at your end?"

"Someone broke the hood ornament and mirrors off my car last night," he cried. "Then keyed the sides. I'm certain it was Taylor or his goon."

"Where was your car?" Isaacs asked as he reached for Mr. Coffee.

"In the driveway. The garage is still full of stuff I haven't unpacked. It had to be him. A warning. Intimidation. I took photos as proof."

"I'm sorry about that," Isaacs said with calming gesture. "The photos are proof of damage but useful only for an insurance claim. They don't prove who did it. So, don't go throwing around his name."

"Why the hell not?" he shouted. "Who else could've done it?"

"Your suspicion is plausible but you have no evidence. A car parked in the open… it could have been a couple of juveniles on a lark. Saying Taylor did it opens you to a defamation case. That said, if it's retaliation then it's also a sign of fear."

"Oh, you're probably right," he conceded. "I talked to him but he won't budge until he faces a court order. The town clerk said the road was abandoned but won't show me the records. I think we should sue him and the township. They're in it together. How soon can we do that?"

"Hold on, hold on," Isaacs said, waving his raised hands. "Don't get ahead of yourself, Bob. Let's assess your documents and consider the next step." Isaacs handed him the cup of coffee. "There is a legal process we must follow. You have more than enough proof to back your title. Suing will be our last resort. Now, let's hear what Boston has found."

Hartwell slumped in the chair with a moody scowl. Isaacs sensed the doctor's resentment that he wasn't in charge of his own case. It struck him as ironic that a man who followed medical protocols had a process-be-damned attitude toward legal procedures. *Boston knows what he's doing but I'll have to help Bob feel he's still a major player.*

"Becker's neighbors don't like the gate across the road," Boston said. "But they aren't going to make it an issue. Each has enough troubles as it is and believe Taylor owns all the land behind the gate. On the other hand, they're all for you in the fight."

"What does that add up to?" Isaacs asked.

Hartwell fidgeted. "It means he threatened them just like he tried it with me. That's intimidation. The sheriff should look into it."

"Hold on," Isaacs said and held up his hand. "We have only third party say-so but no evidence. So, let's stick to what we know. You didn't treat patients without doing all the tests, did you? Here are the facts. The Beckers have vanished. You have documents to prove ownership. You can show the township is uncooperative. You trespassed and was warned off. The rest is speculation, assumption and gossip. The facts may look suspicious but it's not in your interest to get ahead of them."

"But what other conclusion is there?" Hartwell retorted. "We're dealing with a crook!"

"I've dealt with more crooks than you can count." Isaacs removed his rimless glasses and gave the doctor a hard look. "People aren't born crooks. They make a mistake and then try to cover it, which is another mistake. Each cover-up deepens the trouble. Remember Nixon. It wasn't the Watergate break-in but the cover-up that finished him. It's complex. Don't try to practice law. Leave that to the sheriff and the county attorney."

"We're wasting time talking. I say strike him and the town board *now*!"

"No. Here's what we're going to do. Boston will continue to work his contacts and gather as much information as he can. I've prepared a petition to open the road. As the injured party, it's your job to circulate it and gather at least eight signatures. We'll do this by the book."

Chapter 20

"I thought my documents would never get here," Hartwell told Isaacs several mornings later. "They should've come by the first of July, not mid-month." He opened a folder and spread out the contracts and payment receipts that Becker signed. "Now I've got everything to disprove Taylor's claim."

Isaacs reviewed the papers, humming approval in his throat. He nodded and handed his client a petition to open the town road. "If the road wasn't abandoned, you don't need a petition to reopen it. The town board has five members that include the chair, a clerk, a supervisor and two trustees."

"Isn't this a waste time with Taylor chairing the board?"

"No. This is an election year and we are going to engage in power politics. You can't sue until you've been wronged. Taylor and Peterson sound negative. I don't know about the other three. If the board approves the petition, your way is cleared. If it declines, you have a stronger reason to sue."

"In other words, no matter how the majority votes, it's a trap."

"You can say that," he said with sly smile. "Now, when you pitch the petition, stick to the law and the public interest. Don't talk about anybody's motives."

"Okay. I know about petitions," he said. "I circulated a few initiatives in California."

"Good. You'll need signatures from at least seven other residents who live within three miles of the road." Isaacs opened a plat of the township and they picked out the names of potential signers.

Hartwell returned home, newly impressed with Isaacs's craftiness. He guessed that he had misjudged him. Knowing that Taylor and Peterson had already signaled opposition he called the three other members of the town board. Two members weren't at home but their wives promised to relay the message and said their husbands would call later. Marge Greenbriar took his call and asked a few pointed questions. Then she invited him to meet her in the morning.

He arrived at a one-story house in the center of a well-tended orchard. The yard had a small barn and several sheds but there were no tractors nor machinery, no cattle nor poultry. It looked more like a hobby farm than a working operation. Marge stepped outside the house before he got out of the car. The large-framed woman seated him at her kitchen table, gave him a cup of coffee and set out a plate of oatmeal cookies.

"That was a nice piece about you in the *Statesmen*," she said. "A center for wellness and meditation. Like a spa, *huh*? A neat project. So… you've got a petition to open the road."

"Yes, it was a nice piece. I've got the petition with me. I need seven more signatures."

"Tell me why I should sign it," she said. "You've been gone for years. Opening that road will throw the cost of maintenance onto the rest of us." She studied him through half-closed eyes and waited for his reply.

Wow! I didn't see it coming. She gets right to the point. A step ahead of me. A moment in silence passed before he overcame his fluster. "This is important because state law says the township can't close a road if it denies a landowner access. I have documents showing the road was in public use since the 1880s. I know people who will say it was graded and graveled until at least three years ago. As a property owner, I'm also paying for the other town roads, including the one in front of *your* house. As a member of the town board, I want your support so we can resolve this without a court case."

"Well doctor, I know the law *is* on your side," she said, tucking several strands of russet hair behind her ear. "Anyone who signs will be going against Justin Taylor. And crossing him can be difficult, if you know what I mean."

"In what way?

"He's pushy. Definitely not a Minnesotan. I've seen bad things happen that can't be proved. Buildings catch fire. Cattle get sick and die. Machinery breaks down."

"Well, as things stand, I have nothing to lose. My wife of thirty years just died. I've sold my medical practice. Now I intend to open a place by the mineral spring to help prevent heart disease. And from your tone of voice, I think you're unhappy with the way things are." Then he sipped coffee and waited.

"You're right," she said and heaved her ample form out of the chair. "In fact, I'm glad you came along." She reached into a knotty pine cupboard, removed a dark blue flannel bag containing a bottle of Crown Royal whiskey. After pouring a finger of liquor into a pair of small glasses, she handed one to him. "Thank God, you're a man with a spine! Here's to you," she said, touching her glass to his.

"What's your stake in this?"

"I grew up here. So did my late husband. I don't like outsiders stepping on people. Otto, Becker, Purdy and the others were friends of mine. They had to sell out. All legal—*as far as we know*," she said, raising her eyebrows. "Each one had a disaster that sank 'em financially. And when their farms went for auction, Taylor showed up with his checkbook."

"That's what I heard, too."

"Have you ever heard of so many farms going under in a small area over a short period of time?" She stood close to him.

"No. But if it were a disease, I'd call it a pandemic. He offered me twice what the land is worth in return for a clear title. I said no. Aren't you afraid of revenge for backing me?"

Marge tossed off the whiskey and put away the bottle. "Like what? I'm too old to worry. Now, you need at least six more signatures besides mine. I know more than that who'll sign."

"That's great, can you—"

"—I'll call some friends. Let 'em know who you are and why you're coming. I'll call you tonight or tomorrow with their names." Marge put a plump hand on his shoulder. "They'll sign because they're my friends. Because we stick together. And because you're setting an example they'd like to follow."

As they stood at the door, he had a sudden urge to hug her out of gratitude. Instead, he said, "Marge, it is a pleasure to know you. I can't thank you enough for your support."

"Oh, don't mention it," she said, patting his arm. "I'm just doing my civic duty. Go on now, let me make some calls. I'll talk to you later on."

He left, glowing from her support and wondering if she been waiting for the right moment, the right person or the right idea. The article about the wellness center was rippling through Runyon Township and he hoped it was making waves that threatened Taylor's new order. *Well, what goes around comes around.*

Pumped up and hopeful, he felt himself back in control of his life. In fact, he felt so good that he drove a premature victory lap around the eight miles of county roads that enclosed Taylor's property. As he circled the ranch, he had to admit Taylor was the steward of a particularly beautiful patch of southeastern Minnesota.

Hartwell listened to the river's soothing rush while seated on the patio. He wanted to believe his troubles were about to end. The phone rang and Marge rattled off the names of fourteen friends who agreed to sign. All he had to do was drive to their farms and collect their signatures. Sixteen petitioners. Twice the number required by law. Marge had gone out on a limb for him and her word carried the weight he needed.

In the morning, he left the marred Mercedes at the Chevrolet dealer's body shop. Then he rented a Citation with Minnesota plates— the kind modest car farmers could afford. If nothing else, the Chevy would create a positive first impression. He drove at forty miles per hour with the windows down and savored the scent of damp soil, drying hay and sunshine. At that speed, he took in the details of the fields, fence rows and farmyards until he began to feel like a local once more.

A farmwoman directed him to a field where her husband was raking hay. As the John Deere approached, Hartwell watched the rake's rotating steel tines sweep the dried hay into a long windrow. The farmer stopped, idled the engine and yelled. "I hope you win this one. You've got grit goin' against that bag of mean tricks."

"Thanks for your support," the doctor shouted back and handed him the petition on a clipboard. The man signed it and handed it back. They shook hands and the farmer shifted into gear and resumed raking. Depending on the hour and the signer, he met them in dairy barns, machine sheds or the fields. Several wives invited him in for coffee and asked questions about the spa, as they called it. Then they signed the petition for their husbands. Each wished him luck.

Collecting signatures filled the day. By the time he returned to the Chevy dealer, he felt at ease for the first time since he arrived. He felt as if he had been through an authentic reintegration as a Minnesotan. This called for a celebration—a cocktail. Then he called Marge. "Got 'em all," he said in high spirits. "And I've fixed a gin and tonic in your honor. Here's to you. Thank you!" After that, he called Isaacs with the results. "I'm weighing whether to ask any of the immediate neighbors to sign. What do you think?" He heard Isaacs clear his throat.

"Don't. If they didn't object to the gate it's not in their interest to sign. And from what you said, even those who signed are wary. You did a good day's work. Take it as a blessing and let it go."

Chapter 21

The large white GMC pickup rolled through the dusk and into Taylor's yard. Though Duarte could barely see over the steering wheel, he backed the gooseneck trailer into the corral with an expert's skill. He jumped out and opened the trailer's back gate. Three yearling heifers leaped out, wobbled for a moment and then rushed to the water trough. Taylor joined the men.

"*¿Cómo se fue?*" Morales asked about the drive from Texas. Then he spit.

Duarte wrinkled his nose. "*Las reses pasaron la inspección. Pinche policía… pidió sobre los fardos.*" The cattle passed inspection but the fucking police asked about the bales. "*Pero, todo iba bien, Jefe.*" Everything went well. He grinned, baring even white teeth with gold caps.

Morales pointed to the square bales and asked how many. Duarte shrugged and said two dozen. Morales ordered them unloaded. The *campesinos* touched their caps and said "*sí*".

"I don't like it," Taylor grumbled. "They got stopped. None of 'em is legal. The cops will be on the lookout, now. This is givin' me an ulcer. I wanna stop truckin' now that the ranch is payin' for itself. Time we find a new business."

Morales's face darkened. "C'mon, *Jefe. Sí*, she a long drive but my business, *es mio*—"

"—It's not the drivin', it's the risk. These guys got pulled over… I'm in trouble if—"

"—Truckin' make more *dinero* than *reses*, I think."

"Not anymore. I guess ya don't understand..." Taylor sucked a breath. "Money by itself ain't nothin' but paper. Somethin' to get ya somethin' real. Land is real. I bought it with money. Once ya buy and work land, it owns ya. I can explain it to ya but I cain't understand it for ya. It's just that well... everthin' we did in the oil patch was to have a ranch, a piece of the world. Don't ya wanna be part a somethin' real like that?"

Morales's eyes narrowed to black slits. "*Dinero* is real," he retorted, suddenly sick that Taylor wanted out of their deal. "What 'bout me?" He glared at his *compadre* and waited for him to blink. "I do what you want *Jefe*," he said in an injured tone. "You don' ask but I do it. You an' me *compañeros*... long time..." then he sighed and shrugged.

Taylor stuck his hands in his back pockets and his expression softened. "C'mon Nacho. We been through a lot together. Your family gimme a lot of help... *obligado*. I'm obliged. This *rancho* is your work, too. Without you, no *rancho*. We come to Minnesota at just the right time. An' 'cause of you, I got this land so we could raise pure-blood cattle."

"*Jefe, no amo las reses como tú.*" He didn't love cattle the way Taylor did. "An' what for me, *eh*? How you take care of me... *eh*? No more truckin'... *los tipos* in Laredo, they gonna put the *culpa* on me, I think." Morales knew he would be blamed if Taylor quit trucking. He felt his anger running free.

"Lemme figure out what's next for ya. How's that?" he said softly.

"Next? An' what about *dinero*... *eh*?"

"I need you to help run this place. There's time to work this out," Taylor said in a softer voice and turned toward the house. "We'll keep truckin' 'til we make a new deal... *nuevo acuerdo—vale?*"

Morales walked toward his double-wide house, entered and slammed the door. He had comfortable quarters for a single man. A small flag of Texas and another of Mexico hung on one wall. On the opposite side hung a picture of the Virgen de Guadalupe, a gift from his mother. He didn't believe in the Virgen but the image reminded him of how *Mamí* prayed daily before a statue of the Virgen in her home. She claimed Guadalupe had performed several miracles for her, including Nacho's survival from a knife fight that scarred his arms.

"*Jefe*, he don' know how to live. *Pero yo, Ignacio Renaldo Morales Barrón, sé cómo vivir!*" He thumped his chest and said he knew how to live. The money he made paid for a new GMC pickup, good clothes, good times with girls and monthly remittances to support his mother. Because of that, he considered himself a man of honor.

He walked around the room thinking of the years he spent with Taylor. *Jefe* made the plans and he carried them out. That included removing the obstacles. He had never questioned their relationship but now he felt on unstable ground. *Jefe* had been loyal in the oil patch. When he moved to Minnesota, he asked Morales to join him and promised to let him use the farm as a base for a trucking business in return for a share of the receipts. He also promised not to interfere with it. That was fair. Now *Jefe* wanted to end it.

Morales uncorked the bottle of mescal he kept in defiance of Taylor's prohibition of it on the farm. Mescal was a taste of home across the Rio. *Mi identidad como un hombre.* He poured some into a glass. *Jefe no comprende qué podía pasar.* He worried that Taylor didn't understand what would happen if he stopped trucking. He tossed off the drink and stared at the empty glass. *¿Qué puedo hacer?* he asked himself. What can I do?

*
**

Taylor heard the foreman muttering to himself in Spanish as he walked to the mobile home in the grove. *He's a whiner like the rest. Big help in the oil patch. And yeah, his family contacts set up the truckin' business. Truckin' give us both good money. But if it weren't for me, he'd be 'nother Tejano layin' drunk in a Laredo alley. I been good to him. Real good but I've gone too soft.*

He entered the house filled with the clatter of silverware and the slam of cupboard doors. *Dang, Rita's in a horn-tossin' mood. She's been bowed up for weeks now. What's she got into her? Time she started appreciatin' all that I done for her.*

Rita shot him a cold look when he entered the kitchen he had remodeled as an engagement gift. Her joy in it had waned as the months passed. She didn't like the isolation of the farm, hated feeling subordinate to the needs of Charolais cattle. Without an appetite, she felt no desire to cook for him. Not tonight and maybe not any other night. These days, she lived on fruit, salad and yogurt—what he called sissy food.

His daily demand for cooked meat with potatoes, biscuits and gravy set her teeth on edge. She cooked merely to get along with him. So far, married life hadn't matched her dreams or his promises. Justin had women before her but never a wife and living with him was a long step down from domestic life with Gerhard. She swiped at her eyes with the back of her wrist. Gerhard was soft-spoken, gentle and sensitive. Justin wasn't and never would be. She told herself she was stupid to think he would be a comfortable, middle-aged man who'd dote on her. Maddie was right about him. Being his wife was little more than being another farm he's bought. Another employee he ordered around. A new source of money and a soft spot for his dick. She sighed. And then Bob returned—but too late!

She set out a pot of beef stew with a plate of biscuits, butter and jam. Then she tossed a salad for herself and sat at one end of the table. "Justin—your supper's ready," she called and began eating.

He shambled into the dining room, scowled at the salad in front of her and sat down. Without a word, he dished himself a plate of stew and buttered a biscuit. "Ya sick or somethin'?"

"No. Just not hungry."

"Well, if you're not sick, eat more. Have some stew. It'll build up your strength."

"For *what*? You treat me like I'm a… like I work for you—someone you don't have to pay. Is that what you want?"

"Hey, wash off the warpaint. I give you everthin' you wanted. It's time you give me somethin'. Come back to my bed. Merge your money with mine. Things'll go easier 'tween us once ya do. And get rid of Maddie. Her advice is useless. The chickens under the porch know as much as she does. I already know how to get rich."

"She's my friend. My money is my money," she retorted in a sullen voice. Face it, she told herself. There's nothing to say. He wasn't there for her so she didn't expect anything. Instead, she finished eating and began clearing the table.

"What's the matter? Cat got your tongue," he called after her. "Come back. Sit down. Talk to me like a wife's supposed to. What's goin' on?"

"All right, this marriage isn't gonna work," she said in a matter-of-fact tone of voice. "The reality is you want my money. And since you can't have it, you have no use for me and—"

"—An' ya want a *dee*-vorce, that it?"

"Yeah. That's what I want."

"An' then ya gonna marry your old boyfriend, won't ya?"

"No, he's not interested in me. But he's got documents proving his ownership."

"Ya mean he used to own it. So what?"

"He thinks Becker's claim is a fraud. You need to resolve this."

"There's nothin' to resolve—"

"—Oh for Pete's sake! This isn't a Texas oil field. You can't bully your way ahead."

"We'll see about that."

Chapter 22

Searching for Becker had begun to take on the weight of a full-time job, Boston thought glumly as he climbed the stairs to Isaacs' office. Not at all what he had in mind but too late to back out now. He entered the office and declined the offer of coffee claiming he already had a full tank from breakfast. Then they heard footsteps on the stairs and Hartwell appeared. He was grinning for a change and carried a folder and a brown paper sack.

"What's in the bag, Bob?" Isaacs asked, bemused.

"Bourbon. You're looking at a lucky man." He set the bag on the desk.

"Now, why the bourbon?"

"To celebrate. Sixteen people signed the petition. Marge Greenbriar will vote for it and persuaded fourteen friends to sign on. That's twice what we require. Two other trustees won't commit. Peterson is hostile. Taylor is a no vote, of course." Then he reached into the bag and brought out a fifth of Maker's Mark and three plastic cups. "We're getting somewhere. Let's celebrate progress."

"Why was Greenbrier helpful?" Isaacs asked, ignoring the bottle. "What's her stake in this or that of the others?"

"She sees Taylor's money as a threat. So do several others. Some signed because they feel Otto or other friends got the shaft. Others signed out of principle. I guess Marge's word carries weight."

"Anything else?"

"Maybe, maybe not," he said. "I had dinner with Madeline Barnes. She's the Taylor's financial adviser and uncomfortable with him. This is a quote. She said, quote: 'Be careful. Justin is like a grenade—and I think you have just pulled the pin.'"

"All right, gentlemen," Isaacs said in what sounded like a summation. "We've got a valid petition to open the road whenever we choose to use it. At least sixteen residents are willing to stand with us. The financial catastrophes need more investigation. The Beckers' whereabouts is still a mystery. Where do we go from here?"

"Let's subpoena the township records," Hartwell interrupted. "Force them to—"

"—We're not there yet, Bob. Any other ideas?"

"I ought to file that complaint with the sheriff."

"Complaint about what?" Isaacs knit his brows. "You trespassed across his property. His hired man warned you off. Even a lazy lawyer could argue the man thought he was protecting his boss's property. It isn't a crime to carry a pistol as long as he didn't point it."

Hartwell grumbled in frustration. "What about adverse possession?" His voice sharper. "Guys, we're spinning our wheels. Let's get my title on the table. Make him put up or shut up."

"Let's all take a deep breath," Isaacs said with a calming gesture. "As things stand, I arranged a meeting with Taylor's attorney for tomorrow morning."

"To do what? Why don't we just go to court?"

Isaacs removed his glasses and fixed his client with a stern gaze. "Doctor, it is far better for everyone if we come to terms without conflict. It's like preventive medicine. It's better for you if Taylor sees the law and the documents for himself and freely decides he has no case. Otherwise, you face having an antagonistic neighbor going forward."

"I think he's committing fraud," Hartwell said. "I'll bet he killed Norm."

"*Enough!*" Isaacs yelled. "I won't represent you if you continue to utter that kind of unfounded nonsense. Am I clear?"

Hartwell's face flushed red and his eyes seemed to roll back in his head. "All right Morrie. I'll zip my lip. Sorry. I knew Norm."

"Let's see what happens at tomorrow's meeting. Taylor's lawyer if not him is likely to concede when they see your papers. If not, we can go to court. The road is a separate matter. If he concedes ownership, he may open the road. If he doesn't, there is a process that begins with the petition. Meanwhile, will you please take your documents downstairs to the copy shop. Make two copies."

"*Oo*-kay," he said in a long note of concession. "I guess we're finally moving."

"Boston is going to sit in with us tomorrow, if you don't mind."

"I see… Well, it's your call, Morrie." Hartwell gathered the files and went downstairs.

"In case you missed it, Bob resents your presence," Isaacs said. "He is or was in the habit of running things. That's the hard part of retirement. No one to order around except yourself. Meanwhile the world goes on as if you were never there."

"I know the feeling. Sometimes, I'm tempted to meddle in the *Statesman*."

"How does that work out?"

"It doesn't," he laughed. "I promised her a free hand. She raps my knuckles if I meddle."

The doctor returned a half-hour later. The sheaf of original documents had swollen into a collated ream packed in a box. He set it on the conference table.

Isaacs grinned. "Doctor, in light of what we are about to embark on, I think it's time for a dose of the stress medicine in the paper bag. We all could do with a bracer."

The three men met briefly in the morning to prepare for the conference with Taylor and Percy Hickenlooper. Isaacs had already asked Hickenlooper to make copies of Becker's deed and the sworn statement for the adverse possession claim.

"What if he has it?" Hartwell asked.

"It won't stand up against your documents. In a case like this, any good lawyer would rather settle than lose. So, either Taylor realizes

Becker hoodwinked him and admits he doesn't own your land or we go to court with a civil case. No crimes were committed. At least, none that we know of."

"I see… all right, I'm sure you know what you're doing," he said with a long face.

"They know we're coming to prove your ownership—"

"—You mean disprove his lie!"

"I mean prove your title!" Isaacs snapped. "We can't prove it's a lie. Claim is a nicer word more likely to get us to your goal. If Becker were here, you could take issue with him. But he isn't. We'll presume Taylor took his word in good faith. Of course, we want to see the documents. Now, let me do the talking."

Hickenlooper's office occupied half of a new one-story glass and stone building at the edge of downtown Featherstone. Taylor and his lawyer were already seated when they arrived. "Morrie, Boston, nice to see you," Hickenlooper said, extending a pale, soft hand. "Doctor, welcome. You know Mister Taylor, I presume." The cattleman said gruff hellos to Isaacs and Hartwell and cast a wary glance at Boston who took a chair in the corner.

"Percy, you know why we are here," Isaacs began. "So, let's get down to cases. Show us what you have to support the claim of adverse passion."

Hickenlooper swept a hand over his bald head and then opened a manila folder. He passed a copy of Becker's deed and the notarized statement to Isaacs. Hartwell drew his chair closer and examined the paper stapled to it.

"Are these the only documents you have?" Isaacs asked, frowning.

"Yes. It should be enough," he said. "It's Becker's deed plus his sworn statement."

"Y'all callin' me liar?" Taylor challenged, glowering at Isaacs.

"No, not at all," he replied in a mild tone. "However, we have documents that call Mister Becker's claim into question."

"What the hell, Percy?"

"Sit down Justin. Leave it to me. Okay Morrie, show us what's in your hand."

"As we both know, adverse possession is possible if my client allowed Becker to openly use his property for at least fifteen years without objection or recompense. That didn't happen. He rented it for thirty years. But even if he didn't pay rent, Becker had to have paid taxes on it for the last five years. That didn't happen, either. Here are the county tax records showing that Doctor Hartwell paid the taxes every year including this one. Becker had no claim—"

"—Well that's… he signed a notarized statement of ownership by adverse possession."

"We both know he can sign and notarize a bed sheet if he wants," Isaacs said. "These papers are annual contracts between Doctor Hartwell and Norm Becker for the use of his land." Isaacs pushed other papers toward him. "These are receipts for the money transfers that paid the rent. As you can see, adverse possession is legally impossible."

Taylor shifted in his chair. "I offered to buy you out," he said. "I own everything around you. That road will ruin my operation. My operation will make your whatever it is unpleasant. I think sellin' out is the practical solution to both our problems."

"That's beside the point," Isaacs interjected, his voice sharper now. "He has no desire to sell. So, he is entitled to access his property. Denial of access would be theft."

"Okay, cross my land any time you want. But you're on your own as far as risks or injuries. I'm not changing my operation to accommodate—"

"—That won't be necessary," Isaacs said. "The township is obligated to provide access."

"—Everyone knows the road was abandoned an' a private driveway for those farms."

"The neighbors say differently," Hartwell blurted. "Otto was on the town board the last time it was graveled."

"I'm told that was long ago," Hickenlooper said.

"Four years isn't long ago, Percy," Isaacs said. "Town records will confirm that."

"Then you can take it up with the town clerk," Hickenlooper said.

"I did," the doctor shot back. "He said non-residents couldn't see them."

"Aw hell, why don' you just take my word for it?" Taylor said with the expression of a man holding a winning hand. He glanced at Hickenlooper.

"We don't need your word," Isaacs said. "We can ask the court to subpoena the records. We also have a petition to open the road signed by sixteen residents of Runyon Township."

"Take it up with Peterson," Taylor said. "I'm sticking to my claim of possession. Set a court date, I don't give a shit. Are we done with this, Percy? I got cattle to look after." With that, he pushed back from the table and stomped out.

Hickenlooper looked at Isaacs and shrugged. "He's my client but—"

"—You don't have to say it, Percy. We'll see you in court."

Taylor left Featherstone in his pickup with his thoughts churning. "Lawyers ain't worth spit," he growled at the windshield. "All hat and no cattle. Talk, talk, talk for two hundred bucks an hour. If Hickenlooper's brains were ink he couldn't dot an 'I'. He folded. I thought he was better'n that. You don' get nowhere by talkin', only by walkin'. I din't have no troubles 'til Hartwell showed up. Now trouble is compoundin' like interest on an overdue note. He's gonna stand pat on his title. The road is next. No tellin' what Rita knows or who she'll tell. An' then there's Nacho's truckin'. I'm holdin' a pair of deuces against a full house. And Meade is at every meetin'." He barreled into the farmyard dragging a cloud of white dust that didn't stop traveling when he did.

Morales came around the barn and walked toward the pickup.

"Are Pablo and Duarte back?" he hollered as the foreman approached.

"*No. Más tarde.* Duarte he call from Kay-Cee. Here later."

"What's Carlos doin'?"

"He cut alfalfa. How it go?"

"*Mal*! I'm gonna lose. Then the judge will open the road."

"*Jefe*, that place. Not worth it. *No vale nada*."

"I don't want inholdings. No roads, neither. An' if we can't use the sanatorium then we have to stop truckin'."

"So, what you do?"

"Sooner or later I'll hafta let the sonofabitch in if he wants. It don't mean he can go anywhere he wants. For Chrissake, don't let him go in from the yard. For now, let him come in through that swale he used. The inconvenience might change his mind."

"Okay, *Jefe*." Morales grinned. "I make sure he change, I think."

Chapter 23

It was Isaacs' idea to put out a story about the legalities of adverse possession. Such cases were common enough. He suggested a simple statement of the facts in the *Statesman* could educate readers, shape a narrative and might persuade Taylor to concede. Boston's interview with Hartwell was a ragged conversation because the doctor couldn't separate facts from insinuations. He tried to interview the cattleman over the phone but Taylor refused to say anything beyond his ongoing claim. The story appeared:

WHEN YOUR PROPERTY ISN'T YOURS
—Waterford—July 21, 1986.

Dr. Robert Hartwell of Waterford says his family has owned the Runyon Mineral Spring since 1874. According to Justin Taylor, the spring became part of cattle ranch when he bought Norman Becker's farm in May 1985. Mr. Becker's claim of title to the mineral spring rests on thirty years of continuous use.

Acquiring legal title to another party's property is possible through open, continuous, use for at least fifteen years, spending money to improve it and paying taxes on it. The process is called adverse possession or squatter's rights. Mr. Becker left the county after he sold his farm and his whereabouts are now unknown. Dr. Hartwell and Mr. Taylor will present their

documents of title in district court on July 28. Meanwhile, anyone with information about Mr. Becker's
current location is asked to contact the sheriff.

Boston arrived in the courtroom early on the day of the hearing.
He took a seat on a side near the back and meditated on the WPA mural
of a homesteader taking up the land. The theme seemed appropriate
for the morning's case. Then a bailiff entered and turned on the lights.
Isaacs and Hartwell arrived and nodded a greeting in his direction
before sitting at a table before the bench. Hickenlooper and Taylor
trailed in and Boston began jotting notes:

Isaacs and Hickenlooper—lawyers cordial. All stand at *oyez*.
Knatvold looks elfin in billowing judicial robe. Court in session. Judge
studies papers. Pinched expression—as if disgusted by food on plate.
Compares docs for several minutes. Judge looks at attorneys.

"Gentlemen, I have read your briefs," the judge began, lacing
his fingers together. "Mister Hickenlooper, your client claims Doctor
Hartwell abandoned his property and Mister Becker openly used it for
his own purpose, spent his own money to fence it and acquired title
through adverse possession. Your case rests on a notarized statement
Mister Becker presented to your client as his bona fide title to the tract
when your client bought his farm. Is that your position?"

Hickenlooper stood. "That's it exactly your honor."

"Mister Isaacs, your client says his family has owned the property
continuously since 1874. You say its title passed to him through probate.
I see you appended various documents to your brief in support of your
client's cause."

"Yes, your honor," Isaacs said, standing. "We assert that Doctor
Robert Hartwell is the legal owner of the property commonly known
as the Runyon Mineral Spring. The legal description is in the document
before you."

"Mister Isaacs, please summarize the proof of ownership that
rebuts the adverse claim." Knatvold peered quizzically over the top of
his glasses.

"Your Honor, we present an abundance of evidence that
includes the homestead patent to Horatio Hartwell, the probate

documents conveying the property to my client in 1971 and copies of county tax records showing that only my client has paid the taxes on the parcel."

The judge coughed as he sifted the papers. "All right, anything else Mister Isaacs?"

"Yes, we submit notarized contracts between Mister Becker and my client. They show regular contact between them and financial payments for his use of the property. In addition, there are receipts for funds my client advanced to Mister Becker for erecting fences."

"*Hmm* yes, I see those," the judge muttered, nodding. "Mister Hickenlooper, what do you say in light of these facts?"

The lawyer stood, glanced at his client and then looked at the judge. "Your honor, the plaintiff lived in California. He hasn't set foot on the property in decades. In effect, he abandoned it. Mister Becker gained de facto title by using it."

"Mister Hickenlooper, how can the property be abandoned when the record shows Doctor Hartwell paid the taxes? The *onus probandi* is on you."

"Well, *uh*, what I mean is—"

"—Where is your evidence that meets all five requirements of Minnesota Statute five-oh-four point oh-two?"

"Your honor?"

Knatvold glowered. "Where is your evidence that Mister Becker knew his occupation was contrary to Hartwell's intent, that he spent his own money to improve the property, his occupation was open and obvious, he resided on the property continuously and paid property taxes? Where is that evidence?"

"We contend that he did it as an adjunct to his farm operation."

"A contention isn't evidence. All I see is a signed paper that meets none of the legal requirements for adverse possession. Were you a party to notarizing this…?" The judge rattled the paper in front of him. "…this document?"

"Well… *uh*… no, your honor, no I wasn't. I-I accepted it at face value," Hickenlooper stuttered in retreat. "Mister Becker was known as an honest man. We saw no reason to doubt it."

"*Hrmph*! The court will recess for fifteen minutes." Knatvold banged the gavel, gathered the papers and left with his robe flying out behind him.

The lawyers consulted each other while Taylor sat motionless and stared at the judge's bench. Boston wondered what the cattleman was thinking. Then the judge returned, everyone stood for the *oyez* and then sat. Knatvold shrugged his shoulders and adjusted the robe. Then he clasped is hands and stared at the parties like a schoolmaster about to lecture naughty boys.

"After reviewing the law and the documents presented by both parties in the matter of *Hartwell v. Taylor*, the court finds Doctor Hartwell possesses unquestioned title to the property known as the Runyon Mineral Spring. Therefore, the court orders Mister Justin Taylor to cease forthwith all further claims of ownership by word or action. As for you, Mister Hickenlooper, your entire pleading follows a Texas statute and not Minnesota law. I'm tempted to sanction you for that." The judge paused. "However, I will stay that sanction for three months provided you complete a professional refresher course in property law and report to me when you have done so. This court is adjourned." He banged the gavel and left before anyone could stand.

Boston glanced at the courtroom clock. Forty-two minutes to dispose of this case. He watched the Texan leave the chamber and doubted the cattleman would let go of this.

*
**

The decision buoyed Harwell's spirits for a moment. In the aftermath, he felt a weight lifted from his chest. But Taylor wasn't going to remove the gate. Not right away. He made it clear that Hartwell had to prove it was still a public right of way. "How long will it take to open the road?" Hartwell asked as he and Isaacs left the courtroom.

"It won't be like Aladdin saying, 'open sesame'."

"Why not? My title is clear. I've got the petition. I've got a right to access."

"You do, but there are procedural steps that will take some time," he said in a professor's mild tone. "First, you've got to submit the petition. The clerk must validate the signatures as town residents. Then he has to schedule a meeting of the town board and put the petition on the agenda. After that, the board has up to thirty days to meet and vote on it. You need three votes."

"I see…" He exhaled feeling the weight returning to his chest. "Taylor will fight it."

"Every step of the way."

"But once the board votes for the road—"

"—Patience. Even if you get the three votes, the board is likely to give him time to comply with the fencing laws so his cattle aren't on the road. That's another month, at least."

"What if the board turns me down?"

"You can go back to court."

He groaned in disgust. "By God I'll still beat that bastard."

That evening, the town clerk told him to bring the petition to his farm or mail it in, he didn't care which. Hartwell said he would drop it off. *The bastards are going to slow walk me at every step.* As a precaution, he made a duplicate copy of the signed petition in case it accidentally got "lost" as sometimes happened in California.

It was late afternoon when he pulled into the clerk's farm. Even before he arrived, he caught the odor of hogs drifting on the warm, south wind. The metal farm buildings looked new and so did the farmhouse. Evidentially this farmer was doing well despite hard times. The clerk wasn't home but his wife took the packet and gave him a receipt. He called Marge and told her he left the petition. "What do you think?"

"He'll side with Taylor. You've got my vote. I don't know about the other two. They've been inclined to take their lead from him."

"I see… You mean, it's iffy?"

"Yep. That's why I rounded up excess signers. It puts some weight behind you."

"Thanks, Marge. If it weren't for people like you, this would be a hopeless quest."

"Doing right isn't hopeless, just difficult."

Chapter 24

Am I looking at this with tunnel vision—and from the wrong end, Boston wondered. Becker was one of the mysteries but there were others. For some reason, the facts of Hartwell's ownership hadn't changed Taylor's mind. It could be he was just stubborn or it could be something else. With nothing more to dig up on the Beckers, he decided to look into Taylor's past. He groaned. It meant starting a new investigation that would eat up more time. After several hours in the *Statesman's* morgue, he emerged with four brief photocopied articles on Taylor.

The clippings told him little that he didn't already know. After making money as a Texas wildcatter, he bought a farm in 1980 and then some woodlands the next year. His only interview covered rotational grazing in 1984. None of the stories mentioned the sanatorium or Runyon Mineral Spring. A longer story from last year detailed the raucous protests and anonymous threats that followed his purchase of the Wilkes farm.

The only personal information about the cattleman was that he grew up on a Texas ranch, worked in the oil fields of Oklahoma and later struck it rich wildcatting in the Permian Basin in Texas. When oil prices slumped, he sold the oil business and moved to Minnesota to raise cattle. *A nice clean story. A little too clean, a little too neat and missing too much detail. There has to be more to his past.*

Spinning his rolodex, Boston chose his contacts at the daily newspapers in Amarillo and Abilene, Texas and Elk City, Oklahoma.

Then he spent the morning on the phone talking with friends who asked about his life since he left *American Outlook*. He made a simple ask: Did they have background on a wildcatter named Justin Taylor. Three hours later and still no leads.

Thinking he was still on the wrong track, he suspected Taylor didn't do anything that caught public attention. Texas was full of wildcatters that no one had ever heard of. He suspected he was a smaller fish than he pretended to be. He left the desk, rolled his shoulders and walked the quarter mile down the hill to pick up the mail and loosen his muscles if not his mind.

This morning was living up to July's reputation for heat and humidity. The big house trapped heat and he wished for another cold front to clear the air. He opened the windows and set the oscillating fans in strategic spots. Jester lay in front of one, panting. Then, believing the air on the veranda was marginally cooler than inside, he sat in its shade with a glass of iced tea. Sucking on a cube, he considered ways to get closer to Taylor. A colleague in Amarillo suggested calling smalltown editors in the Texas panhandle. They might know the families in the area. Most of the country editors he had met were leery of outsiders and tended to circle the wagons around their communities. He jotted a list of open-ended questions he hoped would entice them to reveal things they withhold from a direct question.

On this hot, drowsy afternoon, even the pickup on the county road traveled slower than usual. Boston raised his arm in greeting but the driver didn't respond. The truck vanished around the end of the ridge. Ten minutes later, it returned headed toward Featherstone at the same dawdling pace. It looked familiar but the county had dozens of GMC pickups. He gathered his questions and went inside to make some calls. The first two hit answering machines. Then a woman at the newspaper in Shamrock, Texas, handed him off to the editor.

"Are you the Meade who writes that column in *American Outlook?*" The editor asked in what sounded like a shout.

"Guilty as charged," he said with a laugh, hoping it would open some doors.

"Well, I like the way y'all look at big events through that smalltown lens. The country needs more of that kind of thinkin'. I'm plumb thrilled to talk to ya."

"Thank you," he said as his hopes rose. From the man's voice, he pictured a white-haired editor shouting into a candlestick telephone in an office where they set lead type on a Prouty newspaper press. It wasn't true, of course, but easy to imagine. He let the editor ramble for a moment before saying he was going to write about a leading local citizen, a Texas cattleman named Taylor who came from Twitty.

"Spell out the name. I don't recollect that handle."

"Justin Taylor." Then he spelled the name.

"*Justin* Taylor? *Hmm*. We had a Justin *Daylor* who used to live here. Lotta Daylors around here." The editor spelled the name. "His pa used to ranch the scrub outside of Twitty. Is that who you mean?"

"That fits what he's told us about himself. He owns nearly two-thousand acres here and raises cattle. Can you tell me anything else?"

"Not much. He went off working in the oil patch around Elk City. Later, he was wildcatting in Odessa or so he said."

"That squares with what we know."

"I guess we're talking about the same fella," the editor said, lowering his voice and sounding relaxed. "We did a piece on him when his pa died. He come home for the funeral bragging about the oil money he made. There was a photo of him, too. Give me your fax number and I'll wire it."

"I appreciate that—"

"—Taylor, *huh*?" the editor said with a snort. "Leadin' citizen, you say? Well, nice to know he's changed more than his name."

"What do you mean?"

"Now, don't quote me, but he got into trouble here when he was younger. A bully—"

"—He's claimed a neighbor's property by squatter's rights—"

"—*Yee*-up. That sounds like him. If he made that big oil field money like he bragged, he never used it to help his pa get outta debt. The old man lost his ranch. That's what killed him in the end. Died of heartache. Leastways, that's my take on it."

"Thank you for your help," he said. "I'll look forward to your fax." Something at last. Our leading citizen might have something to hide.

When Ginger and a gal pal went out for dinner and a movie, Boston invited himself to Jack's house because his brother was grilling Juicy Lucy burgers. After they ate, Ben joined the men on the lawn and listened to Herb Carneal's play-by-play of the Twins battling the Tigers. Now and then, Jack made snide remarks about the White Sox but neither the Chicago nor the Minnesota team was on a winning streak. When Boston tired of the banter, he told Jack what he had learned about Taylor's past from the newspaper editor. His brother seemed unimpressed.

"There's something else."

"*Uh-huh*. With you, there's always something else," he laughed.

"The editor said his real name is Daylor. He faxed me a photo. It's him."

"*Uh-huh*. Because he changed his name, you think he's got something to hide. Now I know what you want," Jack said, rolling his eyes in mock surprise. "Since the deputies have so little to do, you want me to use public resources to call a bunch of Texas sheriffs and ask if he's got a criminal record. That's what you want, isn't it?"

"You know I'd never ask," he smirked, shaking his head. "But now that you've offered to do that, I accept."

"It's not an offer. Got any other information?" Jack turned serious.

"Taylor or Daylor claims he made it big wildcatting near Odessa. I'm talking to newspaper contacts near the oil patch. But we need to look at Oklahoma for any criminal records on him and his foreman, Nacho Morales."

"*We?*" Jack opened another beer. "Tell you what I'll do," he said. "Give me a pretext and I'll make some discrete calls. Has he broken any laws I oughta know about?"

"Maybe. He claims adverse possession of the mineral spring and fenced off the town road to it. The judge just affirmed the owner's title to the spring but the road is still blocked. What's more, the Texas editor said he had priors as a youth."

"All right," Jack conceded, knowing he was sandbagged. "That's not enough to open an investigation. Not yet, anyway. I don't want to cast suspicion without something solid."

"And something else."

He narrowed his eyes. "*Uh-huh*, go on."

"I'm pretty sure someone is stalking me." Then he told him about the cigarette butts and the slow-moving pickup. "No laws broken but it's unsettling. I've got Dad's revolver but... I'm more worried about Ginger than me."

"I can't do anything at this point. Just take precautions. Get a license number or description. Meanwhile, I'll track down Taylor."

The sheriff's department never had enough money or officers to provide the kind of service that Jack wanted. Five years of foreclosures and losses had strained its resources. He knew Boston was on this story because he sensed a crime. And up to now, his nose for a case hadn't failed him. At the same time, Jack couldn't commit to something based on his brother's suspicions. All the same, he called a half-dozen sheriffs in Texas and Oklahoma. If Taylor didn't surface on their radar, he could stop looking.

"Wheeler County sheriff's office," someone answered. Then: "Hold on, I'll get him."

"Hello, Sheriff Meade. How kin we Texicans help y'all up there in the Arctic?"

He laughed. "Send us warmth in January. Meanwhile, I'm tracking down the past of someone here who comes from your county. He calls himself Justin Taylor. We've since learned his name is Daylor. You got anything on him?"

"We got a lotta Daylors out by Twitty on the north fork of the Red. Good folks, most of 'em but they breed like rabbits. What's he done?"

"We're not sure. Still working up a case. So far, he's laid claim to someone else's property and closed a public road to it. He showed up six years ago and started buying distressed farms. He bought nineteen-hundred acres with cash he said he earned wildcatting in Texas. A contact in Shamrock said he had priors as a youth."

"*Hmm. Daylor. Hmm.* I 'spect that was before my time as sheriff. So, if y'all kin wait a spell, I'll ask some old-timers if they recollect him and call. Good enough?"

With Texas calls completed, Jack turned to Oklahoma. "I appreciate you taking my call this late," he said to the obliging sheriff. "I'm doing a quiet background on a local newcomer who says he made a lot of money in the Anadarko Basin."

"Who is he? What's he done?" the officer asked.

"We're still figuring that out. Got anything on a guy named Justin Taylor or Daylor? ...Oh, you do. Can you tell me what it is?" He wrote notes as he listened. "That's good. Thank you. Do you know if he has any associates? Say, a guy named Nacho Morales or any others? ... *Uh-huh, uh-huh,*" he said as he wrote. "Can you fax that up to me. My fax is area code five-zero-seven" and then rattled off the numbers. Then he repeated them. "Many thanks. Meanwhile, I'll call you if I come across anything."

He hung up believing he had learned one thing. Taylor or Daylor hadn't committed a serious crime in Texas. But he was on the radar in Oklahoma. Morales was on their screen over a corpse stuffed into an abandoned bore hole. *Looks like I'm going to be involved.*

Chapter 25

Boston sat in the den straining his notes for overlooked clues from conversations with Larson and Otto. Each blamed his disaster on happenstance or bad luck. That struck him as an excuse to cover their sense of guilt or shame at selling. He didn't believe luck existed. Events had causes that could be discovered. The farmers resented Taylor's buyouts because he offered the best of several bad options. Becker was the only seller who wasn't in financial trouble. He didn't like Taylor but he sold anyway and disappeared. Why he did was a mystery. Was he in a hurry to retire? Or was it an offer he couldn't refuse? Or because he lost all his close friends? Boston threw up his hands with a groan.

"What?" Ginger asked without looking up from reading *The House on Mango Street*.

"Hartwell's case," he said from the den. "I wish I could drop it."

"More likely it doesn't want to drop you," she said. "Lower your standards... quit."

"Oh, thanks a *lot*!"

"It's the Beckers, isn't it? And you won't be fit to live with until you know what happened, will you?"

"Not likely, dammit. I thought this would take a day or two. It's been six weeks. I just got out my *Outlook* column for August and have only a couple pages outlined for the Nielsen book. I need a break!"

"You'll get it when the Beckers turn up or you quit. And I know you won't quit so you won't get a break."

He got up from the desk and went to the turret window where raindrops gathered on the pane and dribbled down the glass. The dribbles would become rivulets on the lawn and eventually merge into brooks that filled the rivers that ran to the sea. The Becker case was like that, he thought. Trickles of fact joined others from Jack and Isaacs to form a small stream. Sooner or later, he thought the facts would lead to Becker. They were either in hiding or dead. But where? All he had was a hunch, and a hunch wasn't evidence any more than a weather forecast was rain.

He sat on the sofa with an arm around Ginger. Heads together, they listened to the rain against the windowpanes. In the gentle patter, he heard everything that needed saying. They were dry, safe and together. He knew they didn't need anything more.

The day broke damp but fair. Boston jogged his usual route to clear the fuddle from his mind. As he trotted along, he recalled Larson's doubts that neither lightning nor wiring nor spontaneous combustion sparked the fire in his barn. That left arson. He wondered if the insurance company considered that. A call to Larson secured a promise to arrange access to his insurance file. Boston dreaded digging into the paperwork. Insurance struck him as a baffling racket of "what if" clauses written by lawyers trained in obfuscation. The convoluted fine print seemed phrased to help the companies justify paying as little as possible—if at all.

In the morning, he drove to the insurance agency's cramped office in Waterford where the genial agent put him in a vacant cube with the file. The paper trail on the barn fire lay buried within a hodgepodge of premium notices and policy changes. Larson kept the barn in good order. Five years before the fire, he installed an automated milking system with upgraded electrical wiring. However, he didn't increase his insurance coverage. Nothing in the paperwork suggested the company did a thorough investigation of the fire's cause.

"How did you determine that lightning caused the fire?" he asked, looking over the cube.

"Process of elimination. No signs of faulty wiring. Not even a tripped circuit breaker. Larson said the barn lights were on when he saw the flames."

"What about spontaneous combustion?"

"Not likely. It was a cool, dry summer. Combustion needs heat and moisture. Larson said the hay was so dry it crumbled. That left lightning—"

"—What about arson? It's not mentioned."

"Well, the fire started during a thunderstorm so—" the agent shrugged.

"—So, you didn't look for arson," he interrupted, annoyed. "Larson said the storm hit after he saw the flames."

"Well, that's what *he* says," the agent replied. "What's the diff now? We paid him. He sold out. The case is closed."

"No, it's not closed. Not in my book. Thanks for your cooperation," he said, clipping his words. His pique at the agent's indifference subsided as he drove. He recognized the agent was a decent guy trying to help an underinsured local and said it was lightning to give Larson the maximum pay out right away. An arson investigation would have dragged out the settlement. Or the investigator confused the convergence of the storm and the fire as its cause. So, the policy paid off, the police weren't involved and the evidence went up in smoke. Game, set, match.

Otto's cattle died from eating water hemlock and he wondered how often than happened. It was another question among many that bred like rabbits. He returned home and scanned the den's well-stocked library that his father curated over the decades. From among its hundreds of volumes of literature, history, science and encyclopedias he chose a battered copy of Peterson's *Field Guide to Wildflowers*. He recognized *Cicuta maculata* immediately. Water hemlock. The text said it was toxic but that wasn't enough detail to assess its effect on cattle.

He called the Alton Veterinary Clinic, a large animal practice at the edge of town. The vet said he would be glad to talk. Entering the veterinary's tidy office, Boston caught a sharp taint of disinfectant mingled with the sweetness of animal feed. A calf bawled out of sight behind a curtain at the back of the building. He hit the bell on the counter. The vet entered a moment later dressed in boots, jeans and a stained lab coat.

"You got a sick animal?" the vet asked, scratching a well-trimmed beard.

"Yeah, after a fashion," he said and introduced himself. "I'm working on a story that involves cattle that died of water hemlock. Or so I've been told. What can you tell me about it?"

"Water hemlock? Deadly stuff. What's your interest?"

"A couple Waterford dairymen. Their cows ate hemlock and died. How deadly is it?"

"Green hemlock can kill a cow in fifteen minutes," he said, adopting the clinical tone of a scientist. "The plant produces an alcohol called cicutoxin that attacks the central nervous system. Causes convulsions like grand mal seizures."

"That fits what I was told," he said. "The owner said his cattle were off the pasture and died of eating baled hay."

"That can't be right," the vet said, knitting his brow. "Hemlock loses toxicity as it matures. Poisoning happens in the spring. That's when cattle eat roots or immature plants. However, the seed heads are green until mid-summer. They can be deadly—"

"—The owner said his herd was off the pasture and eating baled hay."

"*Ope*! Now wait a minute… wait a darned minute," he said, pacing back and forth snapping his fingers. "*Yee-ah*. I recall those cases and…" he rubbed his bearded chin. "Let me see… last year, no, the year before that. A couple farmers near Waterford… *yee-ah*, that story got around the vet grapevine. That's where I heard about it."

"I'm following those cases," he said, hoping he now had an answer. If not *the* answer then he had a theory for an answer. "Is hemlock toxic if it's baled with the hay?"

"No. Doubt it. The toxicity fades as it matures. I think curing hay would evaporate the alcohol and neutralize the toxin."

"What about the green seed heads?"

"They're still potent in August. The time between cutting, baling and feeding would have to be short. Otherwise, I doubt it."

"So, hypothetically, the time of toxicity would be a matter of a days, not months?"

"I think so. Otherwise, the cows might recover."

"That helps a lot. Thanks," he said, leaving with a belief he had something to ask Otto.

"How's it going?" Ginger asked as he poured over a botany book.

"I'm making hay," he said with a grin. "Checking out water hemlock."

"You'll be drinking that if you piss off the wrong folks."

"I only piss 'em off because you gave me the assignment. Now, I have a working theory—with evidence."

"So, tell me your theory," she said, leaning on his shoulders and nibbling his ear.

"The theory is someone sabotaged farmers to throw them into a financial crisis so they would have to sell. Two dairymen were forced to sell after their herds ate hemlock."

"Why hemlock?"

"It's a common, native plant that causes death within minutes of ingestion. A few cattle die of it every spring but not herds of them. A couple more questions. Then I'll know for sure."

Boston called Otto who asked about Becker. They still hadn't turned up, he replied. "I've got a couple questions about your herd. Do you remember when your herd died of hemlock—what month that was?"

"How could I forget? Fifth of August, eighty-four."

"Were they on pasture or off?"

"They were off pasture for two weeks. The grass had dried up. I fed 'em hay. They started dying right away."

"When did you cut that hay?"

"I can't say. It was old hay—last year's hay. What are you gettin' at?"

"I don't think hemlock could be toxic after a year."

"The vet did an autopsy. He said it was hemlock."

"I believe you. And the vet. I think someone added green hemlock seeds to the hay."

Otto fell silent for a long time except for clicking his tongue. "Well now, that makes sense," he said slowly. "That's gotta be how he done it. The cows were fenced in under some trees. I found 'em dead or dying in the morning. He coulda snuck down the fence at night and put the hemlock in the hay. *Yee*-up… that makes sense. Thanks for telling me. At least it wasn't anything I did. Of course, me and you can't prove it."

"I think I can."

Chapter 26

Making a lot of money, especially a lot of money in a hurry, never failed to grab public attention. Boston knew from covering such stories in the past that, if Taylor struck it rich in the Odessa oil field, his name should turn up somewhere in a public record. He threw down his pencil in frustration knowing he was about to take another detour away from the Nielsen book. Get it over with, he told himself and called colleagues at *American Outlook* for their contacts at papers in Houston, Austin and Dallas-Fort Worth. More calls led him to reporters in the oil patch.

He didn't know the reporters at the *Odessa American* and the *Midland Telegram-Reporter*. After fast talking and name dropping, the *Odessa American* reporter recognized his name and took his call. He asked if the *American* had published stories about Daylor or Taylor.

"I don't recall the name," the reporter said. "Got any more info on this guy?"

"He would've been active from the late sixties and the seventies but left before nineteen-eighty. He claims he made a bundle as a wildcatter. In the last five years, he's dropped over a million in cash to buy out seven Minnesota farmers."

"I'll check. Meanwhile, talk to Sam Scott at the *Telegram-Reporter*. He follows the oil patch more than I do."

Scott had a raspy twang to his voice. "*Huh*, so, you're lookin' for a guy named Daylor. Yeah, there's somethin' familiar about that handle. And you're doin' a background investigation—that right? Okay. So you say this fella shows up in Minnesota with a couple million he made from wildcattin'. Gimme your fax number."

"Thanks for that. The number is—"

"—*Hey,* hold on!" Scott gasped. "I don't know any wildcatters who made that kind of money. At least, not in the short haul. Makes me think he mighta struck oil on a moonless night… if ya know what mean."

"I think so. That's how he operates here."

"Tell ya what, I'll check and fax what I find. Here's the number for the Oilfield Crime Team out of Odessa. It's a multi-county operation on account there's so much theft of crude, equipment, bits, tubes, pipe—that sort of thing. A hundred grand worth a month."

"Can you tell me how they do it?"

Scott said the smart ones got jobs inside a company and tipped off pals on the outside when it was safe to steal wellhead oil or equipment. They dumped the stolen oil at a pipeline depot and collected the pay. Or they sold stolen equipment and material to shady operators—like other wildcatters. Sometimes insiders set up a shell company so the operation looked legit. Sometimes they sabotaged a wildcatter and forced him to sell out.

"Thanks, you've been a big help," Boston said and promised to let Scott know if anything came of it. Scott's fax arrived the next day. Justin Daylor worked at several lower-level oil company jobs in the 1960s and then set up Twitty Oil. Twitty bought out Guyver Oil after it suffered large wellhead losses from broken equipment. Daylor sold Twitty to another wildcatter in 1979 and disappeared. *Well, that clears things a little.*

Later that afternoon, Jack took the call from his brother. "That's interesting," he said as Boston passed on what he had learned. "Say, I'm off duty tomorrow. Let's spend the day fishing trout on Windmill Creek. Come in for an early breakfast and we'll make a day of it."

"How can you think of fishing when I have information like this?"

"Yours isn't the only case on my mind. There's trouble in other parts of the county, you know. A day of fishing will help me sort it out.

It'll be good for your overworked brain, too."

Boston agreed because he couldn't dissuade him. Windmill Creek was a spring-fed, bluff country tributary of the Limestone River. Their father had introduced them to flyfishing there when they were boys and they considered it home waters.

"Looks like a good day for a caddis hatch," Jack said as he drove.

"How would you know?"

"It's that time of year. A warm August day brings 'em out."

"A caddis hatch—you're dreaming," Boston snorted. "You're hoping caddis because you don't like fishing with small flies. Fact is, it looks like an ideal day for midges."

"Yeah, that's what *you* always say."

Seeing his brother enjoy the banter was enough to dissuade Boston from mentioning the evidence. Instead, he recalled how their dad had used the tiniest of flies to tease lunkers out from under the banks when no one else could. As much as Boston enjoyed luring and landing trout, fishing wasn't about catching meat but about memories.

Boston parked the Jeep in a pasture under two elms where the stream stumbled from riffle to pool for a half mile through a meadow dotted with oaks and basswoods. Jack studied the water for the kinds of insects the trout were eating. Then each brother made a plan as he rigged up his rod and checked his fly box. Jack walked downstream to fish his way back to the Jeep. "Yep, a perfect day for caddis," he said.

Boston noticed the tiny mayflies lying dead on the water's surface. A brown nose broke the film of slick water and sucked under an insect. He tied a tiny fly onto his leader and cast toward the ripple of a rising trout. As he fished, he considered the sex life of mayflies. The males hatched, mated and then died after an intense one-night stand. Life isn't fair, he thought with a wry smile. After several casts, a trout took his fly and he set the hook. After a running fight, the speckled fish lay gasping on the bank. He laid it in the grass, admired its red and black spots, removed the barbless hook and then slipped it back into the stream.

The graceful rhythms of fly-casting relaxed him as he focused on the currents, the aquatic life and the holes and rocks where trout waited for their next meal. Sometimes, seeing the line roll out in a perfect cast was as satisfying as catching a fish. Soon, he forgot all about Becker, Taylor and evidence as he focused on the world of the river, now and then landing a chunky trout. The brothers returned to the vehicle at midday when the sun drove the wary fish under the shady banks. Neither trout nor brothers would return until the safety of evening shadows. Boston opened the cooler and handed out sandwiches, chips and beer. As they ate, each brother recounted his catches in a familiar and comforting fraternal ritual.

"I know you're antsy about Becker so here's the latest," Jack said, biting into a turkey sandwich. "We don't have access to the Becker's bank accounts but we found out he didn't have a mortgage or any outstanding loans."

"So, they didn't have to sell out under duress like the others."

"No. Now here's where it gets squirrely. He closed his Waterford account over the phone. It was highly irregular and management fired the personal banker when it came to light. He has since moved elsewhere."

"What do you make of that?"

"The personal banker said he closed the account and transferred the funds because the Beckers called from Arizona and were buying a house."

"We've been looking in the wrong direction!" Boston grunted. "Becker didn't commit fraud. Taylor did."

Jack blew out his breath. "I know. We're coming to the same conclusion from opposite ends. Unfortunately, we don't have enough evidence for a case. We have a suspicious character but…" He took another bite of sandwich. "I think we're going be digging a while longer."

The brothers sat on a tarp in the shade and quietly pulled on their beers. Then they lay on their backs with their hands behind their heads. As boys, they had often done that and gazed up into the treetops as they confided their fears and daydreams.

"I found out he had a wildcat oil company near Odessa," Boston said. "He worked for other companies before he started his own. He bought out a competitor when it suffered serious wellhead losses and equipment problems."

"I hear a familiar tune." Jack rolled onto his side to look at him. "It ties in with what I learned." Then he rolled onto his back. "The police in Midland suspect him and Morales of stealing and selling oil and equipment but they never had enough proof. I oughta know more in a week or two. Same with a sheriff in Oklahoma. They suspect Morales of murder but don't have the goods. The Texans tell me he slipped through their fingers a couple times. Bet you a bottle of Jameson the oil he stole financed his land grab."

"Oil money backed with some sabotage and threats. I interviewed several of the farmers he bought out—Arne Larson, Hans Otto and Jarle Lundstrom. Two things struck me."

"And those are…"

"First—they stopped just short of making definite accusations," Boston said, sitting up. "I think they're afraid of retaliation. However, they agree it's suspicious so many farmers in a small area had such bad luck."

"So, they'd like to point the finger but play it safe by hinting it to you."

"Yeah, something like that. I followed up on Larson's fire and Otto's sick cattle. Those are commonplace disasters that don't attract an investigation. Larson's insurance agency never considered arson even though they had scant evidence for other causes. I think it was sabotage."

"What do you think happened?"

"Larson refused Taylor's offer for his farm because he had no desire to sell. He could have weathered the crisis but the barn burned. It wasn't just the building. He borrowed equity to finance the new dairy equipment. His insurance didn't cover all of it and the loss put him out of business. He sold his farm for what Taylor originally offered. Larson said the fire started before the thunderstorm so I think he or Morales used that as cover for arson. But I can't prove it."

"So, oil field tricks—"

"—Yeah. Now, you see those plants along stream… the ones with umbrella-like flowers?" Boston pointed. "That's water hemlock. Otto and Wilkes went under because their herds ate it."

"So, how does it tie in?"

"A vet told me yesterday that green hemlock can kill a cow in fifteen minutes. Water hemlock seeds are still potent in August. I think someone slipped into Otto's corral at night and laced the hay with hemlock seeds. Enough cows died to force him out of business."

"You have been a busy boy," he laughed. "Good thing I dragged you away for some relaxation. Otherwise, it's likely your brain might explode."

"Something about Taylor's cattle operation is off kilter."

"Explain that. It looks successful—"

"—*Looks* is the operative word. Larson's neighbor mentioned it. So did Lundstrom. He lives just up the road from him. Every month, he sees Taylor's rig haul out two or three head. It's gone a few days and returns with bales of hay."

"So...? I don't get it."

"He doesn't need hay. Sometimes the cattle he ships out are the ones that return."

"*Ah!*" Jack rubbed his forehead. "If they're importing hay they don't need then it's a cover for something else. Now, what do you suppose they'd be shipping up from the border... *hmm?*" He winked.

"That's my conclusion. I wonder if Becker saw something he shouldn't have."

"*Hmm.* We'll have to figure out a way to check. Give it a rest for now. You'll need your strength to catch trout."

The men snoozed a while in the shade until the sun was halfway down the sky. Then Jack sat up, yawned and walked to the stream. He rubbed his hands, pleased to see the trout were out from under the banks and feeding again. "I hear splashing downstream. It's caddis. I can see 'em rising. C'mon."

Boston looked up at him from the tarp with his arms behind his head. "I'm coming," he yawned, picked up his rod and fished upstream still thinking about Becker. *The reason I can't find him is because he's dead.*

Chapter 27

A late afternoon phone call interrupted Jack's efforts to tidy his desk at the end of the day. The desk officer said it was the sheriff of neighboring Wacouta County. He was happy to take it because they were friends who paired up a couple times a summer to fish for bass in the Mississippi River backwaters. He hoped this was an invitation to spend a summer day fishing a backwater in his friend's bass boat.

"Afternoon, Jack. Are you missing two citizens named Becker?"

"*Jesus*, yes! Norm and Velva. They left here in May of eight-five. Are they in custody?"

"Not exactly. They're in the morgue. We just brought in what's left of them."

"*Jesus*! Fill me in," He reached for a pencil.

"Two guys found them yesterday evening while fishing a backwater near where we usually fish. They saw the car on the bank and went ashore. By the time they called us it was too dark to go out. Took us all day to bring them in."

"What else can you tell me? It's an odd place to end up."

"No kiddin'. No telling how he did it, but he managed to drive his Buick a good hundred yards off the end of that boggy ATV trail. Their bodies were in the back seat. All decomposed except for bones, hair and clothing. We traced the license and got their names. So, you've been looking for them."

"Yeah, we wanted to question them in a case of adverse possession and possible fraud."

"Since they're your folks, and you've already got a case, how would you like to handle this going forward?"

"Thanks for asking. How we handle it depends on how they died. Have you done any forensic exams?"

"No. We just got them and the car in here an hour ago. That's why I'm asking."

"Our case involves a lot of unexplained angles on several likely crimes. I'd like to send a team to work with you if that's all right with you."

"Sure, it's five-thirty. I'll tell the crew to button it up for the day. What time can your folks get here?"

"I'll send my best detective to work with you," Jack said. "I think you know Mary Kasson. She's a vet and taught me and a lot of others about investigations. She loves the nitty-gritty. None better. That's why she refuses promotions to lieutenant. If you don't mind, I'd like you to put her in charge. She's got the backstory that might be useful. I'd like to send my brother with her. He's working as a private investigator and interviewed all of Becker's neighbors. What he knows might open some lines of inquiry. They'll be there first thing tomorrow.

"Good enough. We'll have a work room ready for them. Anything else?"

"No. Thanks again, I owe you."

Detective Sergeant Mary Kasson was packing up for the day when Jack asked her to see him. The stout, single woman just beyond her fifty-first year had a smooth, young face and sharp eyes for details. She bustled into his office with her mousey hair askew. Dressed in a pants suit, she looked to be every inch the dowdy reference librarian of her former profession. Jack was the man of her life but not for romance. She adored his authenticity, sense of honor and compassion while he admired her clarity and directness. He recapped the call from the Wacouta sheriff.

"*Finally*!—a break in the Becker case," she said. "How do you want to handle it?"

"I arranged for you to lead the investigation. Wacouta is fine with that. Their lab is better than ours so there's no advantage to moving the car and bodies here. Of course, you can bill the department for motel and meals, as necessary."

"Okay. I'll need a couple of my team, too."

"Of course. And I also arranged for you to take Boston if he's willing. He's talked to a lot of people who knew the Beckers. That might open some leads. No telling what you'll find but we need a thorough autopsy. Look for every conceivable cause of death. We also need a motive or several of them."

"Has Boston agreed to go?"

"No. I haven't asked him. He'll find it harder to refuse if you call."

Wacouta was the county east of Alton and bordered the Mississippi River. Among the state's oldest counties, it began around an antebellum steamboat landing at the mouth of the Wacouta River. Wacouta Landing became a village after railroads crossed the river and pushed west. It was now a college town and a decade of gentrification made it a destination for tourists and sportsmen who fished and hunted in the Mississippi backwaters and in the state parks on the bluffs above it.

Boston agreed to Mary Kasson's invitation and they started for Wacouta County in a departmental car. He thought the mousey woman must possess an incredible talent if his brother put such value on her judgment. "If you don't mind my asking, how did you become a detective?"

"When I was a reference librarian, I was engaged to a Saint Paul cop. Someone killed him two weeks before our wedding. When they couldn't find the killer, I went back to school to become a detective. I spent three years looking for the killer. When I couldn't find him, I moved here to start over."

"Amazing! Librarian to detective... that's a radical shift."

"No, not really," she said with a knowing smile. "A reference librarian is trained to take questions and search for answers. We're trained in critical thinking, organizing, cross-referencing and curating information. So do detectives. Same skills but a different application. It's no more radical than a journalist turned investigator—like you."

"You got me there, Mary. I backed into this to help Morrie."

She asked what he knew about the Beckers and listened without interruption as he recapped what he had uncovered. Her probing questions exposed the gaps in what they knew. Now he understood his brother's reliance on her.

"I thought the Beckers had assumed a new identity in another state," he said. "I never anticipated two bodies in a car near a backwater. If they are the Beckers, then my theories aren't worth squat."

"Not necessarily," she said as she parked in front of the new Wacouta County Public Safety Building. They entered a conference room where the Wacouta sheriff welcomed them. While they noshed on a spread of coffee and rolls, a Wacouta detective recapped the bare facets. The car was locked tight and the bodies were side-by-side in the back seat like a couple of teens on a date. A spread of photos showed the bodies had collapsed into each other as they decomposed. The deputies stabilized them with weighted blankets and hauled them out inside the car. The car was more than 300 yards off the ATV trail and they had to winch it through trees and across the soft ground twenty yards at a time. That took most of the day. Then they brought the car to Wacouta and put the remains in the morgue. The deputy asked Mary how she wanted them to proceed.

She wanted to see the bodies in the morgue before the autopsy. Boston followed her and stood back as she put on a surgical mask and gloves. The assistant rolled out the bodies and lifted the cover. Their appearance appalled Boston. He looked away immediately. Then he looked back... horrified. From his interviews, he felt as if he knew the Beckers. Looking at their remains felt like a ghoulish, voyeuristic invasion of their privacy. A sacrilege. He turned away, sick to his stomach, afraid he might vomit. Then he noticed Mary whose composure didn't falter as she peered at the protruding bones, teeth, tufts of hair and patches of dried skin. When she finished, she asked to see the car.

Wild grape, cucumber and creeper vines had begun to reclaim the Becker's Buick Regal. Vines twined into the grille and around the side mirrors. The undercarriage was stuffed with clumps of canary grass and nettles. At Mary's direction, they dusted the car for prints and then opened it. Afterward, she supervised an inventory of the car's loose accumulation of pencil stubs, pennies, cigarette butts, used tissue, notebooks, gum wrappers and other debris from under the seats. They went through the back seat and then the front. Nothing had obvious significance except a single glove and a whiskey bottle. The glove box contained the owner's manual, a service record notebook and an envelope. The trunk had a suitcase with enough clothing for a weekend trip.

Laying the suitcase on a table, she took out each article, held it up, shook it and laid it on a table. She put the men's clothing at one end and piled the woman's clothing at the other. It wasn't much.

"Study the clothing," she said in a teacher's voice as she stripped off the latex gloves. "What do you notice?"

Boston and the deputies walked around the table looking closely at the clothing. "Looks like they were on a short trip," a deputy said. "Not much to go one," another added.

"The suitcase is the right size for a short trip," Boston said, removing his glasses and wiping them. "The woman had enough clothing for a week but not the man." He scratched his head and circled the table again. Then his gray eyes lit up. "Neither pile has any underwear!"

"*Bingo*! Nothing was folded, either," she said. "Just thrown in and the top latched down. Those aren't the clothes you'd pack for a road trip. And you wouldn't pack at all if you intended to commit suicide. That leaves us two obvious causes of death…"

"The car was at the remotest point," a Wacouta deputy said as they gathered around a topographic map of the wildlife refuge. He pointed to the car's location. "The ATV trail is passable in dry weather if you're careful but there's no way that Buick could go that far off the trail on its own."

"I agree," Mary said. "Check the trees for scars. You had to winch it out so it's possible, even likely, they hauled it in the same way. Someone went to a lot of trouble to hide them. Then stage a suicide in case they were found. We know the car was seen leaving in May. I think it's more likely they were killed at their house. The autopsy might tell us exactly when they died though I won't hold my breath."

Mary opened the envelope from the glovebox and removed a sheet of lined notebook paper. She held it to the light and then read the message. "Any prints?"

"One set," the technician said.

"It looks like a suicide note," she continued. "Whose prints?"

"Don't know yet."

She handed the page to Boston and he scanned the handwriting in blue ink:

Sorry for what we did. We can't face jail. It's better this way. Goodbye. Norm and Velva

"What do you think?"

He wrinkled his brow and then shook his head. "Fake. Most farmers have a deep attachment to the property. It's their life. Their identity. The region is full of depressed ex-farmers who sold out. Scribner committed suicide over it. Wilkes drank heavily. But Becker wasn't in financial trouble. Neighbors got postcards from them mailed in Kansas City. Obviously, bogus. Just like this note. It's contrary to everything I learned about them."

Mary scratched her head with the pencil and turned to the Wacouta detective. "Please do the usual dental search. Check with the dentists in Waterford or Featherstone. Test the clothing for residues. I'll be back in a day or two."

"Murder or suicide?" Jack asked when Mary and Boston returned.

"I think it's murder but we won't know for sure until the autopsy. Wacouta is checking dental records. That will take a couple of days. Then we need to know the cause of death. The bodies are decomposed so finding a cause might take a few weeks. Boston says the note we found doesn't square with his knowledge of them."

"So, you think that adds up to murder?"

"Yes," she said. "The car had luggage but that was to give the impression of travel."

"I'm sure it's murder," Boston added. "The Beckers said no goodbyes to the neighbors, never hinted at selling and their car and a U-Haul van left at the same time. We already know the transaction for the van was a cashier's checks to give the killer a cover. He or they must have ditched the van along the way and sent bogus postcards."

"When we're positive it's the Beckers, we'll subpoena their bank records," Mary said. "That should tell us what shape they were in. I don't want to form any opinion until we have the autopsy."

"You can report the deaths," Jack said, turning to Boston. "But please keep it to minimal details until we check the dental records. Okay?"

The Beckers' deaths haunted Boston. He had seen more of their remains than he cared to and the images invaded his sleep. It wasn't that they were dead. What haunted him was deeply personal and troubling. All his questioning and investigating gave him a feeling of a connection that now felt like a loss. It was a strange kind of grieving he didn't understand. Somehow, he cared deeply about someone he had never met. He wrestled with it on the drive into town to file a short story at the *Statesman*. Afterward, he stopped to visit Isaacs and told him what they found.

"I really can't explain how or why I feel this way," he said. "When I was a reporter in Vietnam, I was around the dead every day— GI's, Viet Cong, ARVN soldiers, civilians. That didn't bother me. I suppose it was because I didn't know them. Their deaths were sad but impersonal facts of the war. In fact, at first I was surprised and then ashamed how quickly I learned to look at death with disinterest. I got numb to it. But not the Beckers," he sighed. "I feel as if I have been living with them all this time and...*uh*..."

"I know," Isaacs said gently. "It's your humanity. Though I'm not a practicing Jew like my wife, I know you feel the loss of people whose lives mattered to you. Whose lives infiltrated yours. You cared about them. You are a *mensch*. Let their memory be a blessing."

"Thank you, Morrie. I'll remember that."

The *Statesman* ran a two-paragraph notice of the Beckers' death:

TWO BODIES FOUND IN REFUGE—
Wacouta— July 29, 1986

Wacouta County deputies recovered two decomposed bodies from a car in the Upper Mississippi National Wildlife Refuge. Dental records have confirmed the deceased as Norman and Velva Becker of rural Waterford. The Beckers farmed 240 acres in Runyon Township before selling their farm to Justin Taylor in May 1985. They left without notice or forwarding information. The cause of death is under investigation.

Mr. Becker was born on the family's farm in 1929 and took over its operation at the age of eighteen after his father's death. The farm had been in the Becker family since the 1880s. The late Mr. Becker was an active member of the Farm Bureau, Waterford Masonic Lodge and Future Farmers of America. Friends of the Beckers are planning a memorial. Details are pending.

Chapter 28

Hartwell learned of the Beckers' deaths from Isaacs before he read it in the *Statesman*. It stunned him. He had never seriously believed his friend had defrauded Taylor and now felt guilty for entertaining the idea. Then this. One of the last links to boyhood was dead. The news left another empty spot inside him. He feared becoming a man without anyone but Rita with whom he shared a past—a past he didn't want to relive.

Antsy but low, he walked into town and opened a checking and savings account at Farmer's State Bank. Then he completed transferring funds from his San Francisco bank accounts. Next, he stopped at the Valley Electric Cooperative office to arrange for automatic billing and payment. Finally, he went to the city hall where he filled out forms to become a registered voter, applied for a Minnesota driver's license and ordered new plates for the car. There, he thought, I'm now officially a Minnesotan even if I don't have many connections.

Gretta's Garden had only four customers at mid-afternoon and Hartwell hoped for a few minutes alone with her. If not, then the background chatter of customers might take the edge off his low spirits. Gretta greeted him with a smile and seated him at what was now his favorite table. She recited the day's specials and took his order.

"Gretta, how did you come to start this restaurant?" he asked when she brought the white bean soup and a salad.

"A long story," she said, glancing around before sitting opposite him. "After ten years of nursing, I went to culinary school and got a gig cooking vegetarian in San Francisco. Far-out. Then I came home to see my folks. They're elderly and I wanted to be closer to them. I passed through here by chance and liked the vibe. The town didn't have any vegetarian cafés. I mean, it's a cool river town. Lots of educated people and funky buildings. So, after I got the skinny on it, I moved here and opened this place. It's cool, a little like the way San Francisco used to be. Like you, I wanna give people something that supports their health. You and me are on the same team. I'm pleased to the max you're a regular."

"Down the road, we'll have that conversation about collaboration."

"Right on. I'd like that. I've been thinking of your plans. So, keep me in mind."

"Meanwhile, will you have dinner with me some evening? We could go to a vegetarian place if you'd like—say in Rochester."

"Outta sight! I'd love to try another menu. You name the day and I'm all yours."

He left the Garden shaking his head and feeling happier. Gretta is the un-Maddie. Nothing coy. No mystery. What you see is what you get. An open book. Her cultural vibe isn't mine but she's good company.

Hartwell took his time walking home in the early evening. The constant press of unforeseen challenges sat like a weight beneath his ribs. Now and then he opened his mouth to force air deep into his lungs. He had been doing this ever since Taylor's barbecue. Telling himself that dealing with Taylor wasn't as risky as combat didn't ease the sensation. He knew his pulse had quickened. Then he thought of the blood pressure monitor still packed at home. He didn't' need it, he had told himself. He drew a breath and walked home.

Rita sat in a patio chair as if waiting for him. His heart rose in his throat and he swallowed several times. "*Uh*... well, hello," he said, squeezing out the words against pressure in his chest. "Have... have you been waiting long?"

"Couple of hours, I guess," she said, uncrossing her bare legs. "I needed a quiet place to think. I hope you don't mind."

"*Uh*, no. But I don't understand… why here?"

She stood and walked to him. "Oh Bob," she sobbed and the words stuck in her throat. "It's the Beckers. It's terrible and upsetting—"

"—Did you know them?"

"Yeah, a little. Velva, mostly. I ran into her sometimes at the Piggly Wiggly. A lovely woman. I liked talking to her. She had interesting ideas. They died a horrible death and… I can't shake the idea Justin had a hand in… I don't know, the way things are going… you're the only person I trust. You and Maddie…"

"Sit down… tell me what this is about," he said, trying to summon the calming voice he used as a doctor when a patient's death seemed imminent. "What's the trouble?"

"I'm leaving Justin… I mean divorcing him," she blurted and wiped her eyes.

"I'm sorry… I never guessed," he said lowering himself into a chair and sitting at an angle to avoid eye contact. He breathed deeply against the pressure in his chest. "Seeing you two at the barbecue… I thought—"

"—An act," she spit out the words. "It's over. In a lotta ways it never began. It's going to be rough. I need your support, your shoulder, your kindness. I know I can trust you. We've always been… well, we were always good to each other. I need a friend, a confidant to get through this. Somebody who understands. There's no one like you." She looked directly at him, blinking rapidly. "Please stand by me."

He swallowed hard. An alarm went off in the back of his mind. *Uh-huh. No one like me. She's playing on my emotions. Got me to fuck her at fifteen. Impulsive… but persuasive. Her marriage is none of my business. I've got enough trouble with Taylor. Don't ask why she wants a divorce. Don't get sucked in.* Seeing her struggle, he knew he couldn't turn his back on her and live with himself. He had to ask. She was begging him to.

"You've been married what… a year? What happened?"

"I was a *fool*," she wailed bitterly. "I met him and believed his laid-back, country boy act… He even played guitar. I fell for it. In case you haven't noticed, time isn't kind to women. He's a couple of years younger than me. Still has lots of swagger. I went for him because he made me feel young—younger—not like an old biddy hen. But it was an act. I realized too late he married me 'cause I was a rich widow dying for love. Maddie warned me but I didn't listen. And he's not honest. I'm sure of it."

"I see… dishonest…with other women?"

"No, in business. I'm scared. Scared for my life—and *yours*! Afraid that what happened to the Beckers could happen to us, too."

"You mean, Justin…"

"Yes. He wouldn't do it himself. He'd make an indirect comment to Nacho. You know, a hint to do whatever. It's how they work but—"

"—But what?"

"Well, I pay the household bills and he keeps separate books for the ranch," she said in a calmer voice. "I'm an accountant. So, a ledger is a lot more to me than a page with numbers. One day I looked at the ranch books and what I saw scared me."

"Tell me more." *I'm letting her suck me in.*

"The profit and loss accounts don't square. There's a lot more money coming in than he gets from selling a few cattle each month."

"Didn't he make a lot of money in oil?"

"If he did, it wouldn't show up in those books. Every month, two of his men go to Texas with two or three head of stock. Bulls, mostly. After they return, the ledger shows a slug of money in the sales column. It bears no relation to the price or number of cattle sold, that's for sure. It's gotta be illegal. I don't want to get caught in it. I'm frightened. I want out."

"I can't help you with that, you need a good lawyer."

"I have one. His name is Isaacs."

"He is my attorney, too. Tell him about your suspicions. He used to be a deputy attorney general. He'll know what to do."

"Okay, I will."

"I'm sorry you're going through this," he said in a tone of voice he hoped would wrap up the conversation. "Especially after your happy marriage to Gerhard."

"He was gentle, like you. That's why I married him. Because he was so much like you. We were each other's first loves," she said, reaching for his hand. "I haven't forgotten that."

The touch of her soft, warm hand repelled him like the touch of death. *She scares the shit out of me. It's not about consolation. She's setting me up.*

"I can't help you without making it worse," he said, rising to his feet to end the talk.

"Oh Bob, I need you," she cried. "Need you more than ever." She rose to her feet. "If you ever cared for me, care for me now." She wrapped her arms around him and kissed him on the mouth. "I want you," she said cried. "When I saw you at the IGA, I knew I still wanted you." She pressed herself against him. "If only you had returned two years ago. Then we might've—"

"—*No*! I won't get involved," he hissed. "You've crossed the line. It's time you leave."

"If it's because of Maddie you won't get to first base. I can't say why but you won't. But you and I have so… how close we are."

"Listen," he said, in a rasping voice as he gripped her upper arms and pushed her back. "We aren't close anymore. We were children then… kids exploring sex. We've grown up… at least I hope so. You're married. I won't live a lie for that. Even if your husband is a thug."

"That's why I'm divorcing him. That's why I want you. Because you're good."

"It won't work, Rita. I wish you hadn't come here—"

"—*What*," she snapped. "I trusted you and you… you make me feel cheap—"

"—No, you did that… to… to yourself," he gasped as the dizziness struck him.

"Bob? *Bob*! What's the matter?" she cried as he sank to his knees.

"Call… the—"

Chapter 29

Taylor ground his teeth when he saw the *Statesman* headline about the Beckers. The article troubled him, not for what it said but for what it didn't say. Nothing about the cause of death. Or whether it was murder or suicide. Was that because the sheriff had no evidence to go on or was he being cute? He yelled for Morales and held the newspaper in front of the foreman.

"*Jefe*, I no read *inglés*."

"Somebody found the Beckers but they don't know what killed 'em or how. Dollars to donuts, the sheriff will start askin' the neighbors questions. I'll do the talkin' if he comes here. You just say you don't understand English."

"*Sí, Jefe.* You know what to say, I think."

"I don' know nothin' except I seen the van and their car leavin' one mornin' after he sold his farm'. An' that's *all* I know."

"*Sí, Jefe. Me no recuerdo nada,*" Nacho said he remembered nothing.

"I know I can count on you, like always," he said, putting his hand on Morales's shoulder and smiling. "But we gotta quit haulin' cattle to Texas."

"*¿Por qué? Es fácil, tanto dinero,*" Why, he asked. It was easy money.

"Yes, it's your business but my *rancho*, truck and cattle. You made a deal with the folks in Laredo, I didn't. How you get out of it is up to you."

"You, me, *compadres* long time," he pleaded in a wounded voice. "Don' do this to me! Not right. You gimme *la mano* an' you gimme *el prometido* an' I give you *dinero*," he cried, reminding him they shook hands on the promise in return for money.

"Okay Nacho, enough of this," he said, shrugging. "I'll keep my word. I'll look out for you like always. We've got time to work it out just like we got out of oil trouble."

The men stared at each other, shuffling their feet but said nothing more. Then Taylor turned away and walked toward the house. *Nacho's as dumb as watermelons. Like the other Tejanos… no vision. Useful if he don't think. He'd be nothin' without me or someone like me. Loyal but no imagination 'cept makin' and spendin' money. It's the difference between whites and Mexicans. Why this country is rich and Mexico is a shithole of pobre peones. I dunno. Might hafta cut him loose. Cain't take the risk. Gotta keep clear of his business.*

Morales turned toward the barn and yelled for Carlos. While the two men erected an electric fence, Morales brooded on *Jefe's* change of mind. *Jefe, scared, I think. He take big risk in Tejas but here no. It is Hartwell, I think. Or Rita. Jefe, he used to know what to do. Now, no mucho, I think. I look out for me.*

It was dark when Morales returned to the ranch after an evening in Waterford. The new woman he met at a bar took him home and satisfied him as only a woman could. His carnal satiety faded after he thought of what he had seen and heard afterward on his way to the ranch. It was enough to make him puke in fear. *Muy mal. Jefe, he gonna be mal.*

Taylor's marriage wasn't his business he told himself and he didn't want to say anything. But after what he heard, he knew he had to tell *Jefe*. It threatened them both. And if he didn't tell him now, and *Jefe* found out later, his boss would rip him a new asshole. He pulled into the yard and saw the house was dark and knew Taylor was asleep. He would tell him first thing in the morning but what he knew made for a miserable pillow.

Jefe left early before Morales could tell him. Holding the secret inside made him irritable. He stewed on it while Pablo, Carlos and he moved cattle into the next grazing unit. He preferred silence but the men were talkative and he couldn't ignore them.

"*Vamanos tipos, prisa prisa,*" he barked, telling them to hurry. The morning was turning hot and they had to prep the trailer for Texas. "¡*Carlos, mueve tu pinche culo!*"

Carlos moved his ass, saying, "*Sí, sí, Nacho, Rápido.*"

"*Wetbacks,*" Morales snorted under his breath. He recalled how his father often waded across the river into and out of Texas. He guessed that made the son a wetback. *No importa.* At least the guys took orders without questions. The men closed the paddock and piled into the back of the gray GMC pickup.

Seeing Taylor's pickup parked by the house, he knew he must break the news to a man who sometimes punished messengers. Morales told the men to eat lunch and entered the office.

"Hey Nacho, everything ready for tomorrow?"

"*Sí, todo listo,*" he mumbled. "Duarte and Pablo go."

"Good."

"Jefe... uh—

"—What is it?"

"I hear somethin' you better know. Don' like 'cause you won' like."

"Well, spit it out," he barked. "What in hell is it?"

Then he told him he saw Rita's car parked at Hartwell's house yesterday afternoon when he went to town. He paused to let it sink in. Then he said it was still there at dusk when he returned.

"What the fuck took you so long to tell me?" he roared. "*Huh?*"

"You sleep when I come back. Don' wanna wake you. Then you go early."

"Well, tell me from the beginning."

"When I come home I see her car. I stop. Hear her talk behind the house. Don' see Rita, only hear her."

"Whaddya hear?"

"Her voice, it strong and then soft. Don' hear total. She tell him about *el divorciado.* Then say she want Bob. She trust only him. Say she want him again. He say no. She say she look at ranch books. Think you do something bad. Now she scared."

"That bitch! Anything else?"

"Then I hear *nada* 'til she scream. The ambulance come an' I go."

"Well, she wants a *dee*-vorce."

"What you do?"

"Fight it. She don't get a *dee*-vorce 'til I say so."

"What you need from me?"

"Nothin' right now. Just think on it while you get the rig ready for tomorrow."

Morales walked toward the barn calling for Duarte. As he walked, he considered his future. He thought about all the risks he and *Jefe* ran in the oil fields. Taylor had the white shirt job while he hauled equipment. Then *Jefe* told him where and when to take the oil or equipment they sold at one place or another. They had always split the money equally. Before leaving Texas, Morales used family connections to set up a trucking business. Taylor used his money to buy the farms.

Duarte interrupted his thoughts to say everything was ready for the Texas run. Morales thanked him. He thought of telling Duarte that *Jefe* wanted out of trucking. The little man was something of a comrade. In the end, however, he decided to say nothing—for now, at least.

Morales resumed his brooding. The boss had never liked storing the Texas hay in his barns. As soon as it came in, he wanted the bales emptied and spread for bedding. A few times, they stored hay in the sanatorium before Becker left. That kept it off the farm where no one could get to it. Then Hartwell returned. Now he couldn't use the sanatorium and *Jefe* didn't want to continue the trucking. He couldn't shake the feeling that he had been used. *Compañeros iguales largo tiempo. Then Jefe get what he want. El rancho. Now he want me work like campesino. I gonna tell los tipos in Laredo that Jefe break his promesa.*

Chapter 30

Hartwell was half-conscious when he heard a nurse and doctor talking in low voices. Even before he opened his eyes, he knew he was on a hospital table of some kind. He wasn't certain where he was or how he got there. He recalled being with Rita before he fainted. Then he recalled a blur of EMTs, an ambulance and a round of tests. It felt bizarre. He hadn't been a patient in at least twenty years. And that was for a torn ligament. *I'm a cardiologist, for Chrissake. Now a heart attack. Embarrassing! Oh hell. Get the bad news over with.*

He opened his eyes and looked into those of the doctor standing over him. "Tell me," he snapped, as if to assert control. "How bad was the heart attack?"

"Fortunately, it wasn't," the younger man said. "No sign of coronary disease or any other symptoms. Angina."

"How did I get here?"

"Your lady friend phoned nine-one-one and waited outside the room until we said you were okay. She left five minutes ago. By the way, I'm Ben Elder." Then the doctor asked his name and birthdate and a brief medical history. "Okay, no sign of lost cognition. Are you under any unusual stress?"

Hartwell swung his legs over the edge of the table and sat up. "Stress?" he said with a sardonic laugh. "Stress? My wife of thirty years died in January, I sold my practice in San Francisco, moved here to open a wellness center at the mineral spring, and ran into a cattleman who's doing everything he can to prevent me from accessing my property. Yes! A lot of stress."

"I read the article," Elder said. "Interesting project. That could account for the angina. And as a newcomer, I bet you don't have a network and keep a lot of this inside. I just heard that in your recitation. However, I'm sure you know the drill. I won't presume to prescribe to a veteran cardiologist. I just hope you follow the advice you'd give to any patient."

"Thank you, Ben. I will."

"After you're dressed, I'll give you a lift home. It's after dark."

"Thank you for that, too. Let's have coffee sometime soon."

Rita waited in the bedroom she thought of as her refuge and listened as her husband made his breakfast in the kitchen downstairs. She heard him tell Morales he would be in Rochester for most of the day. Moments later, she heard her husband's pickup leave the yard. Standing at a window, she watched the foreman and Carlos drive into the pasture. Duarte and Pablo were already on their way to Texas. Time now to make a clean break. She and Taylor hadn't talked in two days, which was a relief. And even though Hartwell would never be hers, she felt thankful that he would recover.

The three suitcases she hid in a closet held most of her clothes, jewelry and papers. One by one, she lugged them downstairs and into the trunk of her Mustang. She made a last sweep of her bedroom and picked up her handbag. It held the usual things a woman needed plus a.38 caliber automatic.

She had decided to leave Taylor several months earlier but she waited for the right time. Leaving took on an urgency after Hartwell returned. At first, she thought he and Taylor would came to terms. If they did, she would divorce her husband and eventually be with Bob— she hoped. But not after last night. *He shut me out. That hurt. Damn his straight-laced conscience!*

Her escape plan amounted to nothing but a vague notion. She couldn't stay at the ranch until the divorce was final. That would be hell. But she knew leaving would make him explode. *He or Nacho will come looking. Where can I go? I don't want to vanish like the Beckers.*

She left the yard knowing she couldn't drop out of sight with a sporty red car and her name on a vanity plate. Of course, she could buy a new one. Something modest for cover. The Mustang had good trade-in value but she would still need money for a new car and living expenses. She sat by herself in the lobby of Madeline's office while her friend met with a client behind the inner door. Leafing through *Fortune* magazine didn't keep her mind occupied or quell her fear that Justin might show up. Then there would be a scene. She shivered and couldn't recall when she last felt so afraid. *I've always had someone. Now I'm alone.*

Madeline said goodbye to the client. "Rita, what brings you here?"

"I wanna talk—in private."

"Oh, of course." She beckoned her into the office and closed the door. "You're shaking. Are you sick? Something awful happen?" This wasn't the usually upbeat Rita she knew.

"I've left Justin," she began. "Everything I own is packed in my car. Maddie, I don't know… where do I go from here?" she cried. "What do I do?" Her fingers trembled as she reached into the purse for a tissue. "It'll be ugly."

"Start at the beginning," she said in a soothing voice and removed the silver barrette from her hair. "To be honest, I'm not shocked by divorce. Not from Justin. Or that you have moved out. But I need to know more before I can help you." She folded her hands and waited.

"I was a fool to…" she began. Looking into the dark eyes calmed her. She blew her nose. "You warned me," she said, regaining composure. "But after Gerhard died, well, I told myself I was past the… you know, the sell-by date. I didn't want to end up a lonely old woman. Even a rich one. Justin came along and made me feel young and I… well, you know the rest. I used to get men to do things my way. You know, I thought I could make it work. Well, he's not interested in me—just my money! I'm just another piece of property."

185

"It's good you kept your assets. Otherwise, you'd be in a worse pickle. Anything else?"

"It's worse since Bob came back. I think he blames me for his troubles. He even accused me of having an affair with him."

"Are you?"

"No. Are you?"

Madeline held her gaze and pressed her lips tight but didn't answer. The women stared at each other in silence for a moment.

"Anything more you can tell me?" Madeline asked, now all business.

"Some of this I know as fact and some of it is a guess. But it's hard to sort one from the other." Then Rita told her about the ranch books and how the receipts from cattle sales seemed wildly inflated. "There gotta be another source of money 'cause cattle aren't paying the bills. I'm worried about it."

"Who knows about this?"

She hesitated. "I told Bob. Morrie Isaacs is my attorney but I haven't told him yet."

"Oh for God's sake, you told Bob! *Why?*"

"Because he's an old friend. Because we grew up together, we—"

"—Yes, you've already told me what you shared," she snapped.

"Because I trust him. He's honest and strong enough to stand up to Justin when nobody else will, including *me.*"

Madeline shuffled some papers and screwed the cap onto her fountain pen. Then she offered Rita some coffee to break the tension and wondered what to tell her. Maddie knew her knowledge of marriages and divorces was second-and-third hand from observing her parents and friends. Superficial knowledge at best but not wisdom won from living through it. She looked at Rita, grieved for her sorrow and feared for her safety but didn't offer direction.

"Here's what comes to mind," Madeline said. "Make an appointment with Isaacs. Use my phone. See him today if you can. Ask him what to do. I hear he used to be a prosecutor. Tell him about your suspicions. Then stay at a motel. Go to the Ramada in Featherstone. It's away from here. It's downtown. You'll be safe enough there."

"Thank you Maddie. I wish—"

"—I know. I'd love to have you stay with me but it is the first place he'll look."

"I know," Rita sighed and made an impromptu appointment with Isaacs. Knowing she couldn't stay with Madeline sharpened Rita's desire to stay with her. To her surprise, Maddie was surprisingly funny, even bawdy. When they were together it was like a high school sleepover. It puzzled Rita that confiding in Hartwell had upset Madeline. And again over the possibility they were having an affair. *Maddie can't be serious. Never interested in any man. But then, Bob isn't just any man.*

Isaacs read Rita's agitation from her voice and settled her in a chair. Then he closed his office door and offered her coffee. "I agree with the motel idea," he said. "The divorce takes time. Separation will give you both space to cool off."

"That's not why I'm here. I saw something in the ranch books that scares me." Then she told him her suspicion that Taylor had income not connected to selling cattle.

"*Ah-ha,*" he said as his intuition told him it might lead in new directions. "So, the money comes after every trip to Texas. Have you told anyone else about this?"

"Just Bob and Madeline… because I trust them."

Isaacs ran his hand through his thinning hair and shook his head. "Bob is my client, too. Your problems and his are already badly tangled with your husband. For God's sake, don't talk to anyone else about your suspicions. And that's what they are—suspicions. And don't have any more contact with Bob. If he contacts you, tell him I advised against it—at least until you are divorced and his problems are settled."

Taylor returned from Rochester, entered the house and called Rita's name several times as he went from room to room. Then he went outside. "Hey Nacho, you seen Rita. Do you know where she's at. Her car is gone."

"No. I see her car here when I go to the Otto place. Why?"

He whirled around and rushed into the house. Ten minutes later he strode toward Morales with fists doubled and his head tucked between his shoulders. "Goddamn that bitch!" he bellowed. "She moved out. Took her clothes. Everything. Nobody quits *me!*" His words echoed off the barn. "Nobody! Not 'less I say so. I pay you to look after things. That includes Rita."

"What I do for her?"

"Find her. She won't go far. Not yet."

"Let her go *Jefe*," he begged. "She make you *descontento*."

"I cain't let her go. You told me yourself. She looked at the ranch books. And she knows accounting. She'll figure out that cattle ain't payin' all the bills. She might use it for leverage in the *dee*-vorce. Sure as you're born, she'll use it agin me or give it to the sheriff."

"*O Jesú!* You right, I think."

"I know I am. Go by Maddie Barnes's house tonight. It's on the other side of town by the river. If Rita's car ain't there, check the motel parking lots in Waterford and Featherstone."

"Okay, as you say."

"Another thing. This newspaper man—Meade—he's workin' for Hartwell. Check out his place. Be careful. His brother is the sheriff."

"Already I check. What I do now?"

"Nothin' more yet."

"*Sí, Jefe*," he said as he walked away. Morales knew that *Jefe* wasn't asking him to make her or Meade disappear. He never asked directly because he didn't like violence. Then he remembered all those vacant oil bores... people fell into them and disappeared all the time. Sometimes no one found the body. *Jefe* never had to see it. The police never caught the person responsible. Not that easy to disappear in Minnesota. Instead of worrying about Rita, *Jefe* should worry about *los tipos* in Laredo. *Más peligrosos*—dangerous guys.

Chapter 31

Gretta lived on one of Waterford's quiet backstreets in a two-story Tudor-style house like the one where she grew up in Minneapolis. Waiting on the porch for Hartwell's arrival, she tried to recall her last real date. *Think, Gretta girl. How many years? What are the rules after forty? Have I forgotten how to... Well, be me. Do what comes naturally. He's a good man. Don't want to turn him off.* When the silver Mercedes stopped at the curb, she began a slow, measured walk toward the car.

Hartwell watched her, enchanted as she put one high-heeled foot in front of the other in the deliberate strut he had seen on fashion runways. Until now, he had assumed Gretta's hippy garb was a cultivated image for the restaurant's countercultural vibe. Seeing her now, he realized that *was* her authentic persona. Her lustrous brown hair hung loosely over the shoulders and pendant earrings sparkled among the tresses. The flowing bohemian maxi-dress with flowing sleeves and plunging neckline hid some curves and exposed others. Just looking at her made him feel utterly out of place in a powder blue blazer and a button-down shirt. He groaned silently. *People will think I'm her father.*

"That's a cool outfit," he said as he opened the car door and hoped she would overlook the blazer. Maybe she would think of him as "with-it" by saying things in her lingo. However, he also knew the wrong choice of slang could date him as accurately as a birth certificate. He removed the blazer and casually tossed it into the back seat.

"Thank you," she trilled as she gathered the voluminous skirts over her knees. "I can't remember the last time a gentleman took me to dinner. This is totally rad."

He felt her excitement—at least to eat in a new restaurant if not be with him. Though he knew Gretta was nothing like Felicia or Maddie or even Rita, he couldn't pin down the attraction he felt. It wasn't wholly physical, though she could be attractive. Nor a shared interest in diet and health, though those were important. No, it was something deeper that he couldn't touch. But tonight it was enough to just get acquainted. After that… "Tell me about growing up in the Twin Cities," he asked. "Good memories, I hope."

"Oh yeah, for sure. My folks still live there."

"And you said nursing was a bummer," he added with a quick glance at her low neckline.

"Too much stress. Caring for people by the book didn't feel personal. I was treating problems not preventing them. That's why I went to culinary school. Preparing meals is giving something of myself to others, you know. It's personal, intimate, you get what I mean? A vegetarian diet supports health. It can head off trouble."

"Well, that puts you and me on the same page. I want the wellness center to get ahead of heart disease."

"Right on. Vegetarians of the world unite! You've got nothing to lose but your cholesterol," she crowed, raising her fist. "We must be in a cosmic convergence."

"It seems so," he agreed, amused by her speech. *Cosmic convergence! If anything comes of this, I'll have to update my slang, dress and musical taste. Oh well. She's earnest about diet and health. We're together in that.*

They entered the Thyme & Anise Restaurant with its herbal aromas. Gretta inhaled their bouquet with a connoisseur's appreciation. He felt a tickle in his nose and hoped he wouldn't sneeze. The hostess said, "this way," Gretta grasped his hand and they followed the *maître d* to a table. Feeling her hand in his infused him with unexpected pleasure. For an instant, he thought about the medical and spiritual aspects of touch, the laying on of hands, the kinetic healing that passed from one person to another. What is it, he wondered. Of course, the center should offer various massages. For now, however, it was enough to enjoy her touch.

Facing each other across the table, he tried to see her innate beauty behind the smoky eye shadow and neon lipstick. He thought the make-up hid more beauty than it accented it but that was an opinion shaped by Felicia's minimalist applications. Looking closely, he saw confidence in the hazel eyes that held the pure light of dawn. He knew she was a younger, freer spirit than he. It was exciting but nothing in thirty years with Felicia seemed relevant to Gretta. *Go slow, take it easy, see what happens.*

They ordered Greek Tiger cocktails made of ouzo and orange juice. He ordered *sauvignon Blanc* with the main course. Gretta *yum*-ed and *um*-ed her way through the meal. "This is food from heaven. How could you know it's what I love?" She said the restaurant ambiance made her happy. While they ate and talked, he made two encouraging discoveries. They shared a belief that vegetable-based cuisine could be as savory and as exciting as meat. And she wasn't a moralistic so-and-so who made a religion out of being vegetarian. During the meal, their eyes met often and their voices dropped to a tone just above a whisper.

The moon was high overhead when they left the Thyme & Anise and its light made for intimacy on the drive home. They were halfway to Waterford when he saw flashing red-blue lights cast by several police cars, an ambulance and a wrecker. He pulled onto the shoulder and got out. A deputy approached and Hartwell offered his aid. The officer thanked him and said the victim was already in the ambulance with an EMT. It was too dark to see much in detail except it was an overturned Mustang. Judging by the damage, the car must have rolled at a high speed. Then the officer waved him on.

"You would've helped if you could, wouldn't you?"

"Of course, it's a moral duty. A human obligation, one to another." His response was immediate.

"I'm glad to hear you say it that way," she said. "Some doctors seem pretty detached at times like this. Like mechanics instead of healers."

"Thanks I appreciate your saying so," he said. "Actually, I know a lot of mechanics who aren't detached. They treat cars tenderly the way doctors treat the sick."

She threw back her head and laughed. "You got me there."

He pulled up to Gretta's house and she unbuckled the seat belt. Then she leaned over, cupped his chin in her hand and kissed his cheek. "Thank you for a memorable evening," she said, looking into his eyes with her hand still on his face. "I can't remember when I've enjoyed the food, the company and the moment as much as this. You're for real. I like you."

He watched her walk to the house in the same stately strut. His cheek felt warm where she kissed it and her words rested comfortably inside him. She doesn't have Maddie's mysterious reserve or Rita's blatant come-on. She is who she is. He drove home feeling much younger than he had when he picked her up.

Chapter 32

Rita booked room 201 at the Ramada Inn in downtown Featherstone. The motel was three blocks off the city center and her room on the motel's back side was at the top of an outside stairway. Her car would be invisible from the street. She took an overnight bag with her and left the rest of the luggage locked in her car. The queen-sized bed felt comfortable enough but the room lacked familiar, homey comforts. She missed the grand house she and Gerhard shared with its years of memories. Oh well, she told herself, this is a temporary port in the storm. What did she have now? Her inventory included a handful of friends, fond memories of a dead husband and son, a bitter memory of a soon-to-be ex-husband, no house, no property and no family.

She thought of the Beckers. No one saw them killed and believed they had moved away. Now it seemed that little or nothing stood between her and vanishing now that she understood the farm accounts. However Justin accounted for his money, it had to come from an illicit source. Most likely, it was a continuation of whatever he did in Texas. The cattle sales and the sanatorium were part of it. That must be part of why he and Nacho had been on edge since Hartwell returned. Something about his claim threatens them. With the Beckers dead, the sheriff was sure to question him—if not her. If Justin were ever arrested and tried, she might be compelled to testify. "If I live, I won't lie for him. I'm done with lies."

Two evenings alone in the motel gave Rita the fidgets. She went to Maddie's house for a temporary release. They talked, gossiped, giggled and drank wine. It was nearly eleven o'clock when they finished the Mosel and soft cheeses. Though she felt a little tipsy, she hugged Maddie at the door and got into the Mustang in better spirits. Driving through the moonlight, she believed she could enjoy life again once free of Justin. There was always tomorrow, and tomorrow was always new. She parked in her slot on the darker, back side of the motel. Looking up at her room, she saw the light over the stairs had gone out. Fortunately, the moon cast enough light to climb the stairs and fumble with the key before slipping it into the lock of room 201.

Kris answered the phone at 12:20 a.m. Jack woke as she said, "I'll be right in," followed by rustling in the dark as she put on her scrubs. This wasn't the first time the county hospital called Kris at night. In fact, she was on call all week subbing for a colleague on vacation. He felt her kiss as she left for the emergency room. He rolled over and went back to sleep. Kris returned at 7:30 a.m.

"You look beat," he said, rinsing off his plate. "Want breakfast?"

"Thanks, no. Someone attacked Rita at the Ramada last night."

"Is she all right?"

"No. She has a broken fibula, cuts and bruises. We don't know if she has a concussion. She was raped and thrown down some stairs. I don't have the details. She was conscious but still in the ICU when I left. She gave us a friend's name as a contact but not her husband. I heard they're separated. Her friend is Madeline Barnes in Waterford."

"I heard they were divorcing," he said. As the husband of an ER nurse and the wife of a sheriff, neither had ever found a way to keep the details of their cases confidential. Not and support each other. There were exceptions, of course, but his wasn't one of them. He waited until Kris showered, then he tucked her into bed and drove to his office.

The preliminary report on Rita's assault lay on his desk. Though the deputies were looking into it, he decided to take a closer look into the who and the why. Domestic assaults were often spontaneous and happened at or near the victim's home. This attack was something else. Robbery, maybe. Revenge, perhaps. The preliminary report said the motel's night security guard found Rita unconscious at the bottom of the stairs. No one heard the attack or her fall. Someone smashed her car's driver's-side window, rifled her purse and threw it in a dumpster.

A deputy called the hospital and learned that Rita was alert enough to talk. Jack weighed what little he knew against his knowledge of similar crimes in the county on the short walk to the hospital. Smash and grab attacks were rare. Rapes happened but he didn't recall one during a mugging. The deputies would be thorough but the possible connection to Taylor's separation and divorce required discretion. He entered the three-story hospital that began a century earlier as a hospice run by the Sisters of St. Joseph. The county bought it later and expanded it into a hospital. He entered Rita's room and winced at the sight of the bruises on her face and arms. She lay propped up in the bed with her left leg in a cast.

"Hi Rita. I'm sorry about this. How are you—"

"—I'm shook up mostly, I guess. They say it's a simple fracture. It could be worse."

"We both know it's worse than that. You were raped. I have a few questions off the record if you're willing to talk. I won't be long. Did anyone call your husband?"

"Yeah, but I wish they hadn't. We're separated. I don't wanna see him. Please sit down. That way I don't have to stretch my neck to look at you."

He sat so they were at eye level. "As best you can recall, tell me what happened."

She looked away for a moment and sighed. "It happened fast… I moved out of our house a couple days ago and took a room at the Ramada. I thought a second floor room would be safer. Last night I was with Maddie Barnes in Waterford and got home about 11:30."

"Is that when they attacked you?"

"Yeah. At the top of the outside stairway. The light was out. My room was at the top of the stairs. They hit me as I was trying to get the key in the lock."

"Are there other guests on that level?"

"I don't think so. I didn't see or hear any."

"Go on."

"There were two of them. They punched me and kept punching."

"Did you recognize them?"

"They wore dark ski masks."

"Did they say anything? Recognize their voices?"

"No. I tried to yell but one had his hand over my mouth. They threw me on the floor. and ripped off my panties. Just before I passed out I heard one say '*vamos a chingarla*'."

"Chingarla?"

"It's Spanish for 'let's fuck her.' The Mexicans say versions of *chingar* a lot at the farm. I'm sure it was Nacho and Duarte."

"But you couldn't see their faces."

"No, but they smelled like cow shit. I passed out and woke up here."

"We found your purse. They went through it. Did you have money?"

"A hundred bucks, not more. Did they take the credit cards?"

"Seems so. We found your key still in the lock. Doesn't appear they went into your room. I don't think this was a robbery. Do you think your husband is behind it?"

"I don't know. We haven't had... *uh*, relations for a while but I doubt he would order this. He's never hit me but thinks he owns me. No, I think it was more Nacho's idea."

"Any idea why he'd attack you?"

Rita scratched her injured leg. "I dunno. He and Justin aren't as palsy as they used to be."

"Any idea why?" Jack asked, sensing an opening.

"It's like Nacho has something on him. Or vice versa."

"Any idea what?"

"No, not really... well, something about trucking."

"Okay. I'll have more questions later. Where are you staying after discharge?"

"I'll be with Maddie Barnes, a friend in Waterford."

"Do you need protection?"

"Not from Justin. Just from Nacho or Duarte."

"All right," Jack said. "Be careful."

Chapter 33

The attack on Rita made the rounds of downtown Featherstone by word of mouth a day before the *Statesman* published a short report. It asked anyone who saw or heard anything to call the sheriff. Jack was quoted as saying the attack appeared to be targeted and wasn't a general threat. Isaacs had his own ideas and asked the sheriff's office for a copy of the report. As a woman going through a divorce, the facts might be relevant to her case.

"This is just like old times," Isaacs said as he sat facing his wife in the comfort of his living room with the sheriff's report in his lap. "Contracts and wills pay our bills but a crime adds spice to my life. I've missed that."

"Oh, Morrie," she said. "You're such a Gideon. God made you to go for the truth."

"*Hmm*, thank you," he said. She was faithful to the traditions and rites he had let lapse but he cherished the Torah lessons regarding justice and mercy. He turned to breaking down the assault report into specific pieces.

He set out to understand the dynamic to Rita's divorce and the attack. Were they discrete events or were they related? The attack seemed planned and not spontaneous. Details of the rape didn't point to Taylor. On the other hand, Rita was targeted. If it was two of Taylor's employees, they could have done it at his orders or from other motives. He called Madeline's number and asked to see Rita.

"Hi Morrie," Rita called in a cheery voice when he entered Madeline's sunroom. She sat with her leg propped on a low stool. "Thanks for coming. Be sure to autograph my cast."

"Glad to," he said, taking the proffered Sharpie and signing his name. Her black eye had started to turn yellowish and she had cuts and bruises. "Now seriously, how are you getting along? Rape is a horrific thing."

"I know. But I'm no stranger to sex. I'm not traumatized. Just angry. I'd like some revenge but… Maddie gives me great care," she said, turning a warm smile toward her. "She's spoiling me. I think I'll take months and months to get well!" Then she laughed.

He glanced from woman to woman and noticed the look in their eyes. Whatever was between them, it wasn't any of his business. *Rita is my client, not my daughter.*

"Madeline, Rita and I have a lot to talk about. Please excuse us."

"It's okay, Morrie. I've already told her everything I'll tell you. We have no secrets. I want her to stay," she said, reaching a hand toward her.

"All right. As a matter of protocol, I want only Rita to answer my questions. Both of you are forbidden to repeat anything." He paused until Madeline nodded. "Okay, let's start with Justin's reaction to divorce."

"In a rage," Rita said. "Nobody can quit him unless he says so. I made my plans on the sly and … well, you know that part."

"Then you took a room at the Ramada?"

"Yeah, Maddie's idea. We knew he'd look here first. I mighta gone to Minneapolis or Rochester but wanted to stay close by. It's like him to send Nacho looking for me. I'm easy to find. My license plate says RITA."

"I've read the sheriff's report. They were waiting for you."

"I guess so."

"I know the sheriff's is looking into it. What do you suspect?"

"Justin is angry 'cause I refused to combine my money with his. It's been a sore point since we married. I filed for divorce and moved out because I'm just another acquisition. He thinks I'm leaving him for Bob Hartwell."

"Are you?"

"*For Bob*? Lord, no!" she said, throwing up her hands. "We used to have that chemistry… in high school. There was a moment when… but no, not now." Rita glanced at Madeline. "Bob's a gentleman. He made it clear he has no interest in me."

"That's just as well."

They took a break and Isaacs looked about the room while Madeline prepared coffee and sliced pound cake. It was a comfortable, contemporary house with top-of-the-line furniture and a view of the Wacouta River through the trees. Madeline had collected some fine, original ceramic pieces. While waiting for the refreshment, he smiled to himself as he studied an excellent Renaissance painting of two women embracing.

Afterward, he went over what he had learned from the sheriff's report of the attack. "Do you think they assaulted you on Justin's orders?"

"I don't know," Rita said. "At least not directly. He would know he'd be the main suspect. He uses pressure and intimidation, not raw force. Nacho is loyal but depends on him, too. They have a kind of symbiotic relationship… you know, like fungi and bacteria. He does things to help Justin that Justin never asks for… at least directly. And Justin lets him do his own deals on the side. Nacho mighta done this for his own reasons."

"Why do you think that? What reasons?"

"I've overheard them bickering lately. Over trucking, mostly. That's new."

"You mentioned that before. Is there more?" Isaacs asked in a voice as low and calm as if discussing why the television wasn't working."

"Nacho has a business trucking cattle to Texas and pays Justin for using the ranch as a base. Justin says the ranch is paying for itself and he doesn't want Nacho to continue. Nacho said no. It's his business. It makes too much money to stop."

"Why does Justin want him to stop trucking?"

"Risks. The Missouri cops stopped them but no arrests. Nacho is a citizen but the other three aren't. He's afraid they might be picked up. But I don't think he cares about that. Nacho is hauling something from Laredo in the hay. I think it's connected to the accounts I looked at. They're afraid I know something."

"What might you know that worries him?"

"Justin bought the Becker farm a few months before we married. Everyone talked about that for a while. Then it was quiet until Bob returned. I looked at the farm accounts after they started bickering. The income bears no relation to the number of cattle sold at current prices."

"Above market prices?"

"*Oh!... Waaay* above market by a factor of ten or more. Every month they haul a few bulls or steers to Texas but the accounts show a lot more money than that. So, there's another source of money. They return with heifers and always with a small load of hay."

"Hay?"

"Yeah. A few dozen bales they store in the sanatorium."

"*Ah-ha*," Isaacs said, suppressing a feeling he had received a revelation. *Now we're getting somewhere.* "What happens to the bales?"

"Nacho puts them in the sanatorium for a day or two. Then he goes to Minneapolis."

"Do you know why?"

"No. I've learned not to ask. He has a girlfriend or two there."

"Is it connected to why you were beaten and raped?"

"Maybe. I think Nacho did it in retaliation over trucking."

"Do you need protection?"

"We're protected," Rita said. "I've got a.38 automatic and know how to use it."

"Me, too," Madeline nodded. "I own a Beretta.380. We'll keep them handy."

Isaacs raised his eyebrows. "Please rely on the police. Criminal defense isn't my forte."

*
**

"Mister Isaacs is a fine man," Madeline said after he left. "I like him."

"He's a good man. His modesty hides the heart of a lion. He used to be a deputy attorney general. He's Bob's attorney, too—"

"—Is he married?"

"Why Maddie, are you interested in him?" Rita giggled.

"No, of course not," she said. "I was thinking of you and him. He's a little older and a lot like Gerhard." She went to the refrigerator and returned with two cans of Sprite.

"Maddie, I'm done fooling around with husbands and lovers. No one could be better than Gerhard. Certainly, not Bob. I like him a lot but we are different. No, I'm done pretending I'm still a young bitch in heat. I took a shot at Bob before I left Justin. He turned me down. He's a fine man but… well, he's much too intense for me."

"So, what's next? Are you going to move away—live somewhere else? What are you going to do?"

"I want your advice later. Right now, I want to stay here with you." Rita heaved herself upright. She put the crutches under her arms and hopped across the sunroom to open a window. Then she hopped back and sat, pleased that she could move about on her own.

"I feel… how can I say it? I don't know… I wanna to spend time with you. And then meet other women as friends instead of as competitors. I always judged myself by the men I attracted. Quantity and quality. It was like keeping score—"

"—Like mirror, mirror on the wall, who's the—"

"—Yeah, something like that. I didn't feel attractive in high school unless I had a boyfriend or two or three. Bob was the first. We practiced… had some great… *oops*."

"No, that's okay but you've told me that already."

"His attention made me believe I was beautiful and loveable—"

"—But you are."

"I know that now but I didn't know it then. Not for a long time. I never heard from Bob after he was drafted so, I moved on and married

201

Gerhard. After he died, I wanted some excitement. Someone to tell me I'm beautiful. Justin had devilish swagger that… well, you know the rest."

"I know, I warned you," she said and massaged Rita's shoulders. "I know you're hurting in so many ways. You can stay with me and take your time getting over it," she said and wrapped her arms around Rita's shoulders. "Stay. Just the two of us."

"Thanks," Rita said and reached up to put her hands over Madeline's. "I feel better for letting go of this shit. Anyway, I see how you move between men and women. It's time I learned to do that. I've got enough money so I don't have to work or depend on a man."

"You may change your mind. Right now, focus on healing your heart and your body. After the divorce comes through—"

"—I hope the sheriff puts Justin and Nacho in jail."

"Until then, stay with me. Having you here is better than living alone."

Chapter 34

Finding the cigarette butts below the house had triggered an itchy sensation at the back of Boston's neck. Though he saw no other signs of a watcher, he couldn't shake the feeling that someone lurked nearby. He now glanced at the rearview mirror every few seconds even when he wasn't in traffic. And he checked the Jeep from a distance before getting into it. *I'm overcautious. Maybe. But it saved my hide before.*

Seated on the veranda with Jester lying at his feet, he skimmed his weekly pile of news magazines. Now and then, he marked up items he might work into his column for *American Outlook*. Then Jester growled and got to his feet as a gray pickup passed along the road below and vanished around the end of the ridge. The pickup returned a few minutes later and parked near where he found the cigarette butts.

He quieted Jester and waited to see what the driver would do. A local farmer would get out and check the adjacent soybean field. Ten minutes passed but no one got out of the truck. Boston went inside, returned with binoculars and looked through the veranda's clematis vines. From cover, he saw a man sitting behind the wheel, smoking. No law against that but farmers didn't just sit in their trucks. Returning to his chair, he pretended to surf more magazines but the truck didn't move. It was just after 5:00 p.m., and time for Ginger to return, when the phone rang. He went inside and answered it.

"Both my front tires are flat!" Ginger cried in outrage.

"*What*! Okay. Do you want me to pick you up?"

"Well, *duh!*" Then a moment of staticky silence. "Sorry. I'm not mad at you. I called Benson's Motors. Their guys are on the way."

"All right. I'll be there shortly."

He locked Jester in the house and glanced down the hill at the county road. The pickup remained on the shoulder. Both front tires flat. Not an accident. The reason occurred to him as he went down the driveway. Instead of turning east toward Featherstone, he turned west toward the gray pickup. As he did, the truck started toward him. Boston turned the Jeep sideways to block the road. The pickup stopped, spun quickly and raced away.

Boston chased the pickup to the House of Truth but it was too far ahead to catch up. Seeing the truck's dust plume on the north bound road, he returned to his driveway in case the stalker circled back. *Waiting for me to leave. Give him a chance to…* He waited fifteen minutes and then arrived at the *Statesman* as the crew from Benson's Motors winched Ginger's Subaru onto a flatbed truck.

"What in hell is going on?" Ginger snapped, still seething over her tires.

"I'm not certain but I think Taylor suspects me of helping Hartwell. He knows I've interviewed his neighbors. And the article and editorial about adverse possession don't help him. Neither does the story about the Beckers. He has to know I'm talking to Jack. So, I'm a threat."

"So we're targets," she said to answer a question she hadn't asked.

"It's possible." He told her about the cigarette butts and the pickup he had seen several times. "Someone was watching the house when you called. I think the flat tires were intended to draw me away from the house long enough for… whatever. I drove toward him and he took off so fast I didn't get a plate number." He drove home glancing down the side roads for lurking pickups. Then he went past his driveway and turned around at the House of Truth. His road was clear—for now at least.

***

Ginger got up when Boston left on his run. She said her prayers, worked through her yoga routine and showered. He was usually back by then and fixing their breakfast. But not today. He was an hour overdue on his run. She raced the Jeep along the county road toward the House of Truth. Just where the road climbed over the base of the ridge, she saw him clawing his way up the embankment. The Jeep slid to a stop and she jumped out. Boston leaned on the Jeep, his hair matted with blood and dirt, and staring at her through broken glasses with the blank expression of an amnesiac.

"Oh Mother of God, what happened?" she cried, and opened the passenger door. Then she eased him into the seat. "I've got to get you to the hospital."

"No, home first," he said. "It's not that bad. I need to call Jack."

"It is bad and you can't—"

"—Take me home, goddammit! Sorry, I didn't mean to—"

"—Honestly, you're so stubborn!" she fumed.

"I want to call Jack now, then we can go to the clinic." They entered the house. She washed his face and daubed at his scalp to remove the clotted blood and dirt. He had a large bruise on the back of his head and cuts on his arms and legs where he rolled over rocks on the embankment. She put a bag of frozen peas on his head to reduce the swelling and salved his cuts and abrasions.

"Now... what happened?" she demanded. "And don't say you're okay. You're not!"

"All right," he sighed. "I turned around at the tavern... as usual. Just before where you met me a gray GMC pickup... it came from behind. Heard it accelerate. When I looked back, it was heading for me. I ran to get past the embankment and jump safely... that's when something hit me on the back of the head."

"Any idea who?"

"It's a gray GMC pickup... like the one I saw yesterday. Like the one... it shadowed me when I interviewed Taylor's neighbors. It was him or an employee."

His head throbbed as much from anger as from pain. After two aspirins, he gave Jack a brief report and his suspicion. Then he went upstairs to his old bedroom, removed his father's Smith and Wesson from a dresser and took it to the den. He checked the loads and closed the cylinder. *It might come down to this. A lot can happen.*

"What are you doing?" Ginger demanded as he shoved the pistol into a desk drawer.

"If push comes to shove—"

"—No. *No!* You killed once already. I won't let you kill again."

Chapter 35

To Hartwell's delight, the township clerk posted a meeting notice and an agenda for its August meeting. Isaacs and Hartwell drove together to the Runyon Town Hall. In the red light of evening, the simple brick building with its small belltower seemed as quaint as a lithograph. "My granddad, my dad and I attended this country school," Hartwell said as they entered.

"That's an interesting turn of history."

"Which one of you is Hartwell?" the clerk asked from his seat behind a wooden desk stacked with papers.

"I am." He extended his hand but the clerk ignored it.

"You're last on the agenda. Keep it short. We don't like long meetings."

Isaacs nodded toward the door. "Keep your cool," he told him on the way outside. "We have to jump through the hoops. Judging by his attitude, I think the cook has already baked the cake. Accept it. We'll cross it off the list and go to court. But I could be wrong."

"I doubt it. You haven't been wrong yet."

Marge arrived in a blue Ford pickup dressed in a skirt with a paisley scarf wrapped around her hair. "Ready. Bob?" She gave him a clenched teeth smile like a coach before the kick-off. "This'll be interesting."

He introduced her to Isaacs and asked if the petitioners were going to attend.

"I don't know. Some of 'em signed because they wanted to. Some of 'em because I asked 'em to. My guess is, they'll lay low to play it safe."

"What does Taylor have over people?" Isaacs asked.

"Fear," she answered, planting her fists on her broad hips. "Everyone he bought out had a disaster they couldn't afford. His foreman is the menacing type. No direct threats but he's got a way of creating a worry that something terrible might happen. We suspect he was behind the disasters. It's just that we can't prove it."

"But you're not afraid."

"Not as afraid. I rent out my land so he can't do much to hurt me short of setting fire to my house. He's not that stupid."

"You're certain of that?" Isaacs asked.

"Well, nothing is certain but death and taxes. I better get in. Taylor will show because he's the chairman. He can't vote when it involves his property but he can sway the others."

The final two supervisors arrived together and Hartwell greeted them but they merely nodded and brushed past him. Taylor arrived last and entered without a greeting. He called the meeting to order and they stood with hands over their hearts and pledged allegiance to the flag that promised liberty and justice for them all.

The five members sat in a row behind a long table with Taylor in the middle. Marge took a chair at one end. In quick succession, the board adopted the agenda, approved the minutes and then accepted the treasurer's report. After that, they discussed the reports on the status and condition of the town's roads and bridges. Then they talked about letting contracts to supply gravel and mow the ditches. An hour passed before the board took up the petition.

"I see no reason to rush this," a supervisor said. "I move we table it to another meeting."

"I object," Marge replied. "You delay and it will end up in court." The air in the room went still. No one seconded the motion.

"There is a motion," Taylor said. "Is there a second?" Silence. "The motion fails. We'll hear the petition to open the road. Hartwell, you have the floor."

"Thank you. My family has owned the mineral spring since 1874. The court has affirmed my title and the road has been in public use until recently when a locked gate was installed. Consequently, I am unable to access my property. Fifteen other residents have signed the petition to support opening the road in compliance with state law."

"When was the last time you actually traveled that road?" a supervisor asked.

"My father used it regularly until his death in 1967. I last used it in 1971 and saw it was being graded and graveled, well within the forty-year limit for abandonment. I know of others who will testify it was graded as recently as three years ago. Norm Becker rented my land and used it all the time and kept me posted on its condition."

"Does anyone care to speak against the petition?" Taylor asked, looking left and right at fellow board members. "All right, I will," he said and got to his feet. "When the state closed the sanatorium, the road became the common driveway for the two farms that I bought. He ain't used his property in decades. Openin' the road will split my operation. Then I'll be obliged to build two miles of fence to keep cattle off the road. As a result, my operation will be less efficient and less profitable. If you open the road, I will petition the township for compensation includin' the value of the right of way. That's eight acres at seven hundred an acre plus the necessary fencin' materials and my business losses. I estimate that will exceed ten-thousand dollars."

"Justin makes a good point," a supervisor said. "Our road costs are already high. We can't afford to compensate him. I say vote it down."

"Anyone else?"

Hartwell stood. "If you don't open the road, it constitutes theft of property. I will sue the township for its current market value. That is at least one-hundred-twenty grand, a lot more than the cost of fencing and the right of way."

"All right. Anymore—" but Taylor didn't finish.

"—I move we open the road," Marge said.

"Is there a second?" Taylor asked glaring at the others. "It's been moved that we reopen the road. Is there a second?" More silence. "Hearing no second, the motion fails." Taylor gave Hartwell a smug grin.

"I move to reconsider," Marge snapped, her voice laced with anger. "If you don't, this will end up in court where we *will* lose."

"There is a motion to reconsider," he said. "Is there a second?" Silence. "Absent a second, the motion to reconsider fails."

A supervisor moved to adjourn. The clerk seconded the motion. The chair called for a vote and the meeting adjourned on a vote of four to one.

Marge followed Isaacs and Hartwell out of the hall. "Wait up," she called. "I know you're disappointed—"

"—More than that," Hartwell said. "I'm goddamned angry! This thing was rigged."

"Of course, it was," she replied. "I figured it would be. But the law is clear. The petition gives you legal standing. Remember, people in the township support you."

"We have options," Isaacs said in a calming voice. "We can ask the township to vote on the road in a special election. Or we can go to court. Marge, how do you feel about taking our side if we sue?"

"Count me in!"

Chapter 36

Taylor woke at daybreak. Wife, girlfriend or whore, he disliked passing the night without a woman's warm body next to his. It had been three months since Rita left their bed. *I'll pick a younger one next time. One who needs money. Nacho's right. Better to have a woman you see once a month. Rita's too fuckin' independent. Dangerous. I'm better off without her. I bet Nacho raped her to spite me over truckin'. Bitch deserved it but Nacho... well, cain't do anythin' right now. I'll play that card when the time comes.*

He made himself a breakfast of sausage patties, eggs and hashbrowns. With toast and coffee he felt set for the day. He was wiping up egg yolk with some toast when the phone rang. Exactly 8:05 by the kitchen clock.

"Oh, it's you," he said into the receiver. "Hell no! You cain't go through my yard. Go in the where ya did before."

"That's the long way—"

"—I don't give a shit. It's all the access you get from me. That or nothin'."

"The only terms we'll come to is an open road."

"Won't happen." Taylor hung up and charged out the door yelling for Morales. He found the foreman behind the barn. "Hartwell is hikin' in from the swale."

"No worry *Jefe*," he laughed. "I cover it."

"Good. I know I can count on you." He turned and went back to the kitchen, lit a cigarette and poured a fresh cup of coffee. *Hope Nacho enjoyed fuckin' her. An' I hope she really hated it.*

Hartwell had heard about Rita's attack and the news alarmed him. She didn't deserve that, he thought and it put him into a rage. His first impulse was to visit her and express his sorrow. Then he remembered she was with Maddie and Isaacs told him to stay away. He had a conviction that Taylor was behind it... just like every other disaster in this valley. Thinking of the cattleman set Hartwell to seething for a while before he packed his knapsack for the hike to his land.

He parked his car as before and opened the trunk. The pack had his camera, water and lunch. It also held pruning shears, a fifty-foot carpenter's tape, twine and fluorescent tape. He wasn't trespassing today and saw no reason to stay close to the trees as he had before. This short hike satisfied him as much as trekking in the Sierras because Taylor conceded his title by letting him cross. Thanks to Isaacs and Marge, he had won a skirmish. He was grateful for supporters like Gretta and Maddie and even Rita. He thought about the date with Gretta. *I've still got what it takes to attract a woman. Guess I'm not too old for—*

—A raging, nasal bellow made Hartwell's hair stand on end. Branches crackled in the woods as a bull charged from the trees. Adrenaline surged as soon as he saw it. Speed was his only option in the open. He ran all out. Thundering hooves drowned the pounding of blood in his ears. His lungs burned... he felt light-headed... only a few yards more. Then, with a final burst of speed, he reached the escarpment, grabbed a sapling and leaped. The small tree bent, broke his fall and he landed on the slope beneath the ledge.

The bull stopped at the brink. It bellowed and pawed the ground as Hartwell lay gasping for air. His chest hurt, his ears rang and his heart beat double-time. The tremor in his fingers spread until his body shook. He felt cold. Nothing in combat had terrified him like that.

"Jesus Ex Christ!" he gasped as he lay below the rim waiting for his breathing and heartbeat to slow. "Too close." He lay behind the ledge, grateful to be alive, and rested until he heard the bull wander away. Then he slid down the slope and under the fence to the safety of his property. "The sonofabitch set me up," he muttered as he hiked toward the cavern. *Said he wouldn't be responsible. If the bull killed me, he could call it an accident. End of story.*

It was now mid-August and Hartwell chafed at the delay in opening the road. If nothing else, he could at least measure the site to show the project to prospective architects and contractors. Hiking to the spring, he stopped to take a long drink. Eyes closed, he sat and listened to it gush until the sound entered and soothed him. Once refreshed, he cut a bundle of willow saplings into stakes. Then he jabbed them into the ground at key locations to outline the proposed center. The fluorescent tape and twine outlined the building, the pools, the spring and the old well. With the carpenter's tape, he measured the outlines and recorded them in a notebook with sketch maps showing the relationship between the features. Then he shot photos.

These preliminaries reminded him of prepping for surgery. Instead of X-rays, he took photos and drew sketches. Instead of taking the patient's vitals, he made notes on the site including the thickets of undergrowth around the building, the size of the patio and the location of the cottage foundations. Once the road was open, the contractor could clear the site and remove the old building. Then he could start construction.

The building's core would be a hexagon with abutting wings and enough rooms to treat fifty patients at a time. Besides the mineral waters and meditation spaces, the complex would have private sleeping rooms, an office, a library, a dining hall, small rooms for consultation, meditation and massage, a gym and a commercial kitchen to prepare meals. He hoped to reuse the bricks to maintain continuity with the past. Concentrating on the shape and size of the center pushed the bull to the back of his mind—for now.

Hours passed as he worked around the building site and the day turned hot and humid beneath the overcast. He entered the building's west end and came upon a stack of square bales in the corner. Pushing back his sweaty cap, he wondered again why Taylor was storing hay there. The other barns were closer to the cattle. A closer look at the bales and he realized they were composed of coarse grasses and weeds. *He's not feeding this stuff. None of this is what it seems. It's also a trespass.*

If nothing else, a bale would make a good seat for lunch. He grabbed a bale by its two twine bindings and pulled it from the stack. One twine broke and the compressed hay opened on one side like an accordion. Four small packets fell onto the floor.

"*Ooh shee*-it!" he hissed as his stomach dropped to his feet. Sweat broke out under his arms. Hearing a truck in the distance set every cell in his body to screaming "*run!*" He gasped as hard as he had running from the bull. Swallowing his panic, he glanced toward Taylor's yard and saw nothing. The engine sound faded, but that didn't reassure him. *This is why he claimed adverse possession. Closed the road to keep everyone out. I called his bluff and... Taylor knows I'm here. Maddie said he's a grenade.*

Hartwell's mind moved as rapidly as it had during combat triage. He snapped photos of the broken bale and close-ups of the packages. He considered taking one as evidence. Then he rejected it. Bad idea. Morales might show up. He glanced about wondering how to cover up his discovery. He couldn't leave a broken bale. Then they'd know and come after him. Fixing the bale would be like putting toothpaste back in the tube. Then he remembered his uncle's fix for broken bales. Worth a try.

Laying the bale on its unbroken side, he stuffed the packets back inside it. Each bale had a foot or two of loose twine hanging from the knot. He cut a foot and a half from another bale and tied it to one of the broken ends. Then he tied a loop in the other broken end. Squeezing the hay as tight as he could, he put the loose end through the loop, pulled it tight and tied it off. He pulled several bales off the stack, shoved the lopsided one in the middle and restacked good bales over it. *Bales break all the time. Maybe they won't notice this one. Hah!*

Hartwell wiped his sweaty face with a shirttail. He didn't want to stick around if Morales or Taylor showed up. The air was thick with humidity under the dense overcast and he heard the constant rumble of thunder in the distance. Shouldering the rucksack, he started toward the crevice. With luck, he would reach his car before the rain hit—if the bull didn't get him.

After the first sprinkles, a light, steady rain fell as he hiked. Soaked to the skin, he clambered up the slippery chute and stopped at the cleft in the ledge. Rain spattered on the flat rock as his eyes searched the trees and he listened for the bull. Hearing nothing but rain, he climbed onto the ledge rock and zig-zagged from tree-to-tree back to the car. The bull seemed a minor risk compared to the packets.

Chapter 37

Isaacs went to the office earlier than usual to meet Hartwell. Poor man was out of breath when he called last night. Not hysterical but clearly overwrought. If what Hartwell said was true, and he had no reason to doubt him, Isaacs understood exactly why Taylor was blocking the road and claiming the mineral spring as his. He had no doubt they had stumbled upon a serious felony and wondered where the facts might lead them.

The downstairs door opened and closed. Hartwell was on his way up. "I've got the photos," he began without so much as "good morning." He opened the package and spread out his snapshots of the bales and packets. "I've got a good idea of what's going on. What's my liability?"

"None. We can prove he was using your property without your knowledge. I want you to write out everything you remember from yesterday. Every detail. Use my typewriter if that's easier. That way it will be legible…" he said with a chuckle to lighten the mood.

The doctor spent an hour pecking out a narrative that included the bull and the packages in the bales. Isaacs read it, nodded and took him downstairs to the copy shop where a clerk witnessed his signature and then notarized it. "I'll take it from here," Isaacs said. "As it is, I've got an appointment with Judge Knatvold in twenty minutes. I'll let you know what happens." To his surprise, Hartwell didn't ask to go along.

Isaacs worked up a sweat walking through the muggy air and the air-conditioning inside the courthouse hit him like an Arctic cold front. He stopped to wipe the fog from his glasses. Then he entered the judge's chambers.

The short, gray jurist appeared older than his years. He fussed with his glasses and listened impassively as Isaacs asked for a writ of mandamus ordering the town board to open the road. Then the judge studied the petition and the failure to second any motion except adjourn. Then he looked up from the papers. "Didn't I just settle the ownership of that tract? And despite that, the town board turned him down?"

"Exactly, your honor. The chair and clerk claim it was abandoned. Justin Taylor chairs the board and claims he must be compensated for a loss of property, fencing and inconvenience. My client's property is worth ten times his projected losses."

Knatvold let out a peeved snort like a parent dealing with a willful child. "I believe you Morrie," he said, waving his hand. "Sit down. You've got the statutes on your side. However, this whole business makes me suspicious. There's more here than meets the eye. I want to look at the town records to see what else they're up to. I'll order the clerk to produce them immediately. Then I'll rule."

"Thank you, your honor. Always a pleasure," Isaacs said as he left the chamber.

"Got a minute, Morrie?" Jack asked when he saw Isaacs leave the chambers across the corridor. He closed the door behind them. "Boston keeps me in the loop on Hartwell's case. I know Taylor's real name is Daylor. The eyes of Texas have been upon him for years. He's got a long trail of suspicion but no hard evidence. Have you got anything?"

"His claim to the spring isn't greed. He's hiding something there. His hired man chased Bob off with a warning. When he gave Bob permission to cross his land he didn't tell him he would encounter a bull there. It charged him and he saved himself by jumping off a ledge. That was yesterday."

"Is he filing a complaint?"

"No, I advised him to hold off. He found a stack of bales in the sanatorium. One of the bales broke open when he pulled on it and four packages fell out. We think they are moving drugs. I'll give you Bob's photos his sworn statement."

"*Hmm*. All right mister retired deputy attorney general, what's our next move?" Jack grinned with appreciation. Morrie was one colleague in a million.

"If I were sheriff, I'd get a search warrant for the sanatorium."

"Do you think Taylor is dealing?" He leaned back in his chair.

"Too soon to tell. I doubt he deals directly. From what Rita told me, trucking is his foreman's operation. It looks like he may use the sanatorium as a distribution hub for a network, say in Minneapolis. Hartwell's access threatens it. I suspect the hay and the packets are gone."

"Even if they are, something may linger. The photos give me probable cause for a search warrant. Protecting a drug operation is a motive for murder if, but only if Becker discovered it or Taylor thought he had. Keep that between us for now."

County Attorney Glenda Mercer had the office next to the sheriff's and called in Isaacs as he passed her door. Unlike Jack, the stout, middle-aged woman kept Spartan quarters. The only personal touches included her framed law degree and portraits of Justices Earl Warren, Sandra Day O'Connor, Louis Brandeis and Oliver Wendell Holmes. With a gruff voice, dark suit and closely cropped gray hair, she projected a persona that tended to intimidate witnesses, cops and even judges. Isaacs was fond of her.

"My spies say you've got a township road case," she said with a twinkle in her eye.

"Well, you're ahead of me, as usual," he said, taking the proffered chair. Then she stepped from behind her desk and took a chair facing him. "What's up, Morrie?"

In the terse style he knew she favored, he filled her in on Hartwell's struggle to gain access to his property and the town board's refusal to reopen a public road. He told her the judge ordered the board to send in its records. Then he told her about Hartwell's escape from the bull.

"Are you filing a complaint?"

"Not yet. This business is now more than a dispute over access."

"Go on," she said with a coaxing gesture.

In memorandum style, he told her what the doctor discovered in the broken bale, that he had photographed it and he would give the pictures and a sworn statement to Jack. Isaacs guessed it was heroin, cocaine or marijuana. If the autopsy confirmed someone murdered the Beckers then the drug operation may have been the reason.

"What do you want from me?"

"Nothing for now. I'll leave it to Jack to fill you in when he's ready for a warrant. We both think Becker's death is connected to it."

Mercer's face cracked into one of her rare smiles. "Morrie, deep in your heart you never really retired from being deputy A.G. I'm grateful for that. Thanks for the briefing. You're a kindred spirit."

"Thanks for listening."

"Any time, Morrie. You're always welcome here."

Chapter 38

"So, send 'em," Taylor barked into the phone as the town clerk mewled about the board's minutes. "Quit draggin' your feet. It looks like you're hidin' somethin'." He listened a moment longer. "All right, any chance some of 'em got lost when Otto passed 'em to ya? That's been known to... mebbe the roof leaked... or something. *Jesus*! Use your imagination!" Then he listened and let his anger ebb. "You're a good man. Just send in the records."

"What a *goddamn* mess!" Taylor seethed as he put down the phone. *The clerk is pissing his pants over this.* He stuck a cigarette in his mouth, scraped a match on his thumbnail and lit it. *Everything was going just as I wanted... then Hartwell shows up. The operation is off the rails. Rich bastard has his title. Judge'll make me open the road. That'll cut my place in two. Then there's Rita. She can read accounts an' use it for leverage in the dee-vorce. I can't take the risk.*

He dragged on the cigarette and drummed his fingers on the desk. Everthin's fucked up. Gonna get worse if we keep truckin'. Knew it would happen. Timing's the thing. Got out of oil jist in time. Hartwell had to see the bales. No tellin' what else he saw or who he's told.

Taylor went outside into the evening that had turned soft and mild. This was one of the rare times when he felt like having a stiff drink. He had steered clear of hard liquor ever since adolescence. *Whiskey took the snap outta Pa. Made him a commode huggin', knee-walkin' drunk. That wrecked the ranch. Sober is the only way to stay strong.*

He walked across the yard toward the two mobile homes where the men lived and knocked on Morales's door.

The foreman opened it wearing only boxer shorts and a tee shirt. *"¿Hola Jefe, qué pasó?* He asked what happened? *"You wearin' a worry face, I think."

"The judge wants the town records, *pronto*. He's gonna order me to open the road."

"What you do?"

"De-layin' is the best I can do. Say a month or two. Time to fence the road. That's beside the point. When did you move the hay?"

"Sí. She in the Otto barn."

"No, *cuando*, when?"

"She go this mornin'. Why?"

"Goddamnit! Hartwell seen it. No telling who he's told. Get rid of the goods right now. We gotta get out of it. There's too much risk—"

"—No, no, no. We make *tanto dinero* now."

"No, money is a tool. I want to live raisin' cattle, not dodgin' the law. A good ranch is all I've wanted, Nacho. You know that. It's not the money. It's the satisfaction of ranchin'. Oil give me money to start this place and truckin' give me cash to finish it but I cain't keep takin' all the risk. It's too much. Especially now."

"But the *tipos* who—"

"—I don't care about them. Got no use for 'em. I gotta look out for us. The bull didn't scare off Hartwell. I saw him go in and out of the building. No tellin' what he saw. I went down there afterward. It looked like he moved some bales. I ain't takin' any more chances. The next trip is the last one."

"Jefe, you got cattle but truckin' my business."

"I'll figger somethin' out. I'll take care of you. Just like always. That stuff gives you money but I take the risk. If the shit hits the fan I don't want to be in front of it."

"We quit an' the *tipos* come for us I think."

"Tell 'em the cops are onto us. In fact, I'm pretty sure they are. Tell 'em this whole thing could come apart and take 'em with it."

"Well, you owe me *Jefe*," Morales said, raising his voice to a sullen shout. "You owe big. I make the connection… The Guadalajara *tipos*. They kill us."

"Well, they can try."

***

Isaacs entered the judge's chambers and studied the two men seated before him. Knatvold wore an implacably stern expression. Hickenlooper seemed as submissive as a rabbit and the town clerk fidgeted in his chair like a boy with ants in his pants.

"Gentlemen," the judge began. "I prefer an informal hearing with compliance instead of a formal court ruling. I reviewed the petition and the town's records. It's clear the town graded and graveled the Runyon Spring Road four years ago. There is no record of the board's decision to vacate the road. Nor is there a notice to landowners of their intention to do so. State law prohibits abandoning a road if it denies access to a property holder. The Runyon Spring Road meets all legal standards as a public thoroughfare. Therefore, I *suggest* you remove the gate and let the public use the road. Otherwise, I will issue a court order. It's your choice."

"But your Honor—"

"—Mister Hickenlooper, I understand your client pastures cattle on and around the road. The fencing laws apply. Your client has thirty days to remove the gate and erect fences or otherwise keep his cattle off the right of way. That is all."

"Your honor, I intend to appeal," Hickenlooper said.

"Appeal what?" Knatvold looked up with an indulgent smile. "So far, I made a suggestion. You can't appeal a suggestion. The road's status is supported by town records and black-letter law. This is an unofficial ruling to avoid sanctioning you and your client. I would think you already have enough trouble with me. If you buck me, I'll make it official. Then you can appeal all you want. Until then, the suggestion stands."

"But your honor," Hickenlooper wheedled. "The order forces my client to put up an expensive fence. If we are successful in a later appeal, he will have needlessly spent money for a fence he no longer needs. I'm asking you to stay your, your suggestion."

"Counselor, your request is denied. The town minutes make it clear the road was never abandoned. That means your client is violating state law. If the road isn't open within thirty days, I will charge your client with contempt of court and a violation of several Minnesota Statutes. And I will sanction you, too. I hope that is clear."

Hickenlooper mumbled his thanks and left the chambers followed by the clerk. When Isaacs stood to leave, Knatvold looked up at him and winked.

Chapter 39

The title to the mineral spring was now settled but the notarized statement still bothered Isaacs. It was bogus but the document still seemed relevant to several unanswered questions. A fraudulent claim of adverse possession didn't square with Becker's reputation any more than his suicide. He felt certain Becker's notarized statement tied in with Mary Kasson's investigation of their deaths.

He placed his copy of Becker's statement against a rental contract and compared the signatures. The rental contracts held the signature of a confident man who had learned cursive. The signature on Becker's quit claim looked similar but lacked the fluidity on the rental contracts. Isaacs removed his glasses and pinched the bridge of his nose. The difference might reflect emotion over selling the farm or the haste to get it over with. Or it might be a forgery.

He thought of the forgery cases he had prosecuted. Though he knew what to look for, he needed a specialist to prove it. And he didn't have one. Neither did the sheriff's office. Isaacs considered his options. Would Jack and Boston notice the signature variations. If they concluded it was a forgery, then he had little doubt that was the case. And if that were so, Becker didn't sell willingly and that meant his disappearance was…

Then he noticed the notary on the quit claim. It wasn't the one Becker used at the Farmer's State Bank. Isaacs knew many of the local notaries but not Earl Goodman. He copied the certificate number and called the Minnesota Secretary of State's office to check it against the register. The certificate matched Earl Goodman of Minneapolis.

Why Minneapolis? He called the listed phone number.

"Instant Copy and Mailing," the woman answered. "How may we help you?"

"I'd like to speak to Earl Goodman."

"*Earl*? Earl died three years ago."

"Oh, I'm sorry to hear that. How did—"

"—Someone killed him during a burglary."

"Did anyone report the loss of his notary stamp?"

"I don't know, hold on," she said, and Isaacs heard the woman question someone in the background but her voice vanished in the ambient sound of a copy machine. "No, we didn't. One of the others became a notary. She got her own stamp."

"Thank you, you've been a big help," he said and hung up. Now he felt certain Becker's documents were faked and Taylor or his associate had Minneapolis connections. He called Jack and told him what he had just learned. Jack suggested he meet him and Boston at the sheriff's office in the morning.

Isaacs arrived with papers and photos and Jack made certain the office had an urn of freshly brewed coffee. Boston arrived and the three men sat around a small table.

"I think we are now close to the crime and the killer," Isaacs began in a 'let's get down to cases' tone of voice. "Here is how it looks to me. Taylor and his foreman are involved in an illegal business with connections in Texas and Minneapolis. Probably drugs. The sanatorium is the transit hub."

"Flesh it out," Jack urged, excited.

"I'll get to that in a minute. Look at these signatures." He gave each man a copy of Becker's contract and the quit claim with its sworn statement. "What do you make of them?"

Jack hummed and compared the signatures. Boston held his to the light and slid a rental signature over it the quit claim.

"The affidavit is a forgery," Jack said.

Boston nodded. "Someone tried to copy it, maybe trace over it."

"Now, let's compare it to the suicide note."

"Not even close," Jack said. "Completely different hand."

"What are the chances that Missus Becker wrote it?" the attorney asked.

"Zero," Boston said. "Becker would feel strongest. He would kill her first and then himself. Not the other way around."

"I agree," Jack added. "The note is too short. Those I've seen were longer and specific."

"The notary stamp was a stolen one," Isaacs said. "So, we have prima facie evidence of fraud. Now, let's move on to the photos that Bob took." Then he explained how the packages fell out of a broken bale.

"The trucking operation is the cover for moving drugs," Jack said.

"That's how it looks," Isaacs agreed. "Rita told me they take two or three animals to Laredo each time and usually return with some livestock and a load of bales."

"That's what Lundstrom told me, too," Boston added. "He lives across the road and sees a trailer leave every month with a few cattle. It returns a few days later. Sometimes is has new cattle and at other times the same cattle and always a half a load of baled hay. The rig has hay only on the return trip."

"I think we're close," Isaacs said. "Rita is my client. She used to be an accountant. After looking at the farm books, she noticed the number of cattle sold couldn't account for the influx of cash in sales. They put the bales in the sanatorium for a few days and then used it as bedding in the other barns. Morales goes to Minneapolis after each Texas trip."

"*Ho-lee-shit*," Jack cried. "This is clever. I need to call my federal friends at drug enforcement. We'll need them in on this. And their Texas associates, too."

"Are you satisfied you have enough for a search warrant?" Isaacs asked.

"I'll consult the county attorney. You know how persnickety she is about details. But yeah, I think we have enough. Before I call the DEA, I'll get a search warrant for the sanatorium and take a dog along for a sniff. It's Hartwell's property so Taylor can't object."

"Any risk he'll take off?" Boston asked.

"Doubt it," Isaacs said. "Rita says the ranch is his life's obsession. So far, he's fought impossible odds to get it. He'll fight to keep it."

Chapter 40

Hartwell sat on the steps in front of his house and waited for Jack. He hadn't slept well after the sheriff's call yesterday evening. His photos of the bales and packets plus the report he wrote had provided enough evidence for a search warrant. "This does *not* make you a suspect but it is your property," Jack told him. Then, per protocol, the sheriff would serve him with the warrant and take him to the sanatorium.

The sheriff's Suburban and a K-9 van pulled up to his house. Boston sat in front next to Jack and Hartwell got into the back seat. The sheriff handed him the warrant and explained his rights under the process. The doctor was keyed up and talked incessantly as he spun out theories and surmises. Boston and Jack listened, said little but rolled their eyes to each other in sidelong glances. They turned into the ranch yard followed by the K-9 unit. Duarte and Carlos watched them from the cattle pens. Morales strode toward them with an unwelcome expression on his face.

"What you want?" the foreman challenged.

"I want to see Mister Taylor," Jack said with noticeable sharpness. "Otherwise, you're obstructing police business."

"I'm right here," Taylor shouted from the office door. "It's okay Nacho, I got this."

"I'm Sheriff Meade. I have a warrant to search Doctor Hartwell's property."

"Well, go ahead. He knows the way. You can walk in off County Road 4."

"No. Since you've blocked all legal access to his property, we'll use roadway or the town road."

"*Like hell*!" His face colored.

"This is official business. Are the gates unlocked? If not, I'd like the key. Otherwise, I'll cut the chains."

"God*damnit*... wait here!" He stormed into the office and returned with a ring of keys. "Make damn sure you lock 'em when you're done!" Then he spun on his heel, returned to the office and picked up his naval binoculars.

Jack looked at Boston, raised his eyebrows and shook his head. The Suburban and the K-9 van drove the lane off the escarpment, crossed a pasture and passed through the gate to the sanatorium. The K-9 officer let out a leashed collie she called Brit.

"Doctor, please show the officer where you found the bales. Then come outside and let them work."

He led the officer and her dog through the opening. The corner that had held the bales was now swept clean.

"As I expected," Jack said under his breath. "They moved the hay. I wonder if he used the building when Becker was alive. Awful risky but it keeps the drugs off his property. Gives him some protection. He's been two steps ahead of us."

"Can't we search his barns?" Hartwell asked.

"Not without another warrant. All in good time, doctor. First we need to establish probable cause. I hope we can get some evidence here."

The cracks between the floorboards held dirt, chaff and bits of hay. The officer let Brit off the leash and the dog worked back and forth with her nose just off the floor. Then she stopped and sniffed hard at an otherwise invisible spot.

"*Bingo*. She hit something," the officer called.

Down on his knees with a limber pallet knife, Jack coaxed chaff from between the floorboards and into an evidence bag. Meanwhile, the officer took Brit to the van for a drink and a rest. When he finished collecting chaff into four baggies, he asked Hartwell to lead the handler and Brit through the rest of the building. They finished without making another hit. He intended to give the bags to the lab. If the chaff held traces of drugs, he felt confident of getting a warrant to search Taylor's property.

"So, you'll arrest him now!" Hartwell ordered. "He's been using my property for—"

"—Keep your shirt on, doc!" Jack said with a fierce look. "This is my case, not yours. I brought you because it's your property. Now, you are to say nothing about it. Is that clear? All right, we're done here."

"Satisfied?" Taylor sneered when Jack returned the keys.

"For now. Did you store hay there?"

"Yeah. I used it when I thought I had title to it."

"Where are the bales now?"

"I moved 'em after the judge said it was Hartwell's."

"Where is the hay now?"

"I fed it to my cattle," he said with a smirk. "It's in thousand cow paddies by now. You're welcome to search 'em?"

"I might."

Taylor called Morales into the office as soon as the sheriff left. He doubted that his smug front fooled the sheriff. Not for long, anyway. His gut told him the lawman would be back with another warrant. He looked at his foreman, wishing he'd left him in Texas and regretting their partnership in trucking. However, he had needed a share of Nacho's money to build the ranch. Now he might lose everything if the law came down on him. The drugs weren't his idea. Somehow, he had to put some distance between him and the drugs to avoid taking the fall for them. He had to keep the law looking at Nacho. "You've got problems," he said to the foreman.

"The hay, I think."

"Yeah. The sheriff is fixin' to shut down your operation. I figgered you'd have to close it someday but Hartwell moved up the timetable. The sheriff might be a darky but he's no fool. I cain't do nothin' about a search of the sanatorium. Next he'll get a warrant for my barns, silos—the works. I don' want him to find anything. How soon can ya get the goods to Minneapolis?"

"Tonight, I think."

"Good. When are the boys back from Laredo?"

"They go… *tres días más*," back in three days, he said.

"*Shit*! Three days. All right, I want the barn cleaned. Don't just wash it—sanitize it. I don't want that dog to smell anything but ammonia. If anyone asks, it's something we do every year to prevent listeria. As soon as the boys get back, do the trailer an' truck."

"This mean no more haulin'—"

"—Yeah, like I said. You're done. This load is the last one."

"Stop 'til it safe an' we start again."

"No. The sheriff is on to you. Too much risk. Like I tol' you, I wanna raise cattle."

"*Jefe*, you ahead of police always. This time no different, I think."

"You aren't payin' attention. The Mexican situation is changin'. The narcs are now workin' with the *federales*. Hell, haven't ya noticed… the cartel is unsettled since they arrested Quintero last year. Now his *segundos* are killin' each other for control. They've split into a couple groups. I don't want no part of that. This is where I get off."

"But we chicken-shit players."

"I know. And the cops always start with the bitty ones and work their way up. Things were all right 'til Hartwell come back. I know the dog smelled somethin'. So, time to get out. Wipe out the tracks. Cut your losses. If not, you'll spend a long time in prison."

"*Más fácil dicho que hecho*," he retorted, saying easier said than done. "We *compadres* long time. You owe me, I think."

"I know I owe ya. I ain't forgot all ya done for me."

"So, what I tell Laredo? They come for us."

"Tell 'em the truth. Tell 'em the sheriff will be back to search. Bring in the Feds. Warn 'em the narcs already suspect your truckin'. Tell 'em you're doin' what you can to protect 'em. If you get caught with the stuff, the network will come apart and take 'em with it."

"Quit now an' they kill us."

"Just tell 'em."

"*Siíí, Jefe*," he said as he walked away. ¡*Chíngate* y *chinga tu madre*! he seethed under his breath saying fuck you and fuck your mother. He entered his house, slammed the door and kicked a chair, toppling it. *Damn. Jefe* never lie to me. Now he let me take the hit. Then it came to him. When Duarte returned, he would unpack the goods and take them to Minneapolis as usual. Instead of returning after two days, he would keep the payoff and move on. *Jefe no expect me for two days. I could be in... We compañeros long time. But not now I think.*

Taylor dragged on a cigarette and thought of the years he and the Tejano had been together. Twenty, at least. We were a good team in the oil patch. Couldn't have done it without him and the roughnecks he hired. He was always willing to do what was necessary without being asked. Kept my hands clean. *Loyalty is fine thing but now that my neck is on the line...*

Chapter 41

"Well there it is," Mary said and dropped the Becker autopsies on Jack's desk. She took a chair and he swiveled his to face her. He handed her a mug of hot water and a teabag. They knew each other so well they often read each other's thoughts. At times their minds seemed united somewhere in the ether. That was another joy of working directly with him—each seemed to anticipate the other like dancers moving in harmony..

"Well, name it," he said.

"It's murder. The exact date of death is impossible to determine but we can assume May of eighty-five. They died of poison. It was in the whiskey bottle on the car floor."

"Was it murder by someone else, double suicide or a murder-suicide?"

"Double murder," she said with authority. "The bottle has a fingerprint. Whose, we don't yet know. We've got a pile of circumstantial evidence but this looks well-planned." Mary took a swallow of tea.

"So, we know how they were murdered but don't have the evidence to prove who did it?"

"That's right. The poison was cicutoxin, an extract of water hemlock. It makes cows foam at the mouth and die within minutes. A strong dose could kill a person."

"Why water hemlock?" He didn't doubt her but wanted to hear more.

"No way to trace it," she said, waving her hand. "Strychnine and the other poisons are regulated. Easy to trace the buyer. Besides, any would-be suicide could easily get it. Hemlock is toxic in spring. Just when they died. Someone gathered enough of it ahead of time."

"Tell me how you think this happened." He shook his head in admiration.

"Everyone says Becker was scrupulously honest, didn't like Taylor and had no reason to sell his farm or retire."

"So, reconstruct what happened."

"This thing is buried under layers of deception. Someone reserved the U-Haul in Becker's name a week before they vanished. He was the hold-out in Taylor's scheme to own the valley. Taylor probably tried to force Becker to sell. When he refused, he somehow forced them to drink the poison. Then he or they loaded the van with furniture and drove the car and the van in the early morning so neighbors saw them leave." Mary drew a breath.

"*Uh-huh*. Go on."

"They left the van somewhere and drove the Buick to the refuge. It looks like they winched the car from the ATV trail to the riverbank. The Wacouta deputies found old ruts and two trees that were used to anchor the winch."

"Why go to all that trouble?" He pulled on his lower lip.

"I'm speculating. The river didn't have a spring flood this year but, if it had, the car was close enough to be swept away or covered with debris. They couldn't be sure of a flood. So, they positioned the bodies together to suggest a murder-suicide." Mary wrinkled her brow. "Maybe."

"Keep going. You're on a roll."

"The furniture probably went to an out-of-state charity and the van went to a chop shop. Taylor's crew takes cattle to Texas every month. Interstate thirty-five goes through Kansas City. That made it easy to mail the preaddressed postcards to friends as a cover."

"Yeah," he said, waving his arms in encouragement. "What else?"

"The drugs come from Laredo every month. That's where Morales comes from. He's the connection if we can believe Rita. Now for the tricky part. What is Taylor's role—simply looking the other way for a cut or is he an active agent? And what is Morales's role?"

"Do the drugs tie in with the Beckers' deaths?"

"It's only a guess," she said. "Taylor wouldn't want the drugs on his property. So, maybe he saw the sanatorium as a solution but Becker was renting the property. When Becker refused to sell, they killed him to secure control."

"Any way to prove it?

"No. Not without a confession. I suspect they tried to force Becker into signing a quit claim deed. He refused and they forged his signature. Somehow they induced or forced Becker and his wife to drink the whiskey. But I'm guessing."

"I think you're guessing good," Jack said. "It's possible they didn't think of the adverse possession claim until Hartwell arrived."

"No, I think they used the adverse possession claim to justify the gate," Mary said, dunking the tea bag. "They didn't see the unintended consequences—"

"—And those are?"

"Once Taylor blocked the road, no one could enter the sanatorium without his knowledge or permission. He didn't see that gating the road locked him in as the only suspect."

"Of course! He outed himself by hiding," Jack said, beaming. He got up and walked around the office. "Give me your take on Becker's funds."

"Someone used their personal information to transfer their funds from Waterford to a bank in Minneapolis. The Becker's account at that bank lasted only a month before the funds were put into a cashier's check for someone with identification as Norman Becker."

"This is coming together, Mary," he said with a grin and leaned back in his chair. "It ties in with Boston's digging. A couple farmers lost their herds to hemlock poisoning and had to sell out. It wasn't an accident it was sabotage."

"I'll share the autopsy with him. Afterall, you assigned him to my team. And here is the lab report on the sanatorium. They found traces of cocaine. It isn't enough for an arrest warrant. A good lawyer could claim that vandals or kids used the place to shoot up."

"Thanks, Mary." He scanned the report. "There's enough here for a search warrant of Taylor's place but I want to catch him with the drugs. Without the Beckers we have only circumstantial evidence. Is there anything that directly connects them to the murders?"

"Afraid not," she said. "Not yet. I'll keep looking."

Taylor and Morales know what they're doing, Jack thought scrubbing fingers through his short curls. They moved the drugs quickly and the sanatorium gave them cover and deniability. However, once he closed the road, he was the only party with access to the building. He admitted storing hay. That and the drug residue seemed enough probable cause to search his buildings and vehicles. Even Glenda would sign that warrant. Right now, they needed enough evidence to detain him, Morales and the other three. One of them knew how the Beckers died. He called Boston.

"Didn't you tell me Lundstrom was suspicious of Taylor's operation? Think it's worth talking to him? As I recall, he keeps an eye on their trucking. If that's how they're moving drugs he might help us catch them in possession. Will you set up a meeting? Tonight, if possible."

Jack wore civvies for the meeting and Boston drove him in the Jeep. The tall, ponderous farmer met them on the porch of his white farmhouse. He had snowy hair, a deep voice and a trace of Swedish accent. "Yah, you come in now," he intoned. "Mama, this here is Mister Meade and his brother the sheriff. Let's have us some coffee and bars now."

Boston took the coffee to be polite. Jack sampled a bar, praised it. Missus Lundstrom, you truly know the way to a man's heart."

"You know why we're here," Boston said.

"Yah and you won't print my name or tell others what I say."

"That's a promise," he said. "In fact, the less people know the better."

"Yah well, okay then."

Boston began with the questions he posed to Otto, Larson and the others and his answers were similar to theirs. Lundstrom sold his dairy farm to Taylor in 1980 and concentrated on raising corn and soybeans. It was the Texan's first purchase and he paid in cash.

"You know, if I'da known then what was gonna happen, I fer sure woulda never sold to him. After me, he gobbled 'em up one after the other like he was eatin' peanuts."

"Are you on good terms with him?" Jack asked.

"*Nah*. We don't talk."

"You think there's something funny about his ranch. Tell me more."

"Lemme tell you," Lundstrom said, lowering his voice and shifting in the chair. "It's a strange outfit. He told me once he buys and sells stock in Texas. His driveway is just up the road an' they pass me to get to the highway. I see 'em comin' and goin' haulin' a couple head each time. Every month, they go four days and return with a couple head and a lot of bales."

"What's unusual?" Jack asked, leading him. "Sounds like what you'd expect."

"Sometimes I snoop on 'em with binoculars, you know," he said, looking down as if embarrassed. "Sometimes I seen 'em haul away and bring back the same two or three animals."

"How can you tell?"

"Well, when you raise cattle, you see 'em as individuals, like people, you know. If you know what to look for though, they got their own faces like me and you."

Boston leaned back and took off his glasses. "*Hmm*. I'm not a cattleman... why do you suppose... explain what you suspect."

"Truckin' cattle is hard on 'em, you know. They get knocked around. Hurt. Lotta stress then. Now stress makes 'em lose weight. So them cattle aren't going to any market. They're for show. And the rig always returns with hay."

"Hay... like bales of hay. Is it for feed along the way?"

"*Nah*. You'd give 'em mixed feed or grain. Better for 'em and take less space. Taylor's got more hay than he can use. So, there's something else going on though."

"What do you think that is?" Jack asked with his mouth filled with lemon bar.

"Hard to tell. He's got all the hay in the world. And he don't need it on a long trip."

"Tell me, is there a pattern to those trips?" Jack asked. "Like… first of the month…?"

"Yah. Middle of the month. Gone four days. His rig pulled out yesterday."

"That's good. I'd like you to watch. Call me just as soon as the rig comes back." He handed him a business card. "Call my office during the day. Here's my home number. Call anytime at night. Don't wait. It's important to know the minute you see them."

"Oh yah, fer sure. That all?"

"Yeah. It's a lot. Don't say anything about it to anyone. This has to be quiet."

"What's it about?"

"That's what we hope to find out."

Chapter 42

Lundstrom expected the rig to return from Texas sometime the next evening. As a precaution, he worked as close as possible to the yard for the next two days. When he was away, his wife listened for the rig. He guessed a big crime had happened and he was in the middle of it. Nothing like that had ever happened to him before. Now he sat in the catbird seat and kept the binoculars by a window overlooking the county road. With great anticipation, he ate supper next to the window. It was already dusk when the pickup rolled past his driveway towing the gooseneck trailer. He got up and placed a call.

Duarte drove the rig into Taylor's yard and backed the trailer up to the corral gate. Pablo jumped out, opened a trailer door and prodded the heifers. Two animals leaped out, still unsteady on their feet, and shook themselves.

"*Cómo se fue?*" Morales asked how it went.

Duarte shrugged indifferently. "*Bien—más o menos.*"

"Put the hay in the Becker barn—*pronto*!" Taylor ordered with more sharpness than usual. The men gave him a puzzled look, then nodded and drove off.

"Okay, Nacho. Let's get busy," he said as they walked toward the office. "Will Duarte or the others talk if the cops pick 'em up?"

"No. Duarte, he know. The Laredo *tipos* watch his folks. He don' talk. Pablo an' Carlos, *saben nada*," they knew nothing.

"Tell 'em they can collect their pay in the morning. I don't care where they go. Just get 'em out of here. After they go, we'll hire local help."

"An' what you do when the *tipos* come? For you. For me. What you do?"

"Oh, stop your frettin', Nacho. We're small potatoes. Too much risk for them. They'll leave us alone if we don't talk. Now, go tell the boys."

"*Sí, Jefe,*" he mumbled and went to his mobile home. Seated in the darkened room, he thought about his next steps. *Sí, I go to Minneapolis an' no return..* He muttered a string of expletives in Spanish as if talking to Taylor. They were equals before he got the ranch but now... *Estoy nada, mierda, un pinche Tejano, chingado bracero...* nothing but a shit, a fucking Tejano wetback. "*Jefe, tu hijo de la chingada, tu cabrón!*" he said aloud, calling him a mother-fucking sonofabitch. He drank a mescal and thought of pouring a second. Then he went out to give the other men the news.

The search warrants were already prepared and waiting on the sheriff's desk when Lundstrom called Jack. He thanked the farmer and said he would get the full story in time. Meanwhile, he cautioned him to say nothing. Then he called the office and ordered the team to be ready first thing in the morning. He meant not later than 7:00 a.m. Last of all, he called Boston. "Hey brother, after tomorrow I think you can get back to writing that book. Can you be at my house by six-thirty. Come earlier and we can have breakfast."

At last! An end to this. Boston thought as he put down the phone. "There'll be an arrest tomorrow morning," he said to Ginger. "Save some space for a story that I'll phone in later. It looks like the end of the chase."

"Good!" she said without looking up from her cross-stitching. "Maybe you can get back to your book project so I won't have to listen to you fret and moan about it."

"Hey, I'm not that bad!"

"You should hear yourself when you're alone. Mutter, mutter, mutter."

"All right. You win. By the way, you're on your own for breakfast tomorrow. I'll be out the door at six." The prospect of tomorrow's arrest meant more than the freedom to work on the Nielsen book. It meant closure, a conclusion. No tantalizing loose ends to bedevil him. He couldn't fend off the seduction of becoming involved in the story. Though he knew more than anyone, he couldn't claim objectivity. It was now a story told through his own experience. I did a favor for a friend. I can live with that. He couldn't sleep but for anticipating the arrest.

Taylor rose at daybreak, made coffee and lit a cigarette. It was a cool, fresh August morning that carried the sounds of doves in the grove and cows bawling for calves. He heard Morales and the Mexicans in the yard outside the office joking in Spanish. Being laid off didn't bother them. It was normal where they came from. They have a job one day and then lose it the next but enjoy life either way. He marveled that they always seemed happy with whatever the day brought. Sometimes he envied their easy contentment. If only he had that and the money, too.

Morales entered and Taylor gestured toward the pot on the table. "Help yourself. It's strong enough to walk into your cup."

"*Gracias. Los muchachos están listos,*" he said, the guys were ready for their pay.

"Got it right here," he said, patting three fat envelopes. "All in twenties."

"*Buenos días, Jefe,*" Duarte said, touching the brim of his cap as the men stamped into the office. Carlos and Pablo mumbled, "*buenos días.*"

"*Muchachos, lo siento, pero hoy es el fin de tu empleo.*" Morales told them this was the end of their work.

"*Tu paga incluye un plus.*" Taylor handed each man an envelope and said their pay included a bonus.

Touching their caps on the way out the door, they said *gracias* and adios and *hasta luego.* Then they stood together as each counted his money and then counted it again. With arms around each other's shoulders, they laughed as they walked toward their shared pickup truck. Duarte looked back at the office and touched his cap one more time.

"Well, that's that," Taylor said, finishing his cigarette. "We'll take on a local crew in a week or two. Until then, we'll have to do the work of those three."

"*Jefe*, what we do about… they come for us I think."

"I'll take care of it," he snapped. "This ain't the first contract I've gotten out of. C'mon. It's almost seven. Let's doctor the cut on that bull while it's still cool. Then I'll fix us breakfast and we'll figger out what's next like, like we use to do."

Jefe no comprende, Morales thought and shook his head as he hitched the tractor to the cattle chute. He didn't understand or respect *los tipos* in the cartel. They weren't like shady oil patch operators. *Los tipos* expected total loyalty. No excuses. When the cattle rig doesn't arrive next month, he knew in his gut someone would come for him. He also knew *Jefe* wouldn't run and leave his ranch. That might let him get away safe and free.

He hitched the cattle chute to the tractor determined to leave before *Jefe* turned him in to save himself. He would take the drugs to Minneapolis tonight. Then he would keep the money and head west. Not to Texas, Arizona or California but Colorado had lots of *mexicanos*. He would change his name. If the cartel killed *Jefe*, they might forget him. Seated on the tractor, he fleshed out his plan as he drove the chute to the corral at Becker's barn. *I go tonight. No abrazo. No adios. No vaya con Dios. Yo voy.*

Taylor followed him in his pickup worried the Tejano wasn't going to stick around. *I can tell he's movin' on. He's gonna run. Leave me holdin' the bag. He don' see the whole picture. That's the trouble with those people—they can't see beyond today. Don't know how to build up somethin'. If he runs… an' he will… the Minneapolis folks will come for me. Maybe… He's got the contracts on both ends. I just let him use my truck so… so I can say I don't know how the system works. Might save my neck if the sheriff don't get it.*

Morales backed the chute up to the corral gate, unhitched it without a word and parked the tractor next to the pickup thirty yards away. The injured bull paced about the small corral bothered by the puss and flies visible on its gashed flank. It lowed and tossed its horns as the men waved it toward the chute. Then it saw the opening and rushed into it. The foreman dropped the bar over the bull's neck and locked its head in place. Then he pulled the lever that squeezed the chute's railings against the animal's sides. The bull bellowed and thrashed, rocking the chute.

"*Él loco,* I think," Morales said. "*Qué un diablo.*"

"Yeah," the cattleman agreed as he uncapped the antibiotic. "A crazy devil with good blood lines. Sire some prize calves."

"When you hire hombres?" Morales asked. *La vida de vaquero no es para mí.*" The cowboy life wasn't for him.

"It's a good, clean life, Nacho. Ya oughta give it a try."

"Sí, sí, but... las drogas gimme más dinero an' no mierde de vaca."

Chapter 43

Jack, Boston and a deputy started for the ranch followed by another vehicle with four deputies. On their way, Jack talked through the process of executing the search and bringing the men in for questioning. He doubted that either man would be armed. As much as he wanted a voluntary compliance he had little hope it would happen. Taylor had proved to be a fighter.

"Let me get this straight," the deputy said from the back seat. "There's Taylor and Morales and three Mexican workers. That right?"

"That's right," Jack said. "I hope we can catch them while they are still in the yard. Taylor and Morales are the principle subjects. We want the other three but not at the risk of losing the principles."

"I got it," the deputy said.

The two sheriff's vehicles stopped in Taylor's yard but it was empty except for the white pickup. Jack's knock at the office door went unanswered. He tried the latch, found the door was unlocked and went inside. From the window, he saw the tractor approaching the barn on the Becker farm. He focused the naval binoculars on them and then went outside.

"Okay. They're doing something with cattle in a corral down below. It appears there's no one else around. Their only escape route is through this yard," he said and ordered two deputies to stay behind and begin executing the search warrant. The rest were to follow him into the valley.

"*Oye*, they come," Morales said and pointed to the pair of Suburbans rolling toward them across the empty pasture. His guts clenched in anticipation of a confrontation and an arrest. He watched. The bull thrashed in the chute. *Muy mal*, Morales said to himself as both vehicles stopped behind the corral. The sheriff, Boston and a deputy got out of one Suburban and approached them. Two deputies got out of the other vehicle and stood by the corral with Boston.

"Goddamn-it," Taylor cursed. "What did I tell you." The bull bawled and rocked the chute as the cattleman worked the antibiotic into the infection. Then the bull stood still, breathing heavily, its muscles tensed and waiting. "What do you want now?" he snarled at Jack.

Jack held out a document in a blue wrapper. "Justin Taylor, I have a warrant to search your office, house, barns and vehicles." He extended the warrant but Taylor wouldn't take it. "In addition, I want you and Nacho Morales to come in for questioning about the deaths of Norman and Velva Becker."

"The hell I will. I'm not going with you—"

"—You can go voluntarily or in cuffs. Your choice. Which will it be?"

As Jack moved to detain Taylor, Morales tripped the cattle chute's levers. The antsy bull shot out of the front, ran a few steps and faced the men. The beast lowered its head, rumbled a challenge and pawed up clumps of sod. It lunged forward and the officers scrambled for safety. In the chaos, Taylor bolted for his pickup with Morales right behind him. The bull pivoted. Then, like a bullet, it charged after the runner and quickly closed on them. Morales slipped on a cow paddy and fell beneath the bull as it reached Taylor. The cattleman was grasping at the pickup door when a horn impaled him. His unearthly scream shook Jack to his core. The bull shook its massive head and tossed his owner against the truck. Then it backed up and lowered its head for another lunge.

Jack pulled his revolver and fired, then fired again and again. The .357 slugs hit the vitals and the bull shuddered. Blood dripped from its mouth. Then the beast collapsed slowly onto its knees. A moment later, it rolled onto its side. Dead.

The deputies were frozen where they stood. Taylor wasn't moving and neither was Morales. Jack holstered the revolver with an expression of regret over killing the bull. Two deputies tended to Morales who lay on his stomach. He screamed when they rolled him onto his back. Sweat broke out on his ashen face. Then he fainted.

"He's busted up inside," a deputy said. "Get something for a stretcher."

Jack squatted next to Taylor and found a weak pulse in his neck. There was blood on his lips and his lungs rattled with fluid. "He's alive. Maybe not for long. Call an ambulance," he ordered. They rolled him onto his side and exposed the ragged hole in his back. The grass beneath him was already slick with blood. A deputy packed the hole with the gauze from the first aid kit. Then they laid both casualties in the pickup and drove to the farmyard just as the Waterford EMTs pulled in.

"It'll be a miracle if Taylor pulls through," Jack said. "If he doesn't, I hope the other one can tell us something. Take them to the county hospital," he ordered. Then he sent the deputies to finish searching Taylor's office.

"Taylor had hired hands," Jack said. "Search the barn and mobile homes. If they're not there, call the highway patrol. I recall one of them had a blue pickup with Texas plates. I don't have the numbers. It's a good bet they're on Interstate 35. They're already near the Iowa line. *Move!*"

He picked up Taylor's phone. Madeline answered his call and passed it to Rita. "This is Sheriff Meade. Your *uh…* Justin is on his way to the hospital. A bull gored him. He's unconscious. We're not sure he'll make it."

She gasped and then fell silent. "What can I say? You say a bull got him but… I don't know," and her voice trembled. "I can't say I'm sorry except—"

"—How many men worked for him besides Morales?"

"Three Mexicans. They came together in a pickup from the Rio Grande."

"Do you recall the license number?"

"Yeah, partly. It's a seventy-eight or nine Ford one-fifty with an extended cab. Dark blue with one white front fender. The last plate numbers are five-nine-three."

"Thank you. I want to visit you later today. Do you want your lawyer present?"

"Am I a suspect?"

"No, you aren't."

"Then he isn't necessary. I want to help any way I can."

"Thank you. I'll call ahead of time. See you later." Then he called the highway patrol, relayed the pickup's description and asked them to contact their counterparts in Iowa. He stood outside with Boston for a moment, kicked at the gravel in the yard and exhaled several times.

"Not your fault," Boston said. "They brought it on themselves. You know that."

"Yeah... I know that. Just the same, it's a shitty start to the day. I was hoping for something better. Well, drive me back to the pasture. Let's get the Suburban."

Jack walked up to the bull and Boston thought he looked at it with an expression of remorse. The muscled behemoth lay on its side, a huge inanimate mound of flesh and bone that blow flies had already found. He shook his head and let out a loud sigh. "Twenty years a lawman and I never shot anything in the line of duty until today."

"You're lucky," Boston said. "I can tell you it's better than killing a man."

Chapter 44

Four deputies were going through the office drawers and cabinets when Jack returned. His oldest and most opinionated senior deputy was in charge and he wouldn't miss a trick. They found several sets of account books, address books and other papers. The deputy wondered if Rita could help them make sense of the records.

"Let me talk to her first," Jack said. "She's laid up with a broken leg. Meanwhile, box the records and then search this operation. Pick up any documents in the mobile homes, too. We'll want the Kay-nine unit here."

"What now?" Boston asked as they got into the Suburban.

"What now?" Jack repeated. "I suppose this counts as news. Can you hold the details for a while? I need to bring in the drug enforcement folks. We need to confirm that he and Morales have associates in Minneapolis, Texas and Mexico. They might send someone here to finish them off before they can talk."

"I'll mention it to Ginger."

"All right,' Jack conceded. "Mention it to her. I don't know if Rita is the co-owner of the ranch but either way, it's likely to go into receivership. If he's guilty, the property will be forfeited. Will you call Morrie and fill him in? Oh, and call Hartwell, too. On second thought, don't call him."

"Thank God this is the end for me," Boston said. "When I started in June I thought finding the Beckers would take a few days. I did it as a favor to Morrie. Now it's cost me the whole damned summer. So far, I haven't written even an outline of the Nielsen book."

"Well, now you can write a second book about this caper."

"Oh, fuck you! Just what I need. Where's that bottle of Jameson you promised?"

"All in good time, brother, all in good time."

Boston walked into Isaacs's office and declined a proffered cup of coffee, though it was fresh. "I could use a drink."

"Well, Bob's fifth is still in my desk."

"Thanks, Morrie. I was speaking metaphorically. I rarely drink out of respect for Ginger's sobriety. I stopped by to fill you in. We went to serve search warrants this morning. Before we could do it, a bull gored Taylor and flattened Morales. We think Morales will pull through but we're not sure about Taylor. Jack thinks the cartel might send someone to take them out.

"Have you talked to Bob?"

"No. Jack prefers that we keep him out of the loop for right now. Might save his life."

"I'm grateful to you," he said. "I know this isn't what you signed up for. And I know that it has cost you the summer. I'm sorry about that. But as an old prosecutor, I think you're a damned fine detective. I've never worked with a better one."

Jack returned to his office later and briefed Mary and several investigators. He said there was a boatload of records coming in. If the Minneapolis and Laredo folks heard about Taylor and Morales they might split. He wanted a quick but thorough search of the records so they could bring the DEA up to speed. After that, the narcs might make arrests in Minneapolis and Laredo. Then he called Rita and said he would be there shortly.

"How are you doing?" He asked as he and Mary entered Madeline's living room.

"Please sign my cast—both of you." Rita handed him a Sharpie marker. "I'm getting well fast. Maddie's giving me the world's best care ever," she added, beaming at her. "Is it okay if she sits in?"

"I'm afraid not," he said. "No reflection ons. But it's procedure."

"That's okay, sheriff. Rita will tell me later if she wants to. As it is, I need to shop for supper," she said and she gathered her purse. "I'll be back soon, Rita. You'll be fine."

"She worries about me."

"And for good reason," he said. "We're certain Morales and another man attacked you but can't prove it without a confession."

"I'm sure it was him and Duarte. Nacho tends to take things into his own hands if he thinks it helps Justin, even if Justin didn't ask for it," she said. "That's the way they work. But I think Nacho did this on his own to get back at Justin. It's only a guess."

"Morrie told me you two are armed."

"Yep. We're not taking chances."

"Can you tell us how the farm was managed or operated?" Jack kept his voice soft, as if they were sitting in church. "Are you a joint owner?"

Rita scratched her bare leg. "No, I'm not. And I don't know a lot about running the farm. Not the technical stuff anyway," she said. "But I know accounting. And I know that he never sold enough cattle to account for all the income in his books."

"Why is that?" Mary asked, speaking for the first time.

"Justin was building a herd. He sold young bulls and steers he didn't need but kept the cows and calves. The sale income," she said, making air quotes with her fingers. "The sale income showed up in the books after each trip to Texas."

"Who went on these trips to Texas?"

"Nacho went once in a while with Duarte. Otherwise, it was Duarte and Pablo. Each trip took three or four days. It's a twenty-seven-hour drive to Laredo. Because of the animals, they couldn't stop overnight. They spent at least a day in Laredo and returned with animals Justin bought or if not, they returned with the ones they took down. They always returned with bales."

He nodded. "They ran drugs for the Mexican cartel and hid packets in the bales."

"That fits," she said as if this weren't a revelation. "After every trip, Nacho went to Minneapolis for a day or two. After that, Justin's books showed sale income. That set up made me uneasy."

253

"We're working with the Feds," Jack said. "They say the cartel takes a dim view of quitters. I don't want to frighten you but they may hit your husband and Morales. And they could come after you, too. You are entitled to protection if you ask for it."

"We're armed and we both know how to shoot."

"So I heard. I could arrange—"

"—Thank you, but no. We've talked to the local cops. They have their eye on us, too."

"All right," Jack nodded, impressed by her spunk. "Justin and Nacho will be in the hospital for a while. You'll be a material witness. I don't want you to leave the county without permission. Clear?"

"I'm not going anywhere, I promise," she said, tapping her cast. "Besides, I wouldn't miss the trial for anything."

The Iowa highway patrol stopped a pickup with Texas plates that matched the numbers Rita recalled. There were two men in the pickup and both were held at the police station in Ames. Jack called the border patrol and asked for an officer to work with him. Mary and the bilingual border patrol officer interviewed the men one at a time in the courthouse. Neither seemed to have an overall view of the farm operation. They said Duarte recruited them because they had experience handling cattle. Each said he did as he was told. In the end, it was a tedious exercise in vague non-answers.

"Where is Duarte?" Mary asked through the interpreter. First Pablo and then Carlos shrugged and said, "*No sé.*" Neither man knew. Each said Duarte left them at the Interstate rest stop just before they crossed into Iowa. He told them a friend was meeting him there.

Mary scribbled a note. "Bad news." Of the three, she realized Duarte knew what was going on. If so, he might still be in Minnesota. Meanwhile, the border patrol agent asked Pablo who killed Mr. and Mrs. Becker. After some shifty answers, the agent said it would be better if Pablo told him what he knew, otherwise he might be charged as the killer.

Pablo's eyes widened, and he looked around the small room; then he looked down and shook his head. He said he had never met the

Beckers or been in their house. Not until the night they loaded the Becker's furniture. Duarte told them they were helping the Beckers move to a new home. He didn't know they were dead until later and he didn't know who killed them.

Carlos answered the questions much as Pablo had. He remembered that Duarte, Morales and Taylor went to the Becker's house. Later that night, Morales drove a large van to the farmhouse. Then he, Pablo and Duarte spent the night loading the furniture. The next morning, Morales drove the Beckers' car somewhere and Duarte and Carlos drove the van.

"Hold them as material witnesses," Jack said. "What do you make of it, Mary?"

"They're not American citizens. Immigration says holding them is still up to you. Duarte isn't a citizen, either."

"The cartel doesn't like snitches," he said. "We could lose them if we don't take them into protective custody. Mary, find a translator to help you question them. Let's see if these guys know any of Duarte's other contacts."

"When can we question Taylor and Morales?"

"I don't know," he said. "Check with the hospital. I doubt either man is in any condition to talk. Either way, find out what the doc thinks."

The hospital told Mary that neither man was conscious enough to talk. The cattleman was unconscious and hooked to a ventilator. He had punctured organs and numerous broken bones. It was a miracle he was still alive. His prospects remained unknown. Morales was sedated to keep him quiet. He had a broken back but the prospects for recovery were good.

The detectives dug into the farm records. "Rita had good reason to be afraid." Mary said. "Morales had a strong motive to attack her. Taylor's involvement in drugs was limited to letting Morales use his rig and farm as the transit hub in return for a cut. He abetted but didn't initiate."

As a precaution, Jack assigned a squad of deputies to round-the-clock vigilance at the hospital and monitor who entered and left. Two days later, the hospital said Morales was stable enough to answer questions. The second floor intensive care section was quiet except for the intercom messages. A doctor walked them to Taylor's room where the cattleman lay on his back. A ventilator over his face and an I-V hooked to his arm dripped a solution. The monitor pulsed silent readings every second.

"It's touch and go with him," the doctor said in a low voice as he fussed with something in his coat pocket. "Half his ribs and sternum are broken. The horn punctured the kidney and a lung. There's a huge risk of infection. Survival is iffy. He won't be conscious for at least several days more. Mister Morales has a broken back and ribs. He's in traction but he will pull through."

The foreman lay on his back, his eyes half-closed, and watched them enter. "What you want?" It was a hoarse whisper too weak to be a challenge.

"Well, how are you doing?" Jack asked as if he cared. "Doc says you'll pull through."

"*Sí*. Then you put me in jail I think." He clenched his teeth as he talked.

"We've got a few questions if you're in the mood to talk."

"No talk. I don' have no *abogado*, no lawyer."

"You can have a public defender if you can't afford a lawyer. Pablo and Carlos have one and they told us what they know about how the Beckers died. We want to hear your version."

"Pablo and Carlos? An' Duarte?"

"No. He wasn't with them when the police caught them."

"*Uh, oh*, okay," he said, exhaling slowly. "I wanna defender. An' a *padre, un católico padre*. Then we talk again I think."

He promised to send the priest and a lawyer in the morning. Then he and Mary walked down the stairs to the main floor.

"Did you notice Morales's expression when he heard we didn't have Duarte?"

"No, what about it?"

"Raw fear," she said. "I heard it in his voice. Now he wants a priest. I think he's terrified—afraid Duarte will come for him."

"We've got the deputy so he should be safe for now."

Chapter 45

Morales woke in the morning still foggy from the painkillers but felt better despite the night nurse's interruptions. Immobile, he dreaded the boredom of a long recovery. Nothing but endless hours of television, nothing but time to think… to worry about Duarte… about *los tipos* in the cartel… about what life might be like if it lasted at all. He knew from the start that Duarte's job was seeing that Taylor and Morales lived up to their contract. And if not… if Duarte failed, his parents would die. It's me or them, he thought. Where is he? When will he come for me? He wiped tears from his eyes. *Qué un tonto soy*, what a fool I am, he told himself. *Soy nada ahora. Un pobre tullido. No tengo un futuro sino la muerte.* Nothing but a poor cripple with no future but death.

He thought of the years he and Taylor were *compadres*. When *Jefe* wanted something, he got it because he had brains and Morales did what was necessary. They could have had *la vida rica*, the rich life. *Pero Jefe lo derrochó en vacas y pasto.* But *Jefe* pissed it away on grass and cattle. Now I face the cartel alone. He use me to get what he want. *Chíngate, Jefe. Fuck you. I owe you nada.*

He guessed the sheriff already had the evidence he attacked Rita and moved drugs. Even if he beat those charges, the cartel would come for him. They said so in the beginning. If he avoided prison, he would spend his life looking over his shoulder. At fifty, he felt too old to live on the run.

Jefe gonna die but I live. I say what they want an' they put me in a good prison. Cartel forget me, I think. Jefe, he blame me. But I talk first. Put the culpa on Jefe. Then Morales thought of his mother. He knew Mamí didn't know about his drug business. If he died suddenly, it wouldn't shame her. But if he went to prison, it would. Either way, he knew he could do little. If I die, I want to die honesto—for her honor.

As a boy, he thought she deserved better man than *el viejo*, his father. But she was strong and stood up to his abuse. Then she outlived him and believed it was because of her Catholic faith. He remembered how she prayed daily in the kitchen before a little statue of the Virgin. She said weekly confession made her feel strong again. He decided to confess everything—in case God was real. If he wasn't, then it wouldn't hurt. Either way, he lost nothing. A nurse interrupted his thoughts to admit a bearded man wearing a Roman collar.

"Good morning, Señor Morales. I'm Father Carson," the priest said. "One of the sheriff's chaplains. I understand you asked for me."

"*Sí, padre*. I wanna confess. *Mamí* raise me *católico*… she was regular but…" he raised his eyebrows as if shrugging.

"I understand," Carson said and closed the door partway. He pulled a chair close to him, kissed the cross embroidered on his stole and put it around his neck. "We can start when you're ready."

Morales traced a vague sign of the cross and muttered, "… *en el nombre del padre, el hijo y el espíritu santo… uh…*" He paused and said he didn't remember the words. He thought his last confession was thirty years ago.

"That's all right," Carson assured him. "I'll guide you through it."

His words of contrition stuck in his throat at first. Then he found his voice and the words came more easily. He started with the present and worked backward. First, he confessed to beating Rita, then burning a barn, poisoning cattle, stealing oil and oilfield equipment. He talked faster, unable to stop a long recitation of crimes and petty offenses. He killed a man in Oklahoma and hid his body. Then he helped Taylor kill the Beckers. He confessed to abusing women and men whose names he couldn't remember. He couldn't recall all the lies he had told but said they were many. Each admission made him feel lighter in a way he hadn't felt before. Maybe God is real, he thought.

He did those things because he believed in the man he worked for, because he could make them both rich. Morales said he moved drugs for the cartel in the cattle trailer. And used the sanatorium to hide it from discovery. In return, they divided the money. Ninety minutes passed before he finished and Carson pronounced absolution. Morales lay back exhausted. *Conscience—that is the influence of mamacita. God knows it wasn't el viejo.*

The priest blessed him and left grateful the man had the spirit to make such a confession. A few minutes after Carson left, a balding older man entered the room.

"Good afternoon Mister Morales. I'm your public defender." He took the chair where Carson had sat and laid a scuffed leather briefcase across his knees. "I used to prosecute criminals so I know the tricks and will give your case the strongest defense possible. But that depends on what you tell me."

"*Sí. Qué acusación, qué cargo?*" he paused and then asked, "What charges?"

"The county attorney is still determining that. I believe the charges involve drug trafficking, fraud, and first and second degree murder." He had a wheezy voice and often cleared his phlegmy throat. "Those are state charges. The Feds haven't charged yet."

Morales took a breath and winced in pain. "You see *padre* who leave here?"

"Father Carson… oh, sure. Why?"

"I want a deal for tell you what I tell him?"

"That depends on whether it checks out," he said. "A sin and a crime aren't the same."

"I tell you all what I tell him. I want protection."

"Your first decision is what you intend to plead—guilty or not guilty."

"You represent Taylor, too?"

"No. He is unconscious. I can only represent you."

"I don' live long, I think. You write my confession an' I sign."

The lawyer wrote while Morales talked. Now and then, he interrupted him to ferret out details or clarify a point. Having confessed once already, he spoke without hesitation this time but took an hour. When Morales finished, the lawyer called in a nurse to witness his signature.

"That is what I tell *padre*. Show him and ask if it is true."

"I'm not sure he's allowed to do that," the lawyer said, "… but I'll ask him." He put the confession in his briefcase. "But since you confessed twice and showed remorse, I'll ask for a plea to second degree murder and assault in return for dropping the other charges. It won't get you off the hook for federal drug charges."

"*Lo quiero,* I want it," he said, lying back. "*Mil gracias,*" he added as the man left. Morales let out his breath. *Me siento mejor ahora, tan bueno quitar de esa mierda.* It felt good to get rid of that shit. *What now?* He felt certain Duarte would be his next visitor. The lawyer couldn't do anything about that. But if he was lucky, the confession might get him into a secure prison if not into heaven. And then the cartel would forget him.

An aide entered and checked his vitals. In most circumstances, she wouldn't attract his attention but today he looked at her with appreciation. She was curvy, brown-skinned and spoke accented English that reminded him of someone from long ago.

"*¿Muchacha, hablas español?*" Did she speak Spanish.

"*¡Claro que sí!*" Of course, she replied, her face glowing with a brilliant smile. Hearing it spoken pleased her and she asked how he felt. Was there something she could do for him.

Hearing a woman speak his native tongue reminded him of his mother's home by the Rio Bravo. "*Me daría placer si te quedó y hablar conmigo.*" It would give him pleasure if she stayed and talked with him.

She lingered as long as she could and they talked of small things. After she left, he thought of Taylor, unconscious and near death. *Jefe* was lucky, *afortunado*. But even though he didn't kill the Beckers, he confessed to aiding their murder. Why did I admit that, he wondered. If *Jefe* dies, the *culpa es mio*. My conscience is clean. *Estoy honesto.*

The aide returned later pushing a cart with his supper. Ignoring the soft entrée, he imagined spending a chaste evening with her. He spoke only Spanish to prolong her stay and her innocent friendliness helped him feel like a decent man again—the man his mother wanted him to be. When the aide returned later to remove his tray, they talked for a few minutes more. He saw light in her eyes and held her gaze for several moments, as if absorbing that light was all that was keeping him alive. Then she left and Morales lay back. He drifted into sleep thinking of her as the janitor quietly wheeled in a mop and pail and began swabbing the floor around the bed.

Chapter 46

The bedside phone rang in the middle of the night. "Yes," Jack whispered, trying not to wake Kris. "*What*! I'll be right there." He jumped into the barest semblance of his uniform and rushed out the door. The deputy on the hospital night shift met him in the lobby. "It's my fault," he said. "I screwed up." Jack rushed upstairs to Taylor's room where a doctor awaited him. The cattleman lay in bed with the ventilator over his face.

"He was breathing an hour ago," the doctor said. "A nurse checked every hour. Someone shut off the ventilator. We don't know how it happened. No one has touched anything."

"Was he able to shut it off himself?" Jack went to the ventilator.

"No, he was too immobile. Even so, he couldn't reach the switch."

"Could staff shut if off accidentally?"

"No. Not unless they wanted to kill him."

"I want to question Morales, *now*!"

"Now?" the doctor asked, incredulous. "But he's—"

"—I said now and meant right now!" he snapped in anger. "He may know something," he said, wrestling his temper under control.

Morales lay asleep on his back. A nurse shook his arm but he didn't wake. She felt his wrist for his pulse. "He's dead!" she said in surprise. "He was fine two hours ago."

"Lock down the hospital!" Jack ordered. "*Now*! Call everyone but your critical care staff into the conference room. Get a head count on this shift. I want to know who's missing or who's extra. *Move*!"

The intercom relayed the order and the halls filled with the muffled sound of soft-soled shoes moving quickly but not running. Nurses, aides and doctors stood about murmuring in the conference room. Then Jack and the administrator entered. One by one, the administrator called on the station leads for a head count. All the patients and staff were accounted for. No one had entered all evening except patients who came in ambulances. They were accounted for. The deputy at the entrance confirmed that.

"Is everyone accounted for?" Jack tamped down a sense of desperation.

"All but the janitor," the administrator said.

"Find him!"

The administrator returned twenty minutes later. "We found him," he whispered so only Jack could hear. "He's in the basement. Dead. Someone cut his throat and took his scrubs."

"Did anyone see a janitor on second floor?" Jack asked in a loud voice.

"I did," a nurse volunteered. "I think it was Manuel... it looked like him."

"Describe him,"

"He's about thirty. Short, a brown face. He mops floors at night."

"Manuel is dead," Jack said, now all but certain it was Duarte's work. He was quietly furious with himself because the cartel had outflanked him and killed both suspects in their sleep.

"I'm sorry. It's my fault," the deputy said. "I didn't see him come in."

"Not your fault," Jack corrected. "I think the janitor let him by another door. I want you to stay here. There may be gawkers later. We'll move the bodies to the morgue while it's still dark."

The eastern sky was glowing when Jack left the hospital at 5:30 a.m. He felt drained, discouraged and a failure because... because what? *For Chrissakes, give yourself the same break you gave the deputy.* He longed to talk to Boston but he wouldn't be awake for at least an hour. Even then, he would be grouchy. He went to his courthouse office, curled up on the rug behind his desk and slept until 7:00. Then he called Boston who answered in a grumpy voice.

"Taylor and Morales died in the hospital last night," he said. "Murdered. I think it's the cartel. I know I should call Ginger but you're closer to the story. Just report these facts. Taylor died in the hospital after being gored by a bull. That much is true. And Morales died of internal injuries. Don't mention murder," he pleaded. "It'll tip off the killer."

He hung up and wished he could go home and crawl into bed. Instead, he got a cup of office coffee and sat hunched at his desk while he considered his next move.

"I just heard our suspects are dead," Mary said as she entered his office. Where does that leave us?"

"That's what I want to ask you." He rubbed his eyes and yawned. "Duarte is still missing. As we suspected, he must be connected to the cartel. He's the enforcer."

"The border patrol might have a record on him. It seems likely Duarte's job was keeping both of 'em in line. Otherwise, he would have left with the others. I bet the cartel has something over him."

"Mary, you're a genius, especially this early in the morning," he said and saluted. "So, we'll need to call on the Feds to find Duarte."

Chapter 47

A brief story in the *Statesman* reported the deaths of Taylor and Morales as farm accidents. Their bodies were cremated and sent to their respective next of kin in Texas. The *Statesman* waited a day before reporting the janitor's death. Meanwhile, the FBI, border patrol and various Twin Cities police departments searched for Duarte. A week passed before the border patrol agents arrested him in a Saint Paul safehouse and brought him to Featherstone for questioning and eventual trial.

Two weeks later, Jack went to Isaacs' office to debrief him, Boston and Hartwell on the case. The attorney was still enamored with his Mr. Coffee and made a fresh pot.

"We have as much information as we are likely to get," Jack said. "We grilled Duarte and he confirmed the basic facts in Morales's confession. It's the best we can do."

"Morales killed them, didn't he?" Hartwell refused a proffered cup of fresh coffee.

"No, he didn't. Taylor poisoned them. We found his fingerprints on the whiskey bottle."

"Poison? What kind?" The doctor wrinkled his brow.

"Water hemlock."

"But why?" Hartwell asked. "Why kill the Beckers?"

Jack stretched his arms. "According to the confessions by Duarte and Morales, Taylor and Becker had several arguments when he tried to buy his farm. Sometime later, Becker found hay bales at the sanatorium

267

and confronted Taylor. Morales said they were afraid Becker would talk. So, Taylor took Morales and Duarte with him to Becker's house. Taylor had a pint of whiskey laced with hemlock. He demanded that Becker sell him the farm. When he refused, he poured him a drink. He refused it because he didn't drink. Then Duarte put a gun to the woman's head. They drank whiskey to save themselves, not knowing it was poisoned. Duarte said they writhed on the floor, foaming at the mouth. He called it... ah... *espantoso*... a Spanish word for gruesome. Taylor hid their bodies in the milk cooler for two days while they boxed up their effects and loaded the van in one night. Taylor forged the signatures and Morales took the documents to Minneapolis to be notarized."

"Ugly, ugly!" Isaacs said, his face pinched.

"Duarte and Morales told pretty much the same story," Jack added. "Taylor was the brains and Morales was the brawn in the oil patch. Rita described their relationship as symbiotic in that Taylor never asked Morales to do anything, but Morales did what he thought his boss expected. When Larson refused to sell, Morales and Duarte torched his barn. They sabotaged Purdy's combine and they poisoned the cattle that belonged to Wilkes and Otto. He and Duarte attacked Rita and Boston and slashed Ginger's tires."

Boston poured himself a refill. "Who hired the U-Haul van?"

"Taylor," Jack said. "Morales and Duarte drove the Beckers to the refuge. Taylor followed with a winch. They used it to pull the car to the riverbank. Carlos drove the van and hid it in a shed at a vacant railroad siding. Duarte and Pablo went to Texas the next day while, Morales and Carlos drove the van to Des Moines and left the furnishings at a charity. Then they drove to Kansas City, mailed some postcards and left the U-Haul at a chop shop. Then they rode back to Minnesota with Duarte and Pablo."

Hartwell sat on the edge of his chair, mesmerized. "And the drugs?"

"Taylor had enough money from stealing oil to start a ranch and buy several farms." Jack yawned and stretched. "After that, he needed an interim cash flow. Morales had contacts with the Guadalajara cartel. In his confession, Morales said they fell out over the drugs. Taylor wanted out after he lost the claim to the spring. Morales understood the repercussions of quitting. Taylor didn't. Duarte's job was keeping an eye on both men. When Taylor laid them off, Duarte called someone in Minneapolis who met him near the Iowa line. He killed them in order to save the lives of his parents."

Isaacs removed his glasses. "How did Duarte get into the hospital?"

"There aren't many Mexicans here and they all know each other," Jack said. "Most work at the canning plant or in construction or clean houses. The janitor knew Duarte and let him in. He killed the janitor and took his clothes. Dressed as a janitor, he turned off Taylor's ventilator. Then he suffocated Morales."

"So, that's how it ends," Isaacs said. "*Sic transit gloria mundi*."

Hartwell smiled but with a frown. "Good work but… from what I've seen in California, we can expect more drugs despite this victory."

"Let's enjoy this one," Isaacs said.

Hartwell pointed to Isaacs' desk. "Sheriff, Morrie is holding a fifth of whiskey in escrow for an occasion like this. I hope you can join us for a celebratory shot. What do you say?"

Jack pushed back his shirt cuff and glanced at his watch "Let's see, it's five past noon. I'm entitled to an hour off for lunch. Hell yes, I'll join you."

Isaacs pulled the bottle from his desk drawer and poured a little into the hastily emptied coffee cups. "Gentlemen, a toast to lady justice."

"Hear, hear!" Boston added, and they raised their cups.

Harwell frowned. "You know, as much as I loathed Taylor, I have a sense of loss at his death." He sighed with sadness. "What a tragic waste of talent. I honestly think he wanted to do right by people's health and the environment but—"

"—But he was possessed by his dream," Isaacs said.

"Yes." Hartwell set his empty cup down for emphasis. "It was an adverse possession."

The full story didn't emerge until September, after the DEA moved against the Minneapolis and Laredo ends of the drug operation. It appeared as a series of stories. LOCAL RANCHER HAD CARTEL CONNECTIONS sketched in Taylor's career as a rogue oilman who ran his Minnesota ranch with cash from transporting drugs until Hartwell's assertion of title undermined the scheme. NORMAN AND VELVA BECKER MURDERED was the second story and described Taylor's elaborate attempt to hide their deaths. The last paragraph described the Becker's memorial service that Hartwell and Fredericks arranged. Several days later, the *Statesman* published WATERFORD RANCH BUILT ON FRAUD. It detailed how Taylor built his ranch using fraud, sabotage and intimidation to get the land he wanted. Ginger read the final paragraph aloud over breakfast:

"The Taylor Land and Cattle Company is in receivership. It will be dissolved and the property offered for sale. Because of the fraud involved in the farm's creation, the court has ordered the proceeds from the farm's eventual sale returned to the victims as restitution in proportion to their losses."

"You have a real talent for irony," she said as she folded the paper.

"Thanks. Yeah, if it weren't for the irony, I might hate this work."

"This could be the basis of a crime thriller," she said, tapping the headline with an index finger. "Ever think of that as a new career? It would entertain you."

"No. This is news. I don't need to write fiction to be entertained. I have *you* for that."

She stuck out her tongue. "Yeah well, now you can get back to the Nielsen book. And once that's done, you can write this one!"

"Yeah, if Morrie doesn't call again. He likes doing this."

"So do you."

Chapter 48

Hartwell leaned against the fender of his new Ford Bronco and waited at Runyon Spring Road. A thin sheet of September ground fog covered the Runyon Valley. Two men from the township road crew arrived in a utility truck. They greeted him, selected tools from the lockers and began dismantling the gate. Fifteen minutes later, they hoisted it into the back of the truck. One of the men waved him through the opening and doffed his cap as he passed. The doctor returned a soldier's salute.

"At last!" he cried as months of pent-up emotions burst from him. He drove slowly to prolong the joy. At the road's end, he opened the gate to his property and paused to look back. The road crew had already driven away. Hearing the water gush from the spring, he approached it with a pilgrim's reverence as if visiting a shrine. In his head, he heard Horatio's voice intone, "sacred ground."

He knelt at the spring, cupped water in his hands and drank as if this were a sacrament of communion. Then he cupped water again and sprinkled it over his head like a baptism. He had abandoned religion early in medical school and thought he had forgotten it. But out of memory, he recalled the story of Jesus's baptism and the dove that proclaimed his mission. It made sense now. This spring, this living water, had given him a mission. Yes, it made sense.

After that, he sat by the spring for a long time amid dried bracken and withered flowers. It was enough to be alive. *Wildest year of my life—at least since Korea. I left everything I achieved with Felicia for this. A vision that beats like a pulse.*

He felt he had already paid the emotional cost of the project. Based on preliminary conversations with architects and contractors, the center would cost more than he expected. *Thanks to Morrie, I'm here. And I owe Meade, too. But they can't help me going forward. I need someone like Felicia to help me. I'm not ready for marriage but...* He didn't finish the thought. Instead, he spent the morning walking about the property and cleaning up the patio for the evening's picnic with Maddie.

He had arranged the date as a celebration of the opened road. Her interest had encouraged him and he thought her mystery was what kept them seeking each other. That was the spice of their romance. Tonight, after she saw the spring, he thought he might break through her reserve at last. But it would be complicated as long as Rita stayed with her. But sooner or later...

Madeline accepted his invitation for a picnic at the mineral spring. She had heard so much about it she felt obligated to go since he had been possessed by this vision all summer. *I'm sure he'll be emotional. How could he not be. And he'll expect me to be emotional with him. That's not my style but I can fake some of that.*

Hartwell pulled up to her house in the late afternoon and they set off. First, he drove her all around the roads that had encircled Taylor's ranch. She thought it was his victory lap. Tonight he was happier than she had ever seen him. He was like a boy bursting with joy. "It's beautiful," she said as they drove up the Runyon Spring Road. "The valley looks pastoral in the evening light."

"Yes, it is. Just think how it will affect people on their way to the center. The landscape is inspiring but calming." He parked near the patio where he had already set up a folding table and chairs. The setting offered a long view down the valley.

She provided the wine and he brought sandwiches from Gretta's Garden. They ate slowly, drank the wine and watched the evening fill the low places the way water filled a basin. Crickets chirruped in the evening and the valley seemed lustrous with long strips of golden sunlight and purple shadows.

"Now for the reveal," he said. "Close your eyes." Taking her by the hand, he led her along a raked path to the spring. "Open them."

She gasped. "It is a fairyland! A grotto. Oh… worth the wait to see it. It's special and beautiful but…" She tried to free her hand from his grip but he held on until she gave up trying to free it. Then they walked back to the table just as the waxing moon rose above the low wooded ridge at the valley's far end. The moment seemed suspended in ether. He turned, put his arms around her, and pulled her close to him.

"Don't do that!" she said sharply and turned her face to avoid his kiss.

"I'm sorry, am I rushing things?"

"No. Not exactly," she said, breaking free. "Bob, I enjoy your company. I really do. And I respect you. But don't do that. It will ruin our friendship." She heaved a deep sigh and sat on a folding chair. "It's time I told you." They sat facing each other as the moon rose and bathed them in its silver light.

"But Maddie, it's just… I have feelings for you," he stuttered. "As surprised as you are."

"I'm not surprised. It's that… I'm not right for you, I'm not who you think I am."

"Not right? You're an intelligent, beautiful woman that any sane man would fall in love with. We see so many things alike. We enjoy so much together."

"Yes, and that's part of our problem," she agreed in a tone of resignation. Her face expressed regret.

"I don't understand."

"I know you don't. I really like you. I could love you in a way— but as a friend—not as a lover. You're honest, authentic, courageous but you're a man. I value men who are friends and allies. And I think you could be one. But I can't be your lover, girlfriend or wife."

Hartwell bit his lower lip, confounded. "So… so you're saying you want a platonic relationship. Not a romance or something more intimate?"

"Yes, that's well put. That's exactly it."

"I see... is it something I've said, done, could do to change things. Am I too old?"

"No, no. Nothing like that." She pressed her lips tightly and shook her head. "It's not even about you. It's that I've never been attracted to men." She watched as her words sank in followed by his emotions roiling the surface of his face. And she wondered how he was taking her declaration.

"I had no... no idea..." he said in a long, deflating breath. "I'm sorry, I must have missed something... I didn't see—"

"—You didn't miss anything. I did my best to hide it. That made it easy for you to assume something that isn't... that can't be. I want you as a friend. Believe me, I do. But I can't have you as a lover. And there isn't another man. Can you accept that?"

He sat still, his face flushed with emotional turmoil. All these months of courting and cultivating had seemed inevitable, headed for something permanent, and now... *nothing*! An illusion. Within seconds, he tumbled through feelings of embarrassment, betrayal, shame, stupidity and anger. His chest hurt when he inhaled. He didn't know if he wanted her friendship. *She led me on. Made a fool of me... no... no, she didn't. I did it to myself. I saw what I wanted to see—Felicia.*

He chewed on his lower lip. Then he let out another breath to clear the words stuck in his throat. "I'm very fond of you, Maddie," he said as his voice broke. "Too fond to turn away. You know, after Felicia, I never believed there was another woman for me. Then I met you. You are... it'll take me a while to... to adjust. All through this adventure of the road, I imagined us as a team to bring about the wellness center but—"

"—It's my fault I didn't tell you sooner," she said, her voice soft with apology. "I'm not ashamed of who I am but it's difficult. I couldn't tell you until I knew I could trust you. Even though I trust you, it's difficult." She clasped her hands in her lap. "What I told you isn't the only reason why I left Sonoma."

"I see... go on," he coaxed.

"When I worked for the vintner, I was in my late twenties and still unsure of my... my orientation. I still thought a hetero romance might be possible. You know, a low-key one as a kind of cover. But I wasn't sure and… you know how it was back then. People hated women like me… many still do. I dated a few men but broke it off if they got serious. My boss gave me a big promotion. After that, he started touching me and making it clear I owed him something in return. I told him to leave me alone. When he became more aggressive, I took a self-defense class. Sometime after that, he grabbed me at the office. We argued and he ripped open my blouse in the struggle. I kicked him where it hurts most. He lost control and came after me in a blind rage…" She swallowed hard, her voice trembling… "I reached into my purse… I hope to God I never kill another human being."

Her words hit Hartwell like a rear-end collision. His head snapped, his muscles contracted and then he stared at her with his mouth agape. Madeline… a killer! He shook his head and touched her hand.

"My colleagues heard it from the other room. They called the police. The district attorney called it self-defense but I couldn't stay after that. He was married, a dad, a popular businessman. It wasn't easy… it isn't easy to come out… but I want to be my authentic self. It wasn't safe then. It still isn't safe. Someday, I hope it will be safe. I tell you all this because I feel safe with you. Rita is the only other one who knows."

He released the breath he didn't realize he had been holding. And with it, the hopes he had stored inside. "I had no idea—"

"—Of course not, but people like me are all around you. When you were a kid, weren't there some bachelor farmers living together or maybe a pair of spinster teachers who shared a house? Didn't you think that was odd?"

"It never occurred to me… But now that you mention it, yes. Our dentist was a bachelor. He and another man had a house but, but they acted, *uh*, straight."

"Yes. We have to deny a part of ourselves to be accepted by everyone else."

"I'm embarrassed. And sorry I made you uncomfortable. Of course, I'll keep this in confidence. But how do we relate to each other from now on—or do we?"

"Just as we do now, if you want," she said, with a rueful smile. "We can still go out for dinner, take hikes and see movies. I love doing that because you're great company. Now that you know the limits, we won't have this silent tension between us."

"Yes, but I'll need to deal with my hopes and expectations," he said softly.

"I know. I'm grateful you, especially you, understand what I've gone through—what I still go through."

They fell silent for a moment as the rising moon's light flooded the patio. Then Maddie smiled as if she had a secret. "You are alone now but… when you feel ready for romance, I know of several women who have their eyes on you. None of them are Rita. I also know you and Gretta already have great chemistry. Didn't you say something about collaborating with her on a healthy diet for the center? From what I've overheard, you two are ready to share something more than vegetarian recipes. So, think about it," she said and poured the rest of the wine.

Chapter 49

Ginger had hoped her mother would see her in a new light after Meghan's visit. That she might say "my girl" if not her name. But nothing changed. Mama lapsed into her usual request for "my nun" and Ginger tried to set it aside. Frustrated, she called Meghan and her sister immediately noticed her low spirits.

"Take Boston on the next visit," Meghan suggested. "Something might change if she sees him with you. She set her sights on you marrying him. You two are practically married as it is."

"I never thought of that, thanks!" She returned home that afternoon and told him about the unhappy visit with Mama.

"I'm sorry," he said. "I wish there was something I could do."

"Yeah well, maybe there is," she said, glancing at him from the corner of her eye. "Meg had an idea."

"You're setting me up," he said, knowing she was about to spring a trap.

"Meg suggested you go with me on the next visit. Mama disowned me because we broke up and ruined her dream of marrying into a family with social status."

He shifted uneasily in the chair, knowing she was sandbagging him into something he couldn't refuse. "All right, out with it!"

She huffed in a deep breath. "If Mama sees us together, Meg thought she might think we're married. That would please her. Maybe. After that, she might forgive me in whatever way her mind works."

"I don't know…" he said slowly, running fingers through his hair. "It feels like we're deceiving her."

"A little, but only a little. Meg said I'm practically married to you anyway. That's how she sees us—as all but officially married. I think Father Frank does, too."

He leaned back in the chair. "Okay," he said, letting out his breath. "You've got me surrounded. Yeah, we're kinda married but we're not. I don't want to do this until we've talked this through. We need to be on the same page. I don't want to lie to her."

"Good. Being honest is being you."

"We'll talk… but not tonight. I need to think about this."

It rained the next day and they relaxed on the veranda and listened to the patter. "I want you to visit Mama with me on Saturday… that is, if you're ready."

"Ready—as in ready for that talk?"

"Yeah, *that* talk. The one you've dodged since college—the one about marriage."

He threw her a sidelong glance and then exhaled as if conceding something. Then he reached for her hand. "Ginger, will you marry me?"

"What! Yes, hell yes!" she screamed. "Finally!"

"Let's keep it simple," he said. "We are both divorced Catholics. I don't want this to deny you communion. I know how important it is to you."

"You *have* thought about it, haven't you?"

"Yeah, I have. We both had civil marriages. Technically, those weren't sacraments. If we never had a marriage in the eyes of the Church, we were never sacramentally married. So, we were never divorced. That might start us off with a clean slate."

"Yeah well, don't try to practice canon law—it's too morally twisted," she laughed. "I love the Church for its teachings but not its double standards. We live together in sin. Everybody knows it. No one bats an eye and Frank doesn't deny me communion."

"I know. The question is who will marry us. Personally, I prefer Frank. If he can't, then Pastor Norgaard or a judge."

"I want it to feel sacred and not just a legal proceeding. Don't you?"

"Sacred, yes, of course."

"How about this," she suggested. "Ask a judge to marry us—to be on the safe side. Let's ask Frank if there's a blessing of some kind afterward. Canon law says we can't be married in the eyes of the church without annulments of our previous marriages. And that's a legal pain in the ass I won't put us through."

"I'll settle for something simpler. But let's be clear. Are we marrying because we want each other or because you think it will change Mama?"

"Goddamn your questions! I'll marry because I love you—period. If it makes Mama happy, great. If not, well..." she shrugged.

"All right, I'll ask Mama's blessing to marry you. That's what she's wanted, isn't it?"

"Got you at last!" she said, grabbing his hand. "It's too late to back out."

Mama's eyes widened when they entered her room on Saturday morning. A smile fluttered on her lips though it wasn't clear why.

"Mama, do you remember Boston?"

Her eyes roamed over his face and her lips moved silently. Then she nodded."

He bent down, kissed her forehead. "Mama, I want your blessing to marry Ginger."

"I want to marry him, do you remember that?" Ginger coaxed.

The old woman cocked her head at Ginger and then at Boston. She gave them an enigmatic smile.

"Thank you, Mama."

"So, now you'll finally take my last name," he laughed as they entered the courthouse to buy the marriage license.

"You gotta be kidding," she snorted. "Ginger Meade sounds like a medieval beverage. Why don't you upgrade your lineage and take mine instead?"

With the papers in hand, they walked up the block to the Heath Building and climbed the stairs to ask a favor of Isaacs. Five minutes later, they left with the lawyer's good wishes and a promise to conduct the ceremony as an officer of the court.

A week later, Jack, Kris, their children, Meghan and Jester stood on the veranda to witnesses the ceremony. Everyone wore their Sunday best and Isaacs dressed in his best dark suit. The lawyer faced Ginger and Boston and cleared his throat but, before he could begin, a dark green Lincoln barreled up the hill and into the yard. The doors flew open and two Marine Corps sergeants got out wearing dress blues.

"Hey Meg, I hope we aren't too late," Cletus yelled.

"Almost late—as usual," she shot back.

"Right on the minute," Sean said, pointing to his watch.

Ginger gasped and then tears burst from her eyes and ran down her cheeks taking mascara with them. "Oh, Mother of God! Meg, what...?" but her older brothers smothered her with hugs as she laughed and cried at the same time.

"We waited a long time for this," Cletus said. "When Meg told us about it, we just had to storm San Juan Hill. Okay padre, we're ready."

"I'm not a padre," Isaacs said, amused. "I'm subbing for the judge. If you're ready..."

"I'm so happy to be yours and have you as mine," Ginger whispered that night as they cuddled in bed. "And I'm especially happy Mama will see all her children tomorrow. It's the best gift I've ever had."

Boston rose early and took his coffee to the veranda. Meghan joined him a moment later. With coffee in hand, they watched the day begin.

"So, how is it being married to a spitfire?" she asked with a wry grin.

"It's wonderful. In a way, it feels like we've been married forever. But making our vows, even civil ones, makes it special. Thanks for being here for us," he said, patting her arm. "I've always wanted a big sister. Now I have one. You're an angel and you can take that to the bank. And thanks for calling in the Marines."

Ginger joined them later for a leisurely breakfast. Scrubbed and made up, she put on the simple white dress she bought for the day. He put on a new suit but Meghan remained in her taupe habit.

The green Lincoln, the sheriff's Suburban, Father Carson's VW and several other cars were already parked at the Franciscan Villas when they arrived. An attendant guided them into St. Clare's chapel where Carson prepared the altar for the regular Saturday Mass.

Jack and his family sat on one side among friends from the *Statesman*. The newlyweds sat on the other side with Meghan and the Marines behind them. Mama entered in a wheelchair pushed by an attendant and trailed by a platoon of nuns and aides. The attendants had washed and curled her hair, made up her face and put her in the bright dress Ginger bought for her. They parked Mama's wheelchair next to Ginger and the old woman's eyes remained fixed on her daughter.

"Today is special for the O'Meara family," Carson began. "We are celebrating a family reunion and blessing the vows already made by Boston and Ginger." After the communion, Carson called Boston and Ginger forward and asked them to recite their commitment to each other. Then he gave them a blessing with a few embellishments. As Ginger returned to her seat, she felt Mama grasp her hand and squeeze hard. Ginger held on and smiled through her tears.

The nuns arranged a small reception and, for a golden hour, Mama was the queen of the ball. Though unable to speak, she took everyone by the hand and kissed it several times. When her energies faded, she waved in triumph as the attendants wheeled her back to her room.

"Mama is happy," Meghan said teary-eyed and hugged Ginger and her brothers and then Boston and Jack. "Now we're all one family."

"That's the happiest I've ever seen Mama in my life!" Ginger said, wiping her eyes. "Now *that* is a miracle. And I would drink to it if I could."

"We'll do it for you," the brothers said. "So will everyone else."

"Yes, please do, all of you," she said. "Get drunk at the house if you like."

"Congratulations Ginger," Carson said with a twinkle in his eye. "How does it feel to be an honest woman?"

"Wonderful, but I'll miss the thrill of living in sin," she giggled.

After that, Boston and Ginger visited Mama every week. Though the women never talked as daughter and mother, Mama seemed present at moments and no longer asked for her nun. Neither Boston nor Ginger had any idea what Mama thought but he thought his mother-in-law was already living in a state of grace.

A month passed and Boston rose early as usual. He sat at his desk and gathered some clippings for a manila envelope marked "Runyon Mineral Spring ~ Adverse Possession." From outside the house came the steady patter of the October rain falling on dead leaves. He sealed the envelope and put that into a folder between several others in the filing case. Then he shut the drawer with a sense of completion. It was nearly 7:00 a.m. and time to make coffee when his phone rang. "Meade here," he said in a soft voice. Then he held his breath as he listened to the brief message. "Thank you for calling," he said softly and hung up the phone. Then he climbed the stairs whispering, "Death be not proud, for thou art not so."

"I've been expecting this," Ginger said, after several moments of weeping. She wiped her eyes with the sheet and sat hugging her knees. "Ever since Mama had those small strokes, it was only a matter of time. God is kind. She died in her sleep. I believe her anger dissipated when she saw her dream come true. I'll be all right. She recognized me and died in grace. We're reconciled. My prayers are answered. I can let go."

Acknowledgments

No book is ever written by itself and no honest author can say he or she wrote their story without the help of others along the way. Other people contribute to novels by things I've overheard and used, in unrelated experiences picked up later. And there are the books I've read that gave insight and information. Then, after living with a manuscript for many months, I have lost all objectivity regarding its merits and need the reflective support of others. The story is also the work of those who read clearly, critically and constructively to keep the me grounded and confident. Then the editor and publisher make their contribution. In the end, this book is a team project that is fulfilled when the reader takes it up and gives it his or her particular meaning.

I am deeply grateful Trish Atkinson Pool, Peter Haijinian and Geoffrey Barnard, critical readers whose constructive comments strengthened and sharpened the story. Ralph Winklemeyer and Susan Perry gave me invaluable guidance in addressing certain social and ethnic questions to assure me they were treated as authentically and sensitively as possible. To María Cervantes and Juan Diáz, *muchas gracias* for their critical review to keep the Spanish dialogue authentically colloquial. And a debt of gratitude to the late Robert Cross and his wife Michele, a Wyoming veterinarian and third generation rancher who taught me a lot about grazing cattle.

My eternal thanks to Susan Thurston-Hamerski, my editor, for her support in making me a better writer and this a better story. None of this would be possible without the constant support of my wife, Sue Stavig, who pursues her own form of art while I write.

About the Author

Newell Searle started life on a southern Minnesota farm and attended a vocational high school. He earned a B.A. in history at Macalester College and a PhD at the University of Minnesota. Ditching an academic career, he took up public affairs and discovered a talent for building win-win relationships between unlikely partners. He worked for Cargill Inc., held an executive post in the Minnesota Department of Agriculture and led a national food bank coalition that increased funding for Federal hunger programs. Fluent Spanish, he served as a volunteer consultant to several Mexican food banks. His love of writing began in graduate school and he returned to it in retirement. He found writing fiction liberating but more challenging than history. *Kirkus Reviews* acclaimed his first novel, *Copy Desk Murders*, one of the Best Books of 2023. It is the first in a trilogy followed by *Leif's Legacy,* a winner of the Minnesota Book Award for 2024, and concludes with *An Adverse Possession*, set in southern Minnesota during the 1980s farm crisis. *Saving Quetico-Superior,* a narrative of wilderness protection, received the Federick Weyerhaeuser Book Award. He lives in Minnetonka, Minnesota

Made in the USA
Monee, IL
02 December 2024

70444651R00173